Received On:

JUN 12 2018

Ballard Branch

TO DIE IN VIENNA

D0011954

NO LONGER PROPERTY OF
SEATTLE PUBLIC LIBRARY

ALSO BY KEVIN WIGNALL

TO
DIE IN
VIENNA

KEVIN
WIGNALL

THOMAS & MERCER

This is a work of fiction. Names, characters, organizations, places, events, and incidents are either products of the author's imagination or are used fictitiously. Any resemblance to actual persons, living or dead, or actual events is purely coincidental.

Text copyright © 2018 by Kevin Wignall
All rights reserved.

No part of this book may be reproduced, or stored in a retrieval system, or transmitted in any form or by any means, electronic, mechanical, photocopying, recording, or otherwise, without express written permission of the publisher.

Published by Thomas & Mercer, Seattle

www.apub.com

Amazon, the Amazon logo, and Thomas & Mercer are trademarks of Amazon.com, Inc., or its affiliates.

ISBN-13: 9781477805169
ISBN-10: 1477805168

Cover design by Tom Sanderson

Printed in the United States of America

To Yve and Simon,
who were there for some of it.

Chapter One

Jiang Cheng didn't know Freddie Makin.

Cheng returned to Vienna in September to commence his third year of teaching Applied Computer Science at TU Wien, and over the following month, his routine picked up almost exactly where it had left off before the summer vacation.

He lectured twice a week at TU, oversaw three tutorial groups, and supervised four doctoral students, as well as pursuing his own research interests. He was popular with staff and students alike.

He lived in an old apartment building a relaxed ten-minute stroll from the university. He shopped locally for fresh produce and rarely moved outside of that neighborhood except to go to work. He took great care with his cooking, led an orderly life, read books or watched US sitcoms on his computer, and allowed his obsession with coding and mathematical problems to extend deep into his leisure time. He ran daily on a treadmill in his spare bedroom.

Once every two weeks, on a Sunday (her day off between tours), he was visited by Wei Jun, a guide for Chinese tour groups visiting Europe. They made dinner together and talked, sometimes took a walk, although never to any of the tourist sites, and retired to the bedroom at the end of the evening where they engaged in a perfunctory sexual routine. Early on each second Monday morning, Jun left Cheng in bed and went off to meet her next tour group. Cheng waited for her to go, but got up and stripped the sheets as soon as she'd left.

Despite its proximity to TU Wien, Cheng only went into the historic inner city once a week, to meet Professor Marina Mikhailova who taught Asian History at the nearby University of Vienna. They'd first met at an academic social the previous December and now spent a few hours every Wednesday afternoon playing chess at the Café Griensteidl on Michaelerplatz.

Their table was always reserved for them, and they paid almost no attention to the tourists or to the other handful of regulars, including the thirty-something man who generally sat at the adjacent table reading English novels. Although the older Professor Mikhailova invariably glanced across to note the title of whichever book their neighbor was reading, Cheng didn't appear to see him at all.

He certainly didn't recognize him, and had no idea that he was a freelance surveillance expert, working for a private company in Munich and, beyond that, for persons unknown. He didn't know that the reading man could describe every one of Cheng's tutorial students, that he knew the precise way in which he sliced peppers, the delicate, almost embarrassed way he blew his nose, all his little habits, the way in which he put on his socks, his clockwork bathroom routine morning and night, the heaving of his bony shoulders over Wei Jun's body, the postcoital face that looked exactly as it did after running.

No, Jiang Cheng did not know Freddie Makin, but Freddie knew Jiang Cheng, almost better than he knew himself.

Chapter Two

Cheng was in the kitchen preparing food. It was mid-afternoon and he wouldn't be cooking for at least a few hours, but it wasn't unusual for him to prep this far in advance. He'd made a marinade, and now he was deftly slicing a couple of chicken thighs.

Freddie followed every movement. There was almost nothing he liked more than watching Cheng cook. There was something so graceful about it, like a ballet in miniature. And in some way, it seemed to speak of the meditative quality Freddie wanted in his own life—as with everything else, when Cheng cooked it was as if the rest of the world had fallen away, and he was lost entirely within the moment.

He placed the chicken in the marinade now, turning it three times to ensure it was coated, his movements suggestive of some age-old ceremony. Then he washed his hands and went back to the counter and the ingredients assembled there, but even as Freddie leaned closer to the monitor to see what was next, he felt a slight watery shift in his vision.

He closed his eyes, and kept them closed for a few seconds, but he knew what was coming. As much as he'd been enjoying the cookery demonstration, and as much as he wanted to see what was next, he was about to suffer an ocular migraine, the first in three or four weeks.

He could try to relax, keep his eyes shut, delay the onset. Sometimes it worked, but he knew that more likely than not, within twenty minutes he wouldn't be able to focus on the screens in front of him, that he would see them as if through a kaleidoscope, the constituent parts jumbled into incoherence.

He looked at the monitor again, just to be sure. Ginger. Yes, Cheng was slicing ginger, fine slithers peeling away under the gentle pressure of the knife. But the more Freddie watched, the more his focus slipped and tumbled.

He knew he had no choice but to call it a day and go home. It was an alternate Sunday, no visit from Wei Jun, so he knew exactly how the rest of the afternoon and evening would go for his friend Cheng. It would still be recorded and transmitted anyway, but even four weeks into the new academic year, Freddie knew for sure that there would be no deviation in Cheng's clockwork universe.

Freddie checked the equipment, then headed out. Leo had arranged this apartment, in the same large building as Cheng, and had probably imagined that Freddie would live here as well. But he had always felt it was better to have somewhere else to go, particularly on a long-term job like this—being cooped up in the same place around the clock was a sure way to madness.

And as if he needed a reminder of those dangers, as he left and closed the door behind him, he heard a noise from within the now empty apartment; not just a noise, but someone saying his name quite clearly.

"Freddie."

He knew there was no one there, that it had been a trick of his mind, maybe even a side effect of the migraine. Yet he hesitated, standing by the closed door, wanting to check, because he recognized the voice and knew it belonged to someone long dead. A chill ran down his back and that spurred him to walk on. It was the migraine, only the migraine.

◆ ◆ ◆

He saw no one as he left the building. That had been a brief concern too, just over a year ago when he'd started this job, that Cheng would see him about, start to recognize him. But Cheng didn't recognize people as a rule, not even his own students most of the time, and in this neighborhood and this city Freddie didn't stand out much, just another dressed-down thirty-something, the look of someone working in tech or the media or academia.

It was only a twenty-minute walk to his own place, and the weather was fine and still remarkably warm for late October, so he set off on foot rather than wait for a tram. The aura had already started to dance in front of his right eye, fracturing his vision, but he concentrated on walking and breathing and letting the tension fall away from his shoulders.

There were people around for the first part of the walk, mainly locals—parents with kids, couples, teens in twos or threes, making the most of the afternoon sun. He paid little attention, only vaguely registering them, and more through their sound and presence than through the slightly scrambled images reaching his brain.

By the time he got close to home, he was almost alone, and his own street was completely deserted. It was one of the things he'd liked about it, that it seemed unlived in, full of single professionals and young childless couples who treated it like a dormitory rather than a place to live their lives—he sensed everyone who lived here now would be gone within a year or two.

Inside it was the same, a closed-up silence, the softness of his footsteps on the stairs still managing to produce an eerily whispered echo. And it was only as he took out his key that he heard that rarest of things—noise from inside one of the apartments. He froze, another chill on his spine, but he wasn't hearing things this time.

His vision was starting to clear now, which meant the headache itself would soon follow. He'd have to take painkillers, but he knew also that he had to stay relaxed, and yet as he listened to that noise his shoulders started to hunch and tense, because he *wasn't* imagining it and because it was coming from behind his own door.

Someone was inside his bedroom, clattering about, the sound of a drawer being pulled free and dropped to the floor. Freddie could almost see the intruder's movements, his hearing compensating for the visual disturbance that was still faintly present.

He'd seen a police car a few days ago outside one of the buildings across the street and had heard a couple of people talking about a break-in, one of the rare examples of animation in this neighborhood. But whether it was a burglar or something more troubling, he wasn't sure of the best way to deal with it.

He reached for his phone, but changed his mind, and realized now that his hands were shaking, even the hand that held the key, and there was a tense emptiness in his stomach, one he hadn't experienced in years, one he'd been trying to lose from his memory.

But there was only one thing for it. He raised the key, using both hands to keep it steady, and silently turned the lock. It was a burglar—there *was* nothing more troubling than that, not anymore—but Freddie's heart was pulsing hard and the first little stabs of pain were hitting behind his right eye, and he wasn't sure that this was a wise thing to do, even as he pushed open the door.

Chapter Three

His front door opened directly into the open-plan main room, a combined living area and kitchen with two other doors leading off it, one to the bedroom, one to the bathroom. Freddie didn't keep that much stuff, even after a year here, but what he did have had been turned upside down and scattered about the place, and he could still hear someone going to work on the bedroom.

He didn't give himself the chance for his nerves to win out, walking directly across the room and pushing the bedroom door open. The intruder took a second to glance up from his search, a second for Freddie to get a look at him, dressed in black, dark-haired, but somehow—and he wasn't sure why, yet was sure all the same—looking a little too old and too respectable to be an opportunist burglar.

When he finally saw Freddie standing there, he jumped, but recovered surprisingly quickly, and even as Freddie tried to speak, the guy rushed at him. Freddie recoiled a step backward, but the other was too fast and too powerful, barreling into him, sending him crashing back into the kitchen area and onto the floor, the wind knocked out of his lungs by the contact, his hip thumping hard onto the tiles.

The intruder was gone before Freddie had even registered that he'd been fought off as easily as an adult might cast a child aside. He could hear the steps, louder than his own had been, descending away at speed.

Freddie scrambled to his feet, but stopped with a jolt and grimaced, a pain shooting through his hip, a dull ache in his stomach and chest from being winded. The guy had really hit him hard—he couldn't even remember the last time he'd been knocked about like that. He took a deep breath and limped to the window to get a look down onto the street.

Almost immediately he saw the guy leave the building and head away, talking into his phone, his shoulders hunched, his pace urgent. And then he stopped abruptly, appeared to listen, and even looking down on him from a few floors up, Freddie sensed this wasn't a good development, and he could feel himself willing this man to start walking again.

But he didn't. He turned, slipping the phone into his pocket as he headed once more toward the building. Freddie looked around, trying to think, his thoughts proving stubborn, the pain throbbing behind his eyes. The "burglar" was coming back, had been *sent* back, and Freddie could only imagine one reason for that and it wasn't to apologize for the break-in.

Cheng. This had to be connected to Cheng, which meant there was probably something politically sensitive about this job that Leo hadn't shared with him. He'd have words with Leo about that, but right now there were more pressing matters.

He ran into the bathroom and opened the window, which led out onto a fire escape at the back of the building. He wouldn't get clear in time, he knew it. He left the window, turned the shower on, moved back into the kitchen, glancing to the door—could he already hear steps somewhere below?

If this were Cheng's kitchen he'd have an array of knives to use, but Freddie wasn't much of a cook and barely had anything sharp enough to cut butter. He saw the iron where it had been tipped out onto the kitchen floor—he'd never used that much either, but he picked it up now, standing there for too long, as if wondering where the laundry had gone.

And there it was for sure now, the sound of steps, rapid, forceful. He didn't have a choice but to stick with what was in his hand and hope to catch the guy by surprise. He slipped into the bedroom even as he registered how ridiculous that thought was, even as he heard the lock being worked, the door opening.

The door closed again, gently, and for a few unnerving seconds Freddie couldn't hear him at all. He was conscious of how fiercely he was gripping the handle of the iron, but was afraid to ease his grip in case he dropped it, giving away his position.

And then he heard the other man's breathing, not heavy for someone who'd just run up all those flights of stairs, but at least loud enough to be audible. The bathroom door creaked open and the sound of the shower intensified.

Freddie didn't wait, spinning out of the room, readying himself, but almost stopping when he saw that the guy hadn't gone into the bathroom but was standing in the doorway. It was a couple of steps, that was all, but it seemed too far, and even from this oblique angle, Freddie could see a gun in his hand.

The guy twitched, his instincts kicking in, turned, but the distance had disappeared between them and Freddie swung his arm up now and smashed the iron into his face, the metal plate crunching into his lower jaw with an impact so visceral he could almost feel it himself.

The guy flew backward, bouncing off the frame of the bathroom door, and crashed onto the floor. Even now, Freddie readied to strike again, flooded with adrenaline, his heart pounding, his eyes on the gun, and there was a brief time lag before he realized one hit had been enough—more than enough.

Freddie was breathing hard, much harder than his victim had been breathing just a few moments before, and the throbbing behind his eye told him he was still alive—that fear or anger or simple luck had seen him through this, whatever this had been.

The guy's lower jaw was a mash of blood and flesh and bone, his upper lip and nose still just about intact but steeped in blood too. Freddie looked at the iron—not as much of a mess as he'd expected, given the damage it had inflicted.

He walked into the bathroom, turned off the shower, walked back in, and looked down at the man again. It was a disturbing sight, the way a face could so completely not resemble a face anymore, but still he looked, and then he flinched and almost dropped the iron, because the guy's eyes were open now and blinking hopelessly, the whites just visible, swimming in blood.

A strange noise started to spit and gargle out of the mash of tissue where his mouth had been, and then the hand with the gun started to lift. Freddie kicked out at it, knocking the gun across the kitchen floor. Even then, he grabbed at Freddie's leg, his grip still remarkably powerful.

Freddie yanked his ankle free, and dropped to his knees on the guy's chest. Pulling his head up by the hair, he wound the cord of the iron around his neck and tugged at it with both hands, heaving himself up, lifting the guy off the floor with the effort. The gargling intensified, but Freddie didn't look down at him, just concentrated on pulling until the man was silent.

Only when he was sure did he drop the iron and the cord, and fall to the floor beside the body, rubbing at the palm of his left hand where the flex had cut a burn into it. He made the mistake of dwelling for a moment, wondering what had just happened, but he was quick to slap himself. This wasn't the time for reflection.

Someone had sent this man back to kill him, and it would only be a matter of time before that same someone decided to follow it up. He could worry about what had happened later—for now, he had to get out of here and do whatever was necessary to sort things out with Leo and stay alive.

He climbed back onto his knees and searched the body, still paying as little attention as possible to what remained of the face. Other than the phone, a spare magazine for the handgun, and a key fob for an Audi, there was nothing else.

He put them on the kitchen island, then went and picked up the pistol. It was an M9 with a silencer attached, so maybe he was American, although Freddie seemed to remember Mossad used M9s too, and maybe the French, and even as he speculated, he realized he was thinking only of intelligence services.

He had no reason to think that, except for the current of unease buzzing beneath his thoughts. It was something he'd always insisted upon with Leo—nothing politically sensitive—because he'd struggled to find and maintain some inner peace these five years, and he could already feel it crumbling at the edges now. Leo definitely had some questions to answer.

He put the gun on the island and picked up the phone. It had fingerprint recognition. The guy had held the gun in his left hand, but Freddie thought back to watching him on the street and was certain he'd held the phone in his right. He held the screen up to the light, studying the smudge, reckoning from the size and angle that it was a thumb.

He moved back to the body, lifted the hand and got the phone open on the second attempt. Once he was in, he reset the security to PIN-only, tapping in *1234*, then put the phone back on the island.

He went into the bathroom again and was surprised to see so little blood, only a couple of splashes on the sleeve of his shirt above where he'd held the iron, a single drop on his forehead. It was hard to believe he could have inflicted so much damage and yet be left so unmarked by it.

After wiping away the bloodspot, he went into the bedroom and changed his shirt, looking around as he buttoned the fresh one. The guy had turned the place upside down, yet had somehow missed the fact that Freddie was on the top floor, and so he'd also missed the hatch in the ceiling above the dresser. An easy mistake, even for a professional— it always surprised Freddie how often people failed to look up or down when they needed to.

Climbing up onto the dresser, he pushed the hatch free and pulled down the two silver equipment cases from the attic space, tossing them onto the bed before jumping down. He opened them, moving everything he might need into one case—his camera, all of the small camera units, none of which was bigger than a matchbox, a few tools.

He left the case he was abandoning on the bed, then carried the other through to the kitchen. He put the gun and the spare magazine inside, slipped the car keys and phone into his pocket, swapped his passport and credit cards and headed for the door.

He was trying to work out how long he'd been, wondering whether anyone else would come, whether he should have packed the gun or carried it. And he was still puzzling over this as he opened the door to leave, only just stopping himself in time, alarmed at how sloppy his own thinking was.

These people were serious, professionals, and for whatever reason, they'd targeted him. Maybe they just wanted his equipment or thought he had something on Cheng that they needed, but they'd moved pretty quickly from burglary to wanting him dead.

He put the case back on the island, took a small remote camera unit and fitted it on top of one of the kitchen cabinets in the corner, so discreet that if he hadn't put it there himself it probably would have taken him a couple of days to find it.

Someone would come for the dead man, and when they did, Freddie wanted to see who they were and what they had to say. And he noticed his hands hadn't trembled at all as he'd worked, and the headache had already gone.

Only as he was leaving did it occur to him that for the first time in his life he had just killed a man, or the first time with his own hands at least. He had just killed a man, and he mistrusted how lightly he carried it and didn't want to think about the details that might be embedding themselves even now in his memories.

Chapter Four

Freddie walked in the same direction as the guy had been walking when he'd made the phone call. He'd been crossing the street, so Freddie did likewise, and when he reached the corner he hit the key fob. An Audi SUV flashed back at him halfway along the block.

When he got there, he casually opened up the back and put the case in, checking as he did that nothing else had been left there. Then he got into the driver's seat and took a look inside the glove compartment and the central console. Apart from a pen and a packet of chewing gum in the console, the car was clean.

He took the phone and unlocked it, then went to the contacts list—that was clean too. He went to the call logs but the guy had also been scrupulous about deleting everything there, except for the last number he'd called. Freddie took the pen and wrote the number on the inside of his arm.

He dropped the phone onto the passenger seat and started the car, but at the same time, the phone rang. He killed the engine and picked it up, glanced at the screen and at the digits on the inside of his arm, then answered.

"Yeah?"

"*Yeah?* Why haven't you called it in?"

noticed his hands hadn't trembled at all as he'd worked, and the head-ache had already gone.

Only as he was leaving did it occur to him that for the first time in his life he had just killed a man, or the first time with his own hands at least. He had just killed a man, and he mistrusted how lightly he carried it and didn't want to think about the details that might be embedding themselves even now in his memories.

Chapter Four

Freddie walked in the same direction as the guy had been walking when he'd made the phone call. He'd been crossing the street, so Freddie did likewise, and when he reached the corner he hit the key fob. An Audi SUV flashed back at him halfway along the block.

When he got there, he casually opened up the back and put the case in, checking as he did that nothing else had been left there. Then he got into the driver's seat and took a look inside the glove compartment and the central console. Apart from a pen and a packet of chewing gum in the console, the car was clean.

He took the phone and unlocked it, then went to the contacts list—that was clean too. He went to the call logs but the guy had also been scrupulous about deleting everything there, except for the last number he'd called. Freddie took the pen and wrote the number on the inside of his arm.

He dropped the phone onto the passenger seat and started the car, but at the same time, the phone rang. He killed the engine and picked it up, glanced at the screen and at the digits on the inside of his arm, then answered.

"Yeah?"

"*Yeah?* Why haven't you called it in?"

noticed his hands hadn't trembled at all as he'd worked, and the headache had already gone.

Only as he was leaving did it occur to him that for the first time in his life he had just killed a man, or the first time with his own hands at least. He had just killed a man, and he mistrusted how lightly he carried it and didn't want to think about the details that might be embedding themselves even now in his memories.

Chapter Four

Freddie walked in the same direction as the guy had been walking when he'd made the phone call. He'd been crossing the street, so Freddie did likewise, and when he reached the corner he hit the key fob. An Audi SUV flashed back at him halfway along the block.

When he got there, he casually opened up the back and put the case in, checking as he did that nothing else had been left there. Then he got into the driver's seat and took a look inside the glove compartment and the central console. Apart from a pen and a packet of chewing gum in the console, the car was clean.

He took the phone and unlocked it, then went to the contacts list—that was clean too. He went to the call logs but the guy had also been scrupulous about deleting everything there, except for the last number he'd called. Freddie took the pen and wrote the number on the inside of his arm.

He dropped the phone onto the passenger seat and started the car, but at the same time, the phone rang. He killed the engine and picked it up, glanced at the screen and at the digits on the inside of his arm, then answered.

"Yeah?"

"*Yeah?* Why haven't you called it in?"

He was American. Not Mossad, not DGSE, but American. Freddie didn't know what that signified, whether it was better or worse, and still didn't know for sure if the man he'd just killed, the man he was now impersonating, and the other on the phone, were government or . . . but no, he did know.

"Er . . ."

"No, no, no, don't tell me you didn't do it. This isn't a Bourne or a Bond we're dealing with here. He's a civilian, damn it!"

Freddie felt a little stung, even though it was true. He imagined no one liked to hear they weren't considered much of a threat.

"I, er . . ."

There seemed a barely noticeable shift in the silence that followed, and for the first time the voice on the other end sounded suspicious as he said, "Phillips?"

"No, this isn't Phillips. What do you want with me?"

The line went dead. Like the man had said, Freddie was a civilian, and he guessed he'd just acted like one.

He used the same phone to ring the Behnke office, but of course it was Sunday, and the call ran directly onto the voicemail. He tried Leo Behnke's cell but that went to voicemail too, so he ended the call. He erased the logs, opened the car door, and dropped the phone in the gutter.

He took his own phone now and opened up the feed linking him to the surveillance suite. He was expecting it to be dead and yet still felt a gnawing hollowness in his stomach when he saw it had been shut down.

Scrolling back, he reached the footage of Cheng in the kitchen, still engaged in his preparations for dinner. Freddie was dreading that he'd witness something happening to him, but the screen simply went blank as Cheng diced vegetables.

The question was whether they'd shut down just the surveillance operation or whether they'd shut down Cheng too. And with that thought in mind, Freddie started the engine again and pulled away.

It only took him a few minutes to drive across town to Cheng's neighborhood. He'd planned to do a drive-by, then park up and make his way back on foot, but the drive-by proved enough on its own. A removals truck was parked outside the building and a handful of men were coming and going in a hurry, loading it up.

They were professional, but at the same time, he thought, this was impromptu, even a note of panic about it. There were too many of them to be a regular house-moving team, and most of the stuff was being carried loose rather than packed up. One of them was carrying a desktop computer that Freddie recognized, having spent a large portion of the last year effectively looking at it over Cheng's shoulder.

And as he drove on he felt a little sad, because in a weird way he'd come to know Cheng during that time, had come to like him, to the extent that he'd missed him a little over the summer and had been happy on his return a few weeks ago.

He didn't know what had happened to Jiang Cheng, but he doubted it was anything good, and he'd never really had any idea why Cheng had been under surveillance in the first place. But he knew one thing for sure—something about this job had turned toxic, and the chances were good that the toxicity had been there from the start, even if neither Freddie nor Cheng had known about it.

He left the car a couple of blocks from the Westbahnhof. They'd probably guess that was a bluff, but wouldn't be sure what kind of bluff it was. Freddie walked back into town, bought a suitcase, then clothes and toiletries and a messenger bag. Once the new possessions were inside the case, he walked into a small and anonymous business hotel and booked a room for the night.

There was a pizzeria across the street, so he ate there, watching the front of the hotel the whole time, although he knew no one would find him there, that no one was quite that sophisticated. He was back in his room by nine, the door wedged shut, and for the first time since getting back to his apartment earlier in the day, he allowed himself time to think.

The shock still wasn't so much that he'd killed a man, but that someone had tried to kill him. Would they have killed him anyway if he hadn't gone home too early and disturbed the break-in? Probably. He thought back to them emptying Cheng's apartment, and presumably the surveillance suite too, and he guessed he'd have been hit a whole lot sooner if it hadn't been for that migraine.

In the five years he'd been freelancing for Leo Behnke—mostly corporate work, only the occasional hint of government or NGO involvement, and mostly in Europe, apart from one job in Atlanta, Georgia, and another in Singapore—there had never been any sense of risk or personal jeopardy.

Leo didn't work in the field anymore, but he had in the past, and he'd told Freddie he'd always been terrified of getting caught, of being spotted by the target or by company security, things turning nasty. It wasn't a fear Freddie had shared, not least because it had never occurred to him that he might get caught, but also because the potential consequences had never seemed worth worrying about.

What had gone on today was a different kind of threat, and Freddie knew he had to find out quickly who'd taken out the contract to watch Cheng, where the payments had come from, whether Leo had been given any additional information at all.

If Freddie had stumbled into some intelligence-related work, or if Leo Behnke had led him into it, then he needed to know how serious it was, how high-level the authorization, how likely it was that they would keep coming after him.

Someone had tried to kill him. Someone with an M9 had tried to kill him. The thought was urgent enough to make him put another call in to Leo, and when it went onto his voicemail for a second time the queasiness grew in Freddie's stomach, and was held in check only by the thought that he'd find out tomorrow. One way or another, he'd find out what was happening tomorrow.

Chapter Five

Freddie was woken by the phone on the nightstand ringing. He opened his eyes to see the sickly light of early morning and reached over to grab the receiver.

There was a lot of noise on the line and it took him a confused moment to realize it was Melissa, but she sounded a long way off on a bad line. Then he heard her say something about Talal and he couldn't understand why she was still in denial and talking like that.

"Mel, Talal's dead."

She said something else indistinct. Had she said Talal was there with her? But there was a lot of noise then, a distant explosion. She screamed his name, then shouted something unintelligible, then his name again, afraid and desperate.

"Freddie!"

He shouted back, jumping up, his lungs heaving, and his eyes opened—and he looked around, panicked, trying to see the threat. It was only when he saw that the room was dark around him that he understood he'd still been dreaming.

He turned on the lamp and sluggishly took in the strange hotel room, taking a moment to remember where he was and why he was here. And now that he looked, the phone on the nightstand was nothing like the one in the dream.

He was tired, but didn't want to lie down again, didn't want to risk more dreams. Talal was dead, so were Melissa and Pete, part of his past, and for five years he'd been trying to leave them that way.

His dreams seemed to be his body's way of saying it hadn't worked, that any scratch or cut would reveal that past sitting right there beneath the surface, all his failings, the things he'd done and the people he'd lost.

"Talal's dead," he said aloud, as if Mel were in the room with him or listening in from a discreet distance.

They were all dead. And so was Cheng—the present slipped back into place in his thoughts, a present that required every ounce of his attention.

He got up and looked back at the bed. It looked as though he'd been frantically searching for something in his sleep, and he didn't feel much rested, but maybe it was for the best—he had a lot to do, and an unknown amount of time in which to do it.

He left the hotel without breakfast and took an early Railjet to Munich, lost in his thoughts for most of the journey, but determined to fix those thoughts in the present where they were needed. Cheng's fate was of no material importance to him and yet Freddie kept thinking of him and wondering what had happened, if he'd been afraid, and kept thinking of all his familiar routines.

At one point, he remembered the nervousness with which Cheng would taste a hot spoonful of sauce when he was cooking, like someone creeping to the edge of a diving board, and he smiled at the memory and immediately felt slightly bereft. Perhaps it was hardly so surprising—for the last year he'd been Cheng's intimate companion, even if Cheng hadn't known it himself.

The carriage was quiet, only a few other people in the open-plan compartments, but he could hear a small child now and then, talking animatedly and being hushed. Just after they left Salzburg, the boy walked around the divide into Freddie's compartment and stared at him, smiling.

Freddie smiled back, but the boy frowned in response, and then his mother came along and apologized in German before shepherding the boy away. She was pretty in a natural and unfussy way, and Freddie felt she hadn't actually seen him at all, that her apology had been into the void and that if she'd been asked to describe him, she'd have failed miserably.

It had never much mattered to him before, had even been an advantage, but in some way, he felt he wanted to be visible right now, for a pretty mother to say, "Oh, hello, are you traveling alone, and did someone try to kill you yesterday, and did you kill him instead, and how do you feel about that?"

How did he feel about that? He remembered the splintering crunch of the iron driving his victim's lower jaw into his skull, remembered it like the kind of scene in a movie that might make him gasp or turn away, and yet he didn't seem able to connect with it any more directly than with one of those movie scenes. It would come, he was sure of it.

When he got to Munich, he put his cases in left luggage and took a taxi to the Behnke & Co. office. It was in a shared building, albeit without a main reception, but the door to their office suite was locked. The small vertical window in the door didn't allow him to see beyond the empty reception desk, and he was too conscious of the security camera trained on the back of his head to work the lock.

He took his cell and called the office. He could hear ringing through his phone, but no corresponding ring came from beyond the locked door. He tried Leo again, but still got his voicemail.

What had happened the previous day in Vienna was bad, but this was worse, because it suggested scale, and that in turn made him realize he'd been standing outside the office for too long.

Even so, at a loss, he rang Leo again, and this time, after a couple of rings, someone answered.

"Leo?"

There was no response, but Freddie could hear Petra growling in the background and he smiled because it was something she always did whenever Leo's cellphone rang.

The line went dead, but someone had answered that phone, and Petra would have been doing more than growling if it had been anyone other than Leo. Freddie nodded to himself, happy that he at least had a next move. He kept his head down as he turned and left, avoiding eye contact with the camera above him.

Chapter Six

He headed back down to the street and found the taxi driver who'd brought him still sitting there, engaged in what seemed like a domestic phone call. Freddie got in the back and the driver looked at him, a moment of surprise before taking it as a bonus and ending his call. When Freddie gave him Leo Behnke's address in Grünwald, he looked even happier.

He started to chat as they drove, but Freddie gave the briefest responses he could without appearing terse and eventually the driver gave up. When they got there, the driver pulled up as if expecting the solid metal gates to open so that he could drive through.

Freddie held out two twenty-euro notes. "Thanks, you can leave me here."

Even as the driver took the money, he said, "You don't want me to wait? They might not be in."

Freddie smiled. "They're expecting me."

He got out and walked over to the intercom, pressing the button as the taxi reversed and pulled away into the quiet street. Freddie heard somebody pick up at the other end, but once again, no one spoke.

"Leo, it's Freddie Makin." There was a buzzing and the gate started to slide across the drive, but the line was still open and Freddie said, "Leo, I need you to speak to me."

He could see up the drive now to the large '70s villa sitting in the middle of its lawned plot. Leo's car was in the open garage and he couldn't see any other vehicles, but he didn't like the idea of walking up that drive until he knew there wasn't a reception committee waiting for him.

"Leo?"

"You shouldn't have come here."

The line went dead with a clunk, and just with those few words, things seemed to make sense, of a sort. It was late morning, but Leo sounded sauced.

Freddie started to walk, but kept an eye on the house. As the gate whirred into life and closed behind him, he reached into his messenger bag and put his hand on the gun, not wanting to spook Leo by taking it out, but wanting to be ready all the same.

Petra barked a couple of times as he got close to the house, then again as he rang the bell. He stepped to the side, so he was visible through the window next to the door, and she jumped up at the glass with another bark, but then saw it was him and started to jump around. She was a Doberman and Leo had insisted on her fierceness, but in the four or five times Freddie had been here, she'd always been the same with him.

The door opened, and Petra burst through the gap and jumped up at him. He laughed, taking his hand from the gun to pat her, pulling up short only when he saw Leo standing there in a dark red bathrobe, unkempt, unshaven.

Leo's hair was thin anyway, but this morning it was mussed up too, sparse and wispy, sticking out at odd angles. His bathrobe was heavy toweling, but it was open at the belt and where it hung loose Freddie could see he wasn't wearing anything beneath it. Leo seemed conscious of it now and clumsily tied the belt of the robe, but somehow without managing to close the gap at the front.

Freddie averted his gaze from the wreckage of Leo's body and looked at his bloodshot eyes. He could smell the Scotch on his breath, thick and tangy in the still air.

"God, Leo, what's going on? What are you doing drinking at this time of day?"

"I haven't stopped." He stepped back, the step turning into a stagger. Petra looked up at him with confusion. "You better come in."

Freddie walked through into the living room as Leo closed the door. He sat down in one of the armchairs and Petra trotted in and immediately settled down at Freddie's feet.

Leo didn't follow. Freddie was just about to get up again when he heard him mumbling something and then he came unsteadily into the room. He was about as wasted as it was possible to be while still upright.

"Drink?"

Freddie looked at his watch, not that he needed guidance on the matter, and shook his head. Leo peered around the room, his eyes lighting on a tumbler which was half full. He picked it up, the only movement he managed with any fluidity, and took a gulp before placing it heavily back on the small table and collapsing into the armchair next to it.

His bathrobe fell either side of his fat and hairy thighs, and Freddie lifted his gaze again. He'd seen some unpleasant sights in the last five years, and private behavior that had left him slack-jawed and occasionally nauseous—he'd learned to view most of it with the detachment of a wildlife-documentary maker, but he still didn't want to sit there staring at Leo's genitals.

He focused on the only slightly less appalling sight of Leo's face and said, "Who have I been working for? Who put Jiang Cheng under surveillance?"

For a second, it didn't look as if Leo would answer or that he'd even heard him. But then he nodded, turned, and reached over for the tumbler. He took another gulp, then held the glass in both hands, resting it on his exposed stomach.

"It's done. Didn't you hear?"

"Yeah, I heard, Leo. Someone shut it down yesterday and tried to kill me."

"Did they succeed?" He started to laugh at his own joke, but as the laughter fell away, he lowered his eyes and shook his head. "We're finished. Me, you. Behnke & Co. is finished. I should never . . . And I knew—I should have stopped then. But you know . . ."

"Leo, who's behind the Jiang Cheng job?"

"Who do you think? You should know, more than anyone, *you* should know . . ."

"I know they're Americans, but who? Are they CIA?"

Leo shrugged, like he didn't know or didn't care, but then his eyes became piercing, focused on Freddie as he said, "Who are you?" For a second, Freddie thought he was having some sort of hallucinatory episode, but as little sense as Leo was making generally, this question was more incisive than it first seemed. "Who are you really? Evanston—what was that?" He was visibly running out of steam, as if talking was wearing him out. "Are you one of them?"

"I'm not CIA, Leo, I never was. Is that who these people are?"

Leo laughed. "I don't know! I don't know . . . anything anymore. I'm nobody. A fool. Is he dead? They'll kill us all! You understand? Did they kill him?"

He was talking about Cheng, so Freddie nodded and said, "I guess so." But he also realized he wasn't likely to get anything sensible out of Leo, not unless he sobered him up and he didn't think he had time for that. He decided to change his approach. "Leo, do you keep a work laptop here in the house? Or any papers?"

Leo shook his head and said, "They would have been here already."

Freddie wasn't sure what he meant at first, but then understood. Leo meant the people who'd cleared out Cheng's apartment, who'd come for Freddie, would also have come here if they'd imagined there was anything incriminating to be found. He could have pointed out the obvious, that they didn't know what Leo kept here, but before he could even reply, Petra's ears pricked up and she stirred, springing to her feet, alert.

Leo seemed not to notice, but Freddie listened, and after a moment he was certain he could hear a car, a gentle purr, confirmed as Petra barked once and trotted out into the hallway. A car was coming up the drive, and it was someone who hadn't needed to ring to get through the gates.

Freddie got up and walked to the window, glancing through the blinds, which were open enough to give him a view of the drive without being easily seen. An Audi had just come to a stop in front of the house, one man inside it. Looking down the drive, Freddie could see the gates still open.

He turned, but Leo seemed to have sensed something was wrong and was out of his chair now. As if flushed with a newfound sobriety, he pulled his bathrobe around him and retied the belt.

"Are you expecting anyone?"

Leo shook his head, then looked accusingly at Freddie. "Did you bring them?"

"Leo, what are you talking about? You haven't even told me who *they* are."

"Naturally. Naturally. I know I can trust you. How many?"

"Just one."

Petra started to bark. Freddie glanced back, seeing the guy was out of the car. He looked pretty much like the one who'd come to his apartment. Freddie turned and almost stepped backward when he saw Leo had produced a gun from somewhere and was pointing it at him.

Leo seemed to follow his gaze, but only nodded when he looked down at the gun in his own hand and said, "I . . . am a German." He started to walk out of the room, but doubled back and gulped down the rest of the whisky.

He staggered out of the room then, the dog at his heels, and Freddie moved quickly to where he'd been sitting and retrieved the gun from his bag, even as Petra barked, sounding hoarse with it, and Leo shouted unintelligibly, and then a shot rang out, silenced but still a hammer blow, and Petra squealed and stopped barking.

Another shot, this one from Leo's gun, deafening, and he was still shouting. Freddie had moved toward the living room door, but hesitated, his heart thudding so violently he could feel the blood pumping in his ears. A silenced shot, and then only silence.

Freddie took a careful step back, certain this guy would check the house, and Freddie felt no more confident for having a gun in his hand this time, rather than an iron.

He jumped as a third silenced shot sounded, closer, and a moment later he heard the man speak, and knew he was looking down at Leo as he said, "You stupid son of a bitch."

Freddie felt a small wave of adrenaline kick in on top of all that surging blood, and he was angry, at the guy's lack of professionalism as much as anything else. His voice had given Freddie a fix on where he stood in the hall, and on where Leo had fallen. He checked the safety, and moved quickly into the doorway, raised his arm and fired, even as his eyes focused and he saw that the guy was facing him but staring down at Leo's body.

Freddie's shot hit him in the chest and he staggered back, starting to raise his own gun. Freddie fired again, then a third time, hardly conscious of what he was doing, and only when the guy was down and still did Freddie step clear of the cover provided by the doorway.

Who's stupid now? he thought as he looked down at the body, although he didn't say it aloud, still being possessed of some professional pride. He checked that he was dead. There was no need to check Leo—the first shot had been in the chest, the second above his left eye.

Freddie retrieved the keys from the guy's pocket, but as with the one who'd come to his apartment, there was nothing else, nothing to identify him. He walked over and looked down at Petra and saw that she'd taken a bullet in the chest, a pool of blood on the tiled floor, but that she wasn't dead.

She couldn't lift her head, but she looked up at him with sorry and trusting eyes. The houses here were far apart and leafy and private, but Freddie couldn't be sure someone hadn't heard the gunshots, particularly Leo's. So he had to get out of there, but he lowered himself to the floor and lifted Petra's head into his lap, stroking her as her chest heaved. He couldn't bring himself to look into her eyes again, but he stroked her and listened to her breathing, until the rhythm slowed and finally stopped.

He eased himself free, as if she were sleeping and he didn't want to disturb her, and went in to the living room to get his bag. When he came back out, he looked at the scene, seeing how it would explain itself unless someone were really determined to get to the truth. And if the guy lying there was CIA, any such determination would soon be drained away.

Freddie wasn't sure where Leo's one bullet had gone. All that really mattered was where his own three had ended up. He left, climbed into the Audi, and drove back into the city, mulling over too many questions, mainly questions Leo could have answered if he'd been sober.

The first was whether these people, who'd emptied Cheng's apartment and set about destroying everything and everyone linked to the surveillance operation, were the same as those who'd been paying them this last year.

He had nothing more than instinct to base it on, but his immediate response was that they *were* the same. And although Leo had been vague, Freddie was pretty certain they were CIA or thereabouts, which begged the additional question of why they'd hired a civilian outfit rather than doing it in-house. There were plenty of innocent answers to that question, but also more sinister ones—a need for deniability or an operation that wasn't sanctioned.

And then, finally, there was the most important question of all. What had they been looking for, and what had changed in the last couple of days to make them shut it all down and make it disappear? What could be so important that it wasn't enough to remove Cheng, but that they felt the need to kill Leo too and come after Freddie?

What did they think he knew? And would it make any difference now if they discovered the truth, that he didn't know anything at all?

Chapter Seven

Behnke & Co. consisted of two full-time employees—Leo himself, and a young secretary called Sonja. Freddie had been to her apartment once to pick up some paperwork that Leo hadn't wanted to send electronically. He couldn't recall the exact address, but he remembered the building and the street near the city center.

He left the car a short distance away and walked quickly, scanning the parked cars for any sign that this anonymous gray apartment block was being watched. Although, from what he'd already seen, they were done with watching. The only question was whether Sonja had already been paid a visit or if she'd been next on the list after Leo.

He didn't ring the bell once he got to her door, but listened, then quietly worked the lock. The door opened and immediately stopped with a jolt—the chain was on, which meant she was in, and most likely alive.

He started to ease the door shut again, thinking it might be better to ring the bell after all, but there was a hurried movement and she appeared in the gap, shouting something. He managed to get his foot in the door even as she tried to slam it shut.

She was out of sight now, pushing hopelessly against the door and yelling, "I'm calling the police!"

"Sonja, it's me, Freddie Makin."

"I know who it is and I'm calling the police, so you better get out! What have you done with Leo? And the office? I'm calling the police."

He wondered why she hadn't called them already. Then he looked around, because his real concern right now was that one of the neighbors might hear her and come out to investigate.

Keeping his voice low, he said, "Sonja, I don't know what's happening. Someone tried to kill me. They emptied Cheng's apartment. Americans."

"Americans?"

That meant something, which was a start, as long as he could get inside and talk to her.

"Yes, Americans. Look, Sonja, I have a gun. I took it from the man who tried to kill me. I'm going to pass it through the gap and you can take it from me. Then I'll pull my foot from the door and you can close it."

She didn't respond, but he saw the silence as an improvement. He pushed the gun far enough through the narrow gap that she could see it.

"The safety's on, but even so, try not to shoot anyone, me especially."

For a moment nothing happened, but then he felt her take the gun and the pressure on the door eased a little. He pulled his foot free and the door closed. For another moment nothing happened, a second that stretched beyond itself, long enough that he once again looked nervously at the doors of the neighboring apartments, but then he heard the chain slide free and the door opened.

The couple of times he'd seen her in the office she'd looked glamorous, fair-haired, and athletic—but wearing a uniform executive chic. The time he'd come here, she'd been similarly dressed, as though she'd kept her office clothes on until he'd been.

So he was shocked to see her wearing a loose sweatshirt and jeans, barefoot, with dark shadows beneath her eyes. Until now, he'd imagined she'd gone into work this morning and found something wrong with the office, but she actually looked like someone who hadn't slept in days. Scarily, she was holding the gun but absentmindedly pointing it at herself.

He stepped inside and closed the door behind him, then pointed at the gun, but even that simple movement caused her to step backward. She looked terrified, which meant she knew something.

"Sonja, let me take the gun." She nodded, but was looking at him too, trying to read his intentions, clearly desperate to trust in someone.

"What's happening?"

"I don't know. But I can't lie to you, it's something bad." She nodded again and held out the gun. He took it from her and tried a smile. "I could use some coffee."

"Please, come into the kitchen."

He followed her and put the gun on the small kitchen table, then sat down as she started to make coffee. She seemed disinclined to speak until she was finished, but Freddie wasn't sure how much time he had.

"Sonja, what do you know? Why didn't you go into the office today?"

Without looking at him, she said, "Herr Behnke called me yesterday morning. He told me I shouldn't go into work today, and that if anything happened to him, I should . . ." She turned now, looking confused, and there were fresh tears on her cheeks. "I don't remember. He told me I should . . . but I knew something was wrong. I asked him, and he just repeated that I must not go into work today. I worried all day, and then in the afternoon I called him at home and on his cellphone, but I got no answer."

"I was out there just now. Leo's dead." He didn't bother to explain how recently it had happened.

She looked at him blankly for a second anyway, as if she hadn't heard him but didn't want to ask him to repeat himself, then turned back to the coffee and spoke once more with her back to him.

"I probably shouldn't have, but last night I went to the office. They took my computer, and many things from Herr Behnke's office. They made such a mess." She turned to face him. "I haven't slept at all. Should I go to the police?"

"I think you have to." The resigned look on her face suggested it was the last thing she wanted to do, and once again he wondered if she'd properly heard him a moment before. "Leo's been murdered, Sonja. The police will have to be involved sooner or later."

"How does that help me?" She wasn't expecting an answer and finished making the coffee in silence.

He waited until she'd handed him a mug and sat down opposite before saying, "Who was the client for the Jiang Cheng job?"

"I don't know." She offered a little nod, acknowledging his incredulity even before he'd expressed it. "Last summer, just over a year ago, two American men came, very smart, and for nearly an hour they talked to Herr Behnke. When they left, I asked who they were and he told me it was best I didn't know. The next week, the contract came and I asked if it was from the two American men. He told me not to worry where it was from, and he told me maybe Freddie Makin is best for this job."

"Did he say why? Did the Americans ask for me?"

"I don't think so. The only request they made was that the surveillance operative didn't speak Mandarin."

"*Didn't* speak Mandarin."

"Correct. Herr Behnke also thought that suspicious. He forwarded some of the material to a contractor we use in Hamburg, to translate."

"What kind of material?"

"The tapes from the café, from his apartment when his girlfriend was visiting, some footage of him at the computer. But I saw the transcripts we got back, and it didn't look interesting or sensitive, just everyday things, you know? Herr Behnke stopped sending it after a few weeks."

Even so, there had to be a reason they'd wanted someone to spy on Cheng without understanding him.

She picked up her coffee but appeared unable to stomach it, and put it down again before continuing. "The money came from an account in Liechtenstein. I asked once more who they were, maybe six months ago, but Herr Behnke told me I shouldn't ask questions about this job."

Was that why Leo had been so frustratingly uninformative, because even in his drunken stupor he'd been trying his best not to say too much, as if silence alone might still offer some protection?

"Was there any indication until yesterday that anything was wrong? Did Leo seem nervous, worried?"

"No more than usual. You know how he is. And it was strange, because when he called yesterday, he was so calm. For a moment, I thought maybe he'd been drinking, but it was early in the morning. And he was calm, so relaxed, even as he gave me these very strange instructions about not going to work. It's how I knew something was wrong. Should I go to the police?"

Did she know she was repeating herself? He nodded somberly and sipped his coffee, which was too strong but welcome for that.

"It's probably better if you don't mention I was here. Just say you called him and couldn't get a reply, that someone turned over the office." He thought of the way she'd been confused more than once during their brief conversation. "If it slips out about me, don't worry. It's just easier for me to make my next move if—"

"Your next move?" She looked bemused, then intrigued. "Who are you, Herr Makin?"

"Call me Freddie, please—I'm not even that much older than you." He assumed she was about thirty, so maybe there was eight years in it, but he also knew she hadn't addressed him like that because of the age difference. "And you know who I am. You've seen my résumé. I joined Evanston Electronics right out of college and stayed there until five years ago. There's nothing else to tell."

"You said someone tried to kill you and then you turn up here with his gun. How did that happen?"

She didn't seem so confused now, and he doubted she'd believe him if he told her the truth, that he got lucky because of a migraine, that he took the guy by surprise and smashed him in the face with an iron. But that was all he had for her.

"I went home early, and I got lucky." Before she could counter, he changed course. "I expect they took everything from the office that might have related to Cheng?"

"Yes. Why are they doing this?"

"Sonja, we don't even know who they are. We have no idea why they were watching him or what they were looking for. I'm working on the assumption that in the last few days I've recorded something they haven't liked, but I have no idea what it is, not least because, conveniently, I don't speak Mandarin."

She stared at him intensely, the look of someone wanting a different response, then she picked up her coffee again and drank this time, the mug half empty by the time she put it down.

"What will you do?"

"Right now, I have no idea."

"Will you help me?"

Inadvertently, he'd helped her as much as he could by killing the man in Leo's house, someone who might well have turned up here later in the day.

"Sonja, I'm a surveillance expert, that's all. There's nothing I can do to help anyone. But if you're still alive now, they don't want you dead."

In truth, far from being an expert, surveillance had never really been his thing. And maybe he could help her more if he really wanted to. But he wouldn't, and her chances of survival probably depended on how determined these people were to clear up all the traces of this operation.

Tears broke free and trickled down her cheeks as she said, "I'm scared, Herr Makin—Freddie—I'm scared. Please, there must be some way you can help me."

"No, there isn't, I told you, I—"

"*Please.*" She looked embarrassed to be pleading with him like this, and he just wanted to be out of there.

"Sonja, call the police: they'll be able to help you better than I can." And maybe that was true anyway, but Sonja could see he was washing his hands of her, and she reacted with determined dignity, nodding, wiping her eyes. "If you can wait an hour, give me time to get out of the city, that would help. Then call them, tell them about the call from Leo yesterday, say you're getting worried."

"You're leaving the city?"

He nodded, unsure of why she was so surprised—he'd never lived in Munich anyway, even before the Vienna job.

"Where will you go?"

"I don't know. London, maybe, or . . . I don't know, just some place they won't find me."

"But you said they won't kill more people." She was still terrified, fearing he was lying to her about her own safety, which in a way he was.

"I said they won't kill *you*. They already tried to kill me, and they don't strike me as the kind of people who leave business unfinished." He smiled, then drank the rest of his coffee in a single gulp. "Don't worry about me. But call the police. Leo was a good man."

She nodded her agreement as he stood up, and yet that too was a lie—Leo had been possessed of many qualities, but being good hadn't been one of them.

Chapter Eight

Freddie picked up his luggage and headed to the pizza place in the station, finding a small corner table where he could use his laptop without being overlooked. He didn't know yet where he was headed, but he needed to decide soon because he couldn't keep living on pizza indefinitely.

He ordered first, then opened up the laptop and got a ping almost immediately from the camera unit he'd installed the day before. He put his earpiece in. The camera had started transmitting about an hour ago, so it had taken them the best part of twenty-four hours to go find "Phillips," a suggestion in itself of how busy they'd been with Cheng.

Freddie watched as five men walked into shot. Three were wearing dark casual clothes, heavy-duty, and one of them was carrying a body bag, which he opened out alongside the dead man. The three proceeded to put the body into the bag, economical in both their movements and words. One of them was called Jimmy—he learned that much, but little else.

The other two were in suits, one wearing pale gray, the other in black. The man in black had short brown hair, whereas the one in gray had sandy hair slicked back with gel—he was older and looked more like a Wall Street trader than a CIA guy, which again was what Freddie instinctively took them for.

It was clear just from the way he was carrying himself that the guy in gray was in charge. The two suited men were talking quietly as the other three worked, but Freddie couldn't pick up what they were saying on a first listen.

Then the younger one nodded and said, "I'll get my case."

He walked out of the room and the trader turned his attention briefly to the three men sealing up the body, then walked into the bedroom. While he was in there, two of the others left with the body bag and the one called Jimmy leaned against the island, showing little sign of being much moved by the death of his colleague.

The trader came out and handed him Freddie's other equipment case and said, "Okay, Fernandez, stow this with the rest."

Freddie nodded to himself, noting the full name.

Hello, Jimmy Fernandez.

He could probably do a search on him, but Freddie knew in advance what it would reveal—that Fernandez was attached to a US Embassy or Consulate somewhere in Europe, probably as a driver or something similarly mundane.

Fernandez was young and stocky with a buzz cut, and Freddie noticed he was slow to push himself away from the island and take the case, a faint suggestion of insolence. The trader was in charge, but it didn't look as though he had the complete respect of his team.

Fernandez said something, inaudible again, but the trader responded testily, saying, "You let me worry about that."

Fernandez left, again without much sign of deference, and the trader looked slowly around the room. At one point he even looked directly at the camera but didn't actually see it. Then he turned his attention to the door as the young guy in the dark suit came back in, pulling a small case.

"Good. Once we've gone you can go out and get some provisions, enough to last a few days, but I want you back here within half an hour and I don't want you leaving until I call you in. You can order takeout if you need to."

"Any idea how long—"

"As soon as we track down Makin, you're out of here."

So they were actively searching for him, which for the time being probably meant tracing his movements from his passport, credit card and cellphone, none of which he was using. Maybe in time they'd pick up some trace of this visit to Munich or suspect his involvement in what had happened at Leo's place, but he'd be long gone by then.

"What do I do if he comes back?"

"Let me think . . . You *kill* him. He won't come back, not here, not even to Vienna, but if he does, you make sure it's the last thing he does. He's already seen a lot more than he should have done." Freddie didn't catch the subordinate's response, but the gist of it became clear when the trader spoke again. "That's a 'need to know,' and at the moment, you don't need to know. So just focus on the fact that he's a serious threat to our operations, and will be for as long as he's alive."

"And he killed Phillips."

The trader looked at the floor where the body had been, as if trying to remind himself of who Phillips was.

"Phillips got sloppy, that's what killed Phillips—he allowed a civilian contractor to sucker-punch him with an iron. But I don't care what motivation you call upon. If he comes back here, which he won't, just kill him."

Freddie had heard enough now to know that the trader was the person he'd briefly spoken to on the phone after the break-in yesterday. So he was running this operation, he didn't have the respect of his men, and he seemed pretty keen to have Freddie in a body bag of his own by the end of the week.

It didn't surprise him. Phillips had been sent back to kill Freddie the previous day, so this was nothing new and the shock had settled in now, like the lingering mixture of lightheadedness and tension that came in the hours after a migraine. But knowing for sure that they wanted to track him down wherever he'd gone did give him some idea of the dimensions of his situation.

Freddie watched as the trader left, then as the other man wheeled his case into the bedroom. He came out again almost immediately and then he too left, to buy the provisions that would last him the few days his boss thought it would take to find Freddie.

Freddie switched over to the live feed and saw the young guy, no longer wearing his jacket or tie, tidying up the mess that had been left by Phillips. Freddie was about to watch the earlier footage again, but he saw the waiter heading over with his pizza, so he shut it down and moved the laptop onto the seat next to him.

The pizza was too hot, so he sat looking around the room, thinking about where he was and what had happened and where he needed to go. He'd mentioned London to Sonja, but there were better places to run, and yet even thinking about flight made him weary.

One of the things he'd always admired about Cheng had been his ability to remain completely present within his own life. Freddie only saw now that his admiration for that quality was a reaction to the complete absence of it within his own day-to-day existence.

He'd spent five years running away in one sense or another, and the trader had quite rightly predicted that he would run now. But Freddie didn't want to run anymore, he wanted to stay, no matter what that entailed.

He went back to the laptop again, not to the feed from his apartment, but to the ÖBB website. It seemed there was a Railjet in just under an hour—more than enough time to eat. He bought a ticket.

Because he needed to know what it was he might have seen, and he needed to know who these people were and how persistent they were likely to be—and if there might be any way of stopping them. He felt he needed to know for his own safety, his own peace, but in a strange way he felt he needed to know for Cheng too.

The intuitive thing to do in a situation like this, the thing the trader expected of him, was to put as much distance as he could between himself and the people who wanted to kill him. They didn't know enough about Freddie to understand that his instincts were always weighted toward the counterintuitive, doing the thing least expected; and for a while, before it had all come crashing down, that approach had served him pretty well. So that was what he'd do now, he'd go against every sensible expectation, by returning to the one place they absolutely wouldn't expect to find him.

Chapter Nine

It was dark by the time Freddie got back to Vienna. He remembered a hotel called the Danzig that he'd often walked past, heading from his apartment to the Café Griensteidl, in a pretty good location for all the places he'd need to get to, so he asked the Arabic driver to take him there.

But as they skirted around the edge of the inner city he spotted another place he'd seen before, a glass-fronted cube with a neon sign on top: *the madhouse.* They were stopped at lights, so Freddie pointed at the building.

"What's that place?"

The driver looked and smiled, shaking his head. "A hotel. Mad, you know, it's like crazy. The people there too."

"Okay, take me there."

"But you said Hotel Danzig."

"I know. I changed my mind."

"You want Hotel Madhouse?"

"I want Hotel Madhouse."

The driver laughed, shaking his head again. "I have to drive up and back now to get there, but it's good. Hotel Madhouse for you."

Freddie nodded, laughing along a little too, and it was funnier than the driver knew, because Hotel Madhouse was the last place they'd expect to find him, even if he sent them a postcard from Vienna.

Finally, as they approached the glass-fronted reception, he said to the driver, "You're from Yemen?"

The driver cocked his head, surprised and impressed.

"You can tell?"

Freddie pointed to the various knickknacks hanging from the rear-view mirror, a small enamel Yemeni flag among them.

"I lived there for a little while."

"Really? In Sana'a?"

"Sana'a and Aden. I was doing some work for an aid agency. I left five years ago."

"Me also." The driver nodded sadly, as if some understanding had passed between them. Yes, Freddie was by no means the only one to carry a sadness from that country, or many others that had been similarly cursed. He wasn't even the only one for whom that sadness had been self-inflicted. "Today is different." He stopped the taxi and found another smile as he looked at the building. "So, here we are."

Freddie paid him, and stood with his suitcase and the metallic equipment case, looking up at the hotel with its red neon sign high above. He was about to walk in when the glass lobby door glided open and a dozen somber people in superhero costumes walked out in a line and headed off silently into the city.

He watched them go, then made his way into the dimly lit and slightly chaotic lobby, where people lounged on sofas and beanbags and a brightly painted rocking chair, music was playing, and three young women laughed as they squashed together on the seat inside a photo booth. It all seemed a little too studied for a madhouse, but there was a warmth here that he liked.

An achingly hip Japanese couple were checking in, surrounded by half a dozen pieces of luggage. Behind them, waiting in the middle of the lobby floor as if scared of being caught up in any of the activities around him, stood a bewildered businessman with a small wheeled suitcase and a briefcase. His company had obviously booked him in here, but in his ill-fitting navy suit and patterned tie he looked desperately out of place.

Freddie turned casually and saw his own reflection in the glass door. With his plaid shirt, slightly scruffy hair and the beginnings of a beard, he fitted in with the rest of the clientele more than he did with the uneasy business traveler, superficially at least.

"Hi, welcome to the Madhouse!"

Freddie turned in response to the cheery voice and saw that an extra person had appeared at the reception desk—a young woman with a floppy purple Mohawk and multiple piercings in each ear, wearing what appeared to be the informal staff uniform, a Breton stripe sweater.

She'd been addressing the businessman, who stepped forward and spoke so quietly that Freddie could only hear the other receptionist talking to the Japanese couple. Then he heard the girl with the purple hair confirming in English that the businessman was only staying one night.

Freddie zoned out a little, until he heard her say, "Yes, either elevator." He turned and saw that the man had wheeled his case across the lobby to head for his room.

"Hi, welcome to the Madhouse!"

Freddie smiled, because she was talking to him, and he walked across to the desk.

"I don't have a reservation, but I was hoping you might have a room."

"Sure, let me check. How long for?"

Move on every couple of days—that was the standard procedure for being on the run.

"A week, I think, to begin with. I might need longer."

"Okay." She stared at the computer. He noticed she had a name badge: Eva. He glanced across at her colleague, a ring in his nose and young enough still to have slightly pimply skin. According to his name badge, he was called Arnold—Freddie wondered if they made up the names they wore.

Eva frowned, keeping her eyes on the screen as she spoke. "We only have one of the big rooms free for a week. I could put you in a smaller one, but I'd have to move you after two days to a different room."

"A big room's fine."

"Great!" She smiled, having fun with him. "Maybe you need a big room, for all the parties." She put a form on the counter. "Can you fill this in, and I need your passport and a credit card. We can take—"

"Sure, you can take the full payment for the week, and I'll settle extras on top. Parties can be expensive."

She laughed, because he suspected they both knew he wasn't the partying kind, but then she went back to the computer and said, "So, if you're paying in advance . . . I can give you a better rate. And hey, breakfast is included, in the restaurant just through there."

He looked over his shoulder, beyond the people lounging on sofas, through to a busy restaurant. Even as he looked, he could see a Breton-clad waiter carrying a pizza to one of the tables—hopefully it wouldn't be the only thing they served.

"Looks good." He went back to the form.

"You wanna eat tonight?"

"No, I don't think so."

"Okay. Well, there's a bar on the rooftop too, if you wanna drink, make friends, you know, hang out."

He hadn't heard her saying any of this to the businessman, so he guessed he was fitting in, and that the cover would be a good one. He'd be able to walk wherever he needed to go from here too.

She copied his passport and took the payment as he filled in his details, and when he handed the form back to her she looked at it and nodded to herself. "Alfred Robbins. Do they call you Alfie or . . ."

"Freddie. My friends call me Freddie."

"Great. I'll put that in the system." She typed a rapid little rhythm into the computer, then smiled at him. "So, welcome to the hotel, Freddie. I'm Eva, this is Arnold. If there's anything you need, let us know." Arnold nodded to him and went back to pointing at a map for the Japanese couple. Eva handed him his keycard. "You're in room 520."

"Thanks."

As he turned, one of the elevators opened and a group of young guys who looked like an indie rock band spilled out of it. One of them was singing to himself, another tapping on his fake leather jeans as though playing the drums.

Freddie took their place and made his way up to the fifth floor. The room was big, like she'd said, but one wall was entirely glass, looking out across the museums to the Hofburg and the inner city. He smiled as he stood there taking in the view of the city by night—there was hiding in plain sight, but this took the concept to another level.

Maybe the hotel name was appropriate, because he could feel a prickling restlessness under his skin, and this had not been a sane decision. But then, he could see clearly now that nothing in the last five years had been entirely sane either.

After standing there for a few minutes, he pressed the button next to the bed to lower the blinds, then got to work. He opened up his laptop and checked the live feed from the apartment—there was no one in view, but the bedroom light was on.

Freddie took the spare magazine he'd found on Phillips. He emptied and reloaded it, slipping a tracker in place of the fourteenth bullet. He was gambling that the guy in his apartment now would also have an M9, and that he wasn't likely to use it any time soon.

He went back through the feed then, seeing what he'd missed and how the new resident was filling his hours of idleness in Freddie's old place. For a long time, the guy sat at the kitchen island looking at his laptop, but with the back of the machine to the camera, preventing Freddie from being able to see anything of what he was doing. He wondered if it could be worth trying to install anything on it, but doubted he'd get the opportunity.

He fast-forwarded, and went back to normal speed when the guy put his laptop to one side and got up. He went across to the kitchen counter and started to prep ingredients, with the look of someone who loved food and enjoyed cooking, and a couple of times he looked a little exasperated as he searched in vain through the cutlery drawer.

Freddie watched for a little while, but felt himself becoming more and more forlorn. How many hours or even days over the last year had he watched the ritual of Cheng lovingly preparing his dinner? It had been like an act of meditation in itself, just to watch him. But Cheng was almost certainly dead.

He forwarded through the rest of the footage and then shut it down and got ready for bed. He lay there in the dark, and could just make out a faint beat coming from the rooftop bar a couple of floors above, but he could also feel sleep sweeping down on him.

It had been a long day, a long two days, and those that lay ahead wouldn't be any easier. A proper night's sleep was the very least he'd need if he didn't want to end up like Cheng, like Leo, like Phillips. He thought of them, and tried not to think of the more distant dead as, reluctantly, he fell away into the dark.

Chapter Ten

Throughout the twelve years Freddie had officially been an employee of Evanston Electronics, his stress dream had always taken the same form. Irrespective of what had been happening in the present, he'd always found himself dreaming of being back in the exam room at university. The dreams always started realistically, of being surrounded by people he'd known in college, hearing the instruction to turn over the exam paper, realizing to his horror that he hadn't studied and knew nothing about the questions being asked. Inevitably, the dream then spiraled into surreal territory, finding people from the present sitting at neighboring desks, sounds of distant explosions or a plane apparently hurtling toward the exam room, crumbling teeth, being unable to move. And then the desperate swim toward the surface that was waking up, gasping, drained.

In the five years since, he'd wished time and again to find himself back in that exam room, but he had dreamed only of Yemen, and always of the same pivotal incident. When he woke on his first morning at the Hotel Madhouse, it was because he'd woken himself, shouting "No!" and jumping up, scrabbling free of the duvet and the bed, before the slow welcome realization that it had only been a dream, that he had not been back there, that it was long gone.

The Yemen dream, like the exam dream it had supplanted, almost always started in the same way, and was so realistic that it fooled his unconscious mind every time. They were driving, Melissa next to him in the back, Pete up front, and Talal, their young driver and interpreter, behind the wheel. The radio was playing and Talal heard something he liked and turned it up and started to sing along, much to their amusement.

And then they arrived at the makeshift roadblock and Talal talked to the gunmen with their scarves covering their faces, and they called someone, and another man came out of the nearby building, and even with his face hidden in the same fashion, Freddie could see that it was Abdullah, and he felt a clench in his stomach because he could see in Abdullah's eyes that something had changed, that something bad was about to happen.

It was usually around then that the dream broke down, that he would see his parents, or that Abdullah would still be there but the setting had changed to Freddie's childhood home, or it would not be Melissa next to him but Chloe, her eyes full of fear and anger, or Freddie would be running through the streets, then taking flight and hurtling over the buildings, before crashing back down in a fatal explosive dive.

He didn't know whether it was the right thing to do, and had never sought or been offered advice on the matter, but he always tried, when he woke from such a dream, to remind himself in simple terms of the facts, of what had really happened, of the incident as it had actually played out. Did it reduce the frequency of the dreams? He couldn't be sure, but it had become part of his routine, like a morning meditation.

He sat on the edge of the bed now, the blood sluggish in his veins, and thought of Talal turning off the radio as they approached the roadblock. He thought of Pete saying to Freddie, "Any of these look like your man?" and then laughing—"What a stupid question!"—because of the scarves. And yet it hadn't been stupid at all, because Freddie could still see Abdullah's eyes above the scarf that covered his face and recognized him even from the memory of it. He remembered the heat crushing against them as soon as the windows were lowered, the air-con failing to keep it at bay. He remembered the taste of Melissa's blood as it spattered his face.

And of course, he reminded himself that Chloe had never been in Yemen, and deconstructed the guilt-ridden reasons for his subconscious mind substituting his fiancée's face for Melissa's. It was as if it hadn't been enough to be responsible for the deaths of his friends, but that he also needed to carry the burden of betraying Chloe too.

He leaned over and pressed the button, the blinds whirring up slowly to reveal the glass wall and the city laid out magnificently before him under a uniform pale gray sky. This was what he had to deal with now—the present—and for all he knew, within the next few days there would be something else to supplant the Yemen dream.

Reaching for the laptop, he opened it up and looked at the feed. It was nine o'clock and the guy in Freddie's apartment was already sitting at the kitchen island on his own laptop. Astonishingly, given that Freddie knew he wouldn't be going anywhere today, he was wearing a crisp white shirt and a tie.

Freddie looked back a couple of hours earlier on the feed and saw the guy emerging from his room at a minute or so after seven, wearing just boxer shorts and carrying his shoulder holster as he walked into the bathroom. He stayed in there for twenty minutes, came out again and back into the bedroom, emerging after another fifteen minutes wearing the clothes Freddie could see him in now. He made himself breakfast, ate it, cleared up, then went to work on his laptop, the shoulder holster nearby.

Freddie smiled, because he could just tell, the way he'd learned to tell, that this was a creature of precise habits in front of him. If he was right about that, he'd pay him a visit just after seven the next morning and see what he could find out. But there was plenty he could do before then.

He picked up the phone and rang reception. It rang for a while before a woman answered with the air of someone who'd only just noticed there was even a phone there.

"Hello?"

"Hello, I was hoping I could order some breakfast?"

"Of course. The restaurant's open right now."

"No, I mean room service."

"Oh." She laughed a little, at her own confusion or his misunderstanding. "We don't do room service. It's just not our thing, you know. But it's a great vibe in the restaurant."

"Then I guess I'd better come down."

"You won't regret it. Is there anything else I can help you with?"

"No. Thanks."

He showered, dressed and headed down.

The lobby was even more chaotic than it had been the night before. There was a pop-up shop selling ceramic artwork and half a dozen people waiting to check out. A woman with a shaved head and Arnold, who'd been behind the desk with Eva the night before, were processing the departing guests in a fashion that was relaxed enough to explain the line and the look of resignation on some of the faces. He heard the woman say, "Sure, it's a great vibe," and guessed it was the one he'd just spoken to on the phone.

He drifted through into the restaurant and a young guy with film-star looks approached him with a smile.

"Hey! Good morning. Breakfast?"

"Please. Room 520."

"Sure." The guy tapped it into the terminal on the restaurant reception. "Freddie, yeah? And breakfast is included in your rate. So, the buffet is there, but how about something from the kitchen?"

"Some eggs maybe, scrambled. Some bacon, mushrooms."

"Sounds good. Coffee, tea?"

"Coffee, please." Freddie looked around the restaurant, which was lively, no doubt helped by the absence of room service. A row of tables by the side wall were empty apart from the businessman from the night before, but they gave a good view of the room, so he pointed to one of them. "I'll sit just over there."

"Okay, make yourself at home. I'll be with you soon."

Freddie nodded. He noticed the guy's name badge—PEDRO—it was surely one of the hotel's in-jokes that all the staff made up their names.

He grabbed a glass of juice and some cereal and took it over to the table next but one to the businessman, who was making his way glumly through a bowl of muesli. And when he sat down, he noticed the Japanese couple from the night before sitting over by the windows, looking immaculate and poised and self-contained in a way that Freddie envied somehow.

Elsewhere in the room were plenty of people in twos and threes, his age or younger, the look of people who worked in media or fashion or the arts. But there were a fair number who were older and more conventional too, most of them wearing permanently bemused expressions. It still felt like the last place anyone would look for a surveillance contractor on the run.

A ringtone sounded, building in volume, and the businessman answered. The person at the other end was loud enough for Freddie to be able to tell that he was annoyingly cheery, even if he couldn't make out the words. The businessman laughed, but it was paper-thin, and his voice when he spoke was edged with office resentments.

"I'm glad it's provided some amusement, but I have to tell you, Martin, I think David got Sally to book me into this place on purpose." He was English. "And what if the client had wanted to come and meet me at the hotel? The Austrians are serious people—they wouldn't see the funny side."

Freddie started on his cereal.

"No, I'm checking out as soon as I've had breakfast. Meeting's at twelve, flight's at six." He listened to his colleague's response and laughed again, no humor in it at all this time. "Not in a million years, and I won't be letting him book my hotel again either."

He ended the call and Freddie could sense him looking around, as though he wanted to share the experience with someone else. Freddie was the only person nearby and he was concentrating on his cereal, giving no purchase. Finally, the businessman looked ostentatiously at his watch, puffed the air out of his cheeks and stood up to leave.

The whole overheard phone call and the businessman's overblown dissatisfaction had the odd effect of making Freddie appreciate the place a little more. Clearly, the Austrians did see the funny side, and beneath the slightly strained wackiness of the place, Freddie felt a genuine friendliness. And ironically, it was only in being on the receiving end of that relaxed warmth that he realized it had been missing from his life, probably for most of the last five years.

He only regretted that he hadn't visited this place before, that he'd waited until now. But he shook off the regret, as he'd been trying to learn to do, and focused instead on the moment, and on Pedro heading toward him with a tray and an easy smile.

Chapter Eleven

Later that morning, he went back to the surveillance suite. He wanted to see what they'd taken and what they might have left behind. He didn't hold out hopes of learning anything crucial, but he had to do something, and Cheng seemed like the place to start—he'd been the reason for Freddie being here and the reason for him being in danger now.

He didn't expect to find anyone waiting for him, but as he neared the building he loosened the straps on the messenger bag. He breezed into the lobby without hesitating, and took the elevator to the fourth floor. Only when he saw the corridor was clear did he take the gun from the bag and walk along to the apartment that had been his place of work until a couple of days earlier.

He thought back to the nerves he'd felt on finding an intruder in his own apartment and was surprised by how calm he felt now. He didn't even listen at the door first, but slid the key into the lock and pushed it open, the gun at the ready in his hand.

And, as it happened, he was right not to be nervous. The place had been stripped, not just of all the surveillance equipment, but everything—chair, desk, kettle, coffee mugs, even the jar of instant coffee he'd been using. It was as if they were already planning to put it back on the market.

Freddie strolled around the empty rooms, his footsteps echoing lightly. It had been his workplace rather than his home, although he'd spent longer here than in the apartment, and yet he couldn't get any sense of his own presence in these rooms. Without the surveillance equipment, the place didn't even feel familiar.

The thoroughness with which they'd emptied it was a concern, and Freddie thought of Sonja in Munich, and wondered if she'd gone to the police, because he was thinking she probably wasn't safe after all. Maybe he'd inadvertently bought her some time by killing the guy at Leo's place, but the stripped-back emptiness of these rooms seemed to speak of a determined and risk-averse cleanup operation.

Freddie was also a part of that particular to-do list, of course. If there'd been any doubt before, he certainly didn't entertain any now— they'd bring the same thoroughness to bear on finding and silencing him too, even though, ironically, he'd seen about as much as Sonja had.

He slipped the gun back into the bag and made his way down the stairs to the floor below, and along the short corridor to Cheng's apartment. There was no one about, so he pulled the gun again and used the key he had to open the door, ready to shoot first if he found anyone waiting for him. But as soon as he stepped into the stillness of the hallway, he knew he could relax.

He'd been inside this apartment half a dozen times and the real shock was that it felt no different—he'd seen the computer being taken out, but the bulk of that removals operation had apparently been focused on the surveillance suite. He moved from room to room, an environment he knew intimately, and was surprised by how little was missing.

He knew the surveillance units would be gone, but he replaced a couple of them with new units, one in the smoke alarm in the entrance hall, another overlooking the desk and the bookshelves. It was unlikely anyone would come back here now, but if they did, he wanted to know.

The desk had been stripped of Cheng's computer, notebooks, paperwork, but books had been taken from the shelves and spread out neatly, like a table display in a bookstore, as if there had never been a computer there. Everything else in the apartment appeared untouched—all of Cheng's clothes, his treadmill in the spare room, foodstuffs and the many specialist utensils and pans he'd used to prepare them.

The vegetables and other ingredients for Sunday evening's uneaten dinner were gradually shriveling away on the kitchen counter. Freddie checked the fridge and saw the chicken there, soaking in its marinade, and he wondered if Cheng had put it there or one of the people who'd come for him.

At first glance, it was almost as if Cheng had simply stepped out for a while, to go and buy some ingredient he'd forgotten or to take a walk around the neighborhood. Cheng was more than likely dead, so it was all the more disconcerting that his presence still seemed to inhabit this space more than Freddie inhabited his own.

And as he stood looking at the wasted ingredients, he wondered what he'd hoped to find here. Cheng was gone, and the people who took him wouldn't have left anything that would offer him a clue as to why. That was the important question—what had Freddie seen in this apartment, or what did they think he'd seen?

With that thought in mind, he sat down at the kitchen counter, took out his phone and opened the feed to the camera in his own apartment. His new friend was almost mirroring him, sitting at the island, studying his laptop, occasionally using the trackpad or the keyboard, but in a way that suggested he was killing time rather than engaged in specific work.

Even with that limited view, Freddie's apartment looked bare and characterless compared to the one he was in now. Freddie looked around as he shut the feed off, once again struck by the sense that Cheng's personality, contained and simple as it had been, was all around him here.

Briefly, he wondered why they hadn't emptied this place too, but he thought of the way they'd used books to replace the computer on the desk and saw it immediately. Cheng's existence here couldn't be erased, so they'd make his disappearance part of a narrative. They *wanted* it to look as though he'd just stepped out, because when his body was found, as Freddie was sure it would be, this uncooked meal and everything else in the apartment would be part of the story, part of the mystery.

Freddie was different. He'd been a ghost in this city anyway, and now they had to make it look like he'd never been here, because he was the start of the trail that led back to them, whoever they were. It should have troubled him even more to think of it, yet there was something faintly life-affirming about it, as if he'd been swimming underwater for a long time and had just burst back through the surface. They wanted to kill him, and so desiccated had Freddie's life become, that this felt like an affirmation in itself.

Chapter Twelve

He made his way slowly toward the hotel, his mind running through his limited options. He could have a little talk with the person currently living in his apartment, but if he was CIA, Freddie couldn't imagine much coming of it. He could try to find out what Cheng had been up to, but if Freddie didn't know the answer to that after watching his every move for the best part of a year, he wasn't sure who else might.

Then there were his own contacts from the past, but he was reluctant to explore those channels, even if they were still open to him. And it probably wasn't the wisest move to trust in people who might be linked to the outfit who'd tried to kill him.

Except for one, perhaps—Drew Clarke, their former CIA contact in Sana'a. If he could trust anyone, it was most likely Drew, but even the thought of getting in touch with him made Freddie's heart beat with a sickly rhythm. There were too many bad memories, and they were always too close to the surface. So, contacting Drew would be a fallback position, but if it was at all avoidable, he'd avoid it.

He turned into a narrow, covered arcade that cut between streets, and stopped at a small vegan café where Cheng sometimes ate. It only had space for about a dozen customers, as well as a few extra small tables outside, so Freddie had never eaten in there before for fear that even Cheng might finally recognize him as someone familiar.

There were a couple of women eating at one table, another woman eating on her own, and a young guy in the back corner who was drinking a lurid green juice as he worked at a laptop. A waitress who looked Turkish or Eastern European came out and smiled at Freddie, gesturing for him to take a seat.

He took a quick look at the menu, inevitably imagining what Cheng might have ordered, and went for a fried plantain dish together with a goji berry smoothie.

The waitress smiled in response and said, "You'll enjoy it."

Once she'd left him, he opened up the feed on his phone and looked at what was going on in his apartment. The poor guy had at least left his laptop. He was on the phone, walking around the island in the kitchen, out of shot for a few seconds as he strolled into the living area, then back.

Freddie didn't have the sound on, but looking at the guy's face, the smiles, and the way he was talking, he guessed it was a wife or girlfriend. Or perhaps someone he wanted to be his girlfriend—there were a couple of moments when he smiled a little bashfully. This was a man in love, looking younger even than his fairly youthful years.

Freddie shut off the feed as the waitress came out with his smoothie, but then something occurred to him. As well as being transmitted automatically to the client account, all his feeds on Cheng had gone to Freddie's own cloud account, the same one he was using for this feed from the apartment. The content for each feed was stored for around twenty-four hours before overwriting, but if the people who'd stripped the surveillance suite had shut off the feeds, maybe it hadn't overwritten, and so he still had around a day's footage he could access.

He went back into the account and scrolled back to Sunday morning, and smiled and felt a little sad all at once as he saw Cheng running with his easy composed gait on the treadmill in the spare room. This was a dead man before him, still on the treadmill, oblivious.

But Freddie had the footage, that was the key thing. From around mid-afternoon on Saturday he had a whole day he'd be able to study. And the fact that he was looking at it now meant they didn't know about Freddie's cloud account, although that was hardly surprising—not even Leo had known about it.

It wasn't much to go on, and thinking back over Cheng's final twenty-four hours in the apartment, Freddie couldn't recall anything out of the ordinary, but it would still be worth going over the footage once he was back at the hotel. Even if he didn't find exactly what had brought about this sudden development, there might still be clues, clues he'd missed simply because he hadn't known to look for them.

He shut the phone off and waited for his food, looking out at the people coming and going in the arcade beyond. The food was good when it came, but for some reason he couldn't quite fathom, he became forlorn again as he sat there, and by the time he finished, he couldn't wait to get out of the place.

He continued on his way, a meandering route back to the hotel, passing the slightly esoteric stores common in this little district—one with a window display of tarot cards and paraphernalia, a sex shop, a vinyl record specialist, another selling T-shirts emblazoned with the names of punk and rock bands.

He stopped, retraced his steps to the sex shop, and went inside. There was a girl behind the counter with multicolored spiked hair and wearing a metal bra, a kind of steampunk erotic fantasy. She looked dangerously bored and he almost felt like advising her to apply for a job at the Hotel Madhouse.

Instead, he said, "Hi, I want some handcuffs."

She smiled grudgingly. "Then you've come to the right place."

A couple of minutes later, he was on his way out again, with a surprisingly robust pair of cuffs. And that purchase seemed to focus him a little more and he walked more purposefully now, even though he wouldn't get to use them until the next morning.

When he got back to the hotel, he found the lobby quiet for the first time. He headed directly toward the elevators, but stopped when he heard someone call his name.

"Freddie! Hey!" He turned. It was Eva with the floppy purple Mohawk, behind the desk with Arnold—he was beginning to wonder if Arnold ever slept. "What have you been up to?"

He smiled and walked a few paces closer to the desk. He'd never been in a hotel quite like this one.

"Oh, just had to go and meet someone, then stopped for lunch on the way back. Going up to do some work now."

She pointed at the empty sofas and beanbags, the outsized painted rocking chair.

"You could work down here."

"Maybe not today. I'll need to concentrate."

Arnold nodded agreement and said, "Oh, then it's no good down here—there are just too many distractions."

Eva shrugged, but brightened then. "Can I read your palm?"

"Read my palm?"

"She's very good. She read mine and she got loads of things right."

"But she knows you, Arnold."

"Trust me, she's good."

"No, I'm not, I'm just learning. Can I?"

Freddie nodded, stepped up to the desk, and put his hands out. "Which one?"

"I can do both." She took his hands in hers and closed her eyes, her thumbs moving across his palms. "You have soft hands."

"Is that part of the reading?"

She laughed but didn't answer, and continued to trace her thumbs over the lines on his hands. Apart from Phillips barreling into him the other day and grabbing at his ankle, he couldn't remember the last time anyone had touched him.

"You're very selfless in love."

Freddie was aware of Arnold nodding off to one side, but he kept his eyes on Eva, impressed by how seriously she was taking this. He noticed for the first time that she was attractive, the bone structure of a model, and he felt shallow for having only seen the purple hair and the piercings in her ears.

"Yes. You're very selfless in love. You gave someone up."

He almost pulled his hands free and had to fight the urge. She didn't know anything about him, and maybe she was taking it seriously, but these were the kind of random comments that most people could relate to from some point in their lives.

"Maybe. Can you tell why?"

Her thumbs slid across his palms, the warmth and the pressure strangely comforting. "No. There's no trauma. No bad energy." And Freddie smiled, because he knew for sure now that she was just guessing. "There have been problems, but right now you're in a good place, and it's going to get even better." She opened her eyes and smiled. "How was that?"

"I told you she was good."

Freddie looked at Arnold, then back to Eva, but she looked deflated and said, "I know. I'm still learning. But I could tell that you have lots of good energy. Izzy says I can always tell about people's energy."

"Izzy?"

"My girlfriend. She's really good, not just at palm reading. Isn't she, Arnold?"

"I think you're better."

As they talked, the door slid open and a twenty-something couple came in with carry-on suitcases, although Arnold and Eva didn't seem conscious that the new arrivals might have anything to do with them. It was Freddie who acknowledged their presence first.

"Well, thanks, Eva. I'd better let you check these people in."

She released his hands reluctantly and with a smile, as Arnold said, "Hi, welcome to the Madhouse."

Freddie raised his hand in a wave and made for the elevator. He had a gun in his bag, two days ago he'd garroted someone after smashing his face in with an iron, and yesterday he'd shot someone three times and comforted a dying dog. If she was still picking up good energy after all that, she could probably rule out a career as a fortune teller.

Chapter Thirteen

When Freddie got back to his room, he stood for a minute looking out over the city. The sky had remained uniformly gray all day but it had stayed dry. Now, as the afternoon was drawing to a close, some sun had broken through, casting the grand buildings before him in a golden light.

He'd been living in Vienna for over a year, but so narrow had been the focus of his life that he'd never really noticed what a beautiful city it was. He was seeing it through fresh eyes now, as a tourist might, and he was a little besotted.

Eventually, he moved over to the bed and opened the laptop. He brought up the feed from Cheng's apartment and started to work through it, concentrating particularly on what Cheng had been looking at on his own computer.

It had been one of the trickiest parts of the operation. Freddie had managed to install a keylogger into Cheng's keyboard, so that a record of whatever he'd typed could be sent to the clients, but because of Cheng's background and his expertise, it hadn't been safe to install software onto the machine itself.

Freddie had managed to position a camera inside a light fitting so they could film over Cheng's shoulder to see what he was looking at. It wasn't a perfect image, but it showed the pages he was visiting clearly enough, and the clients would have been able to enhance any particular image that aroused their interest.

The trouble was, as Freddie looked through the footage, he couldn't see anything that might arouse the interest of anyone but Cheng. Lots of things interested Cheng, from news sites to Chinese art and archaeological studies, to business and company reports, to environmental stories and the usual array of tech and mathematical sites.

On first glance and out of context, it was hard to believe anything there might have led them to want the surveillance operative killed. It was possible, of course, that the something he was supposed to have seen might have popped up in the days of footage he no longer had access to. And it was possible it wasn't something on the computer at all, although the rest of Cheng's routine over his final twenty-four hours in the apartment was even more innocuous than his web browsing.

Eventually, Freddie gave up and switched over to the feed from the lone camera unit in his own apartment. The tie had come off and the shirtsleeves were rolled up, and the new resident was sitting at the island eating what looked like some sort of stir-fry. The laptop was still open off to one side, and occasionally he looked over at it and maneuvered the trackpad.

Freddie felt sorry for the guy, being stuck there waiting while the trader and Jimmy Fernandez and the rest of his colleagues were presumably doing their best to track Freddie down. And little did he know that he'd be the first to find out where Freddie was.

The more he thought of it, Freddie couldn't even imagine where the others could be looking for him. Sure, they'd have put a trace on his credit card, but would surely have realized by now that he wasn't using that card anymore. He was confident enough that his tech wouldn't give him away, and if they were planning on exploring past locations and contacts, they'd come up just as short.

For a little while, maybe a week, maybe a month or more, he could be reasonably certain they wouldn't track him down, but that didn't mean he could just disappear and forget about it. If the business surrounding Cheng had been serious enough, they'd keep searching, and no one could stay hidden forever.

It was dark by the time he turned off the computer. He looked out briefly at the light-strewn view in front of him, the grand buildings illuminated by floodlights, then headed down to get some dinner.

The reception desk was empty as he walked past, and once again, the restaurant was heaving. A bald guy with a full beard met him as he walked in.

"Hi. Can I help?"

"I'd like to eat. Table for one."

"You have a reservation?"

"No, but I'm staying in the hotel. Room 520."

According to his name badge, the bearded man was called Marius, and he responded with a facial expression that suggested this couldn't be more difficult.

"520. Can you wait here just one minute? If I can get you in, I'll get you in. As you can see, the restaurant is *really* popular."

Freddie nodded, and Marius disappeared into the melee. When he came back, he was smiling.

"Freddie? Come with me."

Freddie followed him to a single table that was wedged between two groups of six. He ordered and ate amid the combined voices and laughter of a dozen people—and the laughter and voices of all the people beyond—lost in his own little cocoon of silence.

As he was leaving, Marius spotted him and said, "Tomorrow?" Freddie nodded without much sense of what he'd be doing tomorrow, although guessing he'd probably still be alive and would therefore need to eat. "I'll keep you a table."

"Thanks. See you tomorrow."

He walked into reception, passing a few women on the sofas and beanbags, all in high spirits with glasses of white wine. He saw that Eva was alone at the front desk.

He smiled as he made to walk past, but she called over to him. "Sorry about earlier." He changed course, but made clear his confusion. "Arnold doesn't think you enjoyed me reading your palm. He thinks you were just too polite to say no."

"Arnold doesn't know me very well. I've never had my palm read before, and I try to be open to new things, you know. It was interesting."

"Really?"

"Really." He pointed at her badge. "Is your name really Eva?"

"Of course." She smiled crookedly, as if suspecting a trick question.

"It's just, everyone here has such unusual names—Arnold, Marius, Pedro—hipster names, you know?"

"So maybe you could work here too. Freddie." He shrugged, acknowledging she had a point. "What *do* you do?"

"I'm a technology contractor. It's not very interesting, but it's easy, and I enjoy it, I guess." He tried to add up how many lies he'd included in that simple reply.

"I thought it was probably a tech company. Arnold thought you were in advertising."

"Like I said, Arnold doesn't know me very well."

For some reason he couldn't quite figure out, she looked a little bashful, smiling as if embarrassed by a compliment, although he hadn't made one that he knew of.

"You *do* have good energy." Now it was Freddie who smiled, but she was quick to add, "I know you think you don't, but really, you do."

"I'm glad you think so, Eva. Whatever kind of energy it is, I'm taking it upstairs."

"To the bar?"

"Not tonight. Early start."

"Okay. Good night, Freddie."

"Good night, Eva."

He walked over to the elevators, but as the door to one cabin opened, the three women who'd been drinking white wine in the seating area came trotting over and joined him. They all had long blonde hair and were dressed more for high-end clubbing than the hipster vibe of the Madhouse.

"Which floor?"

"To the top," said one of them and pointed upward, in case he didn't get it. Freddie pressed for the fifth and seventh floors.

A second said, "Yeah! Take us to the top, baby." Their glasses were still half full, and they didn't seem particularly drunk.

But when the elevator stopped on the fifth, the one who hadn't spoken tried to leave, and Freddie tapped her on the shoulder and said, "This is me. You're the next stop."

She turned and looked disappointed. "Aren't you coming too?"

"Not tonight."

Maybe they were drunk after all. They waved and called goodbye as the doors closed. He wouldn't have joined them any night, but particularly not when he had to be up early, to confront an armed man, to take him prisoner and interrogate him and find out why they wanted him dead.

Chapter Fourteen

Freddie had liked the fact that his apartment building, the street in which it sat, and the streets beyond were all devoid of much in the way of local community. He'd rarely seen most of his neighbors, but he now realized that this was because he hadn't generally been up and about before seven in the morning.

Having earned two or three guarded greetings from some of those former neighbors, people who naturally didn't recognize him, he checked his phone and headed outside to walk once more around the block. It was good to be in the cool air anyway, and under the pale gray sky—a chance to clear his head.

He'd slept badly again, and though he didn't remember his dreams he was certain of what had been in them. In the shower, closing his eyes to let the water run over his face, he'd seen Mel, the way she'd looked at him that day, the look of distilled terror in the fleeting seconds after Pete and Talal had been shot. He'd seen it exactly as it had been, the plea in her eyes, desperate for him to do something, and he had not been able to shake that memory in the hour since his shower, nor the feeling of faint nausea and self-loathing that came with it.

He was a hundred yards from the building when he checked his phone again and saw that the feed had kicked into life and the guy was just heading into the bathroom. Freddie turned, walking casually so as not to draw attention, but once inside he ran up the stairs, taking two or three at a time, and then as he caught his breath again at the top, he looked at the feed once more.

The bathroom door was still closed, but conscious of how easily he could mess this up, Freddie went back through the footage, making sure the guy hadn't already come out. And only once he was confident and his breathing had settled did he take the gun from the messenger bag and slip the key into the lock.

He smiled as the door eased open, because he hadn't been mistaken, and could hear the shower running and some indistinct tune—the poor guy was actually singing, something unfamiliar but upbeat. He deserved credit for remaining in high spirits after what had effectively been two days of solitary confinement.

But as Freddie moved into position against one of the kitchen counters, he wondered what his own years of near solitary confinement had done for him. It was perhaps why he'd enjoyed talking to Eva and Arnold so much, because it meant nothing, and yet his life had been devoid of such conversation for as long as he could remember. Or since Yemen, anyway.

He took the handcuffs and the spare magazine and slipped them into his pockets, then lowered the messenger bag to the floor and checked the gun's safety was off. The guy would come out facing him, and there was a risk he'd try to duck back into the bathroom, or that he'd rush him, so Freddie had to be ready to shoot if necessary. Not that he wanted to shoot anyone else, and nor was he confident of hitting the guy with a non-lethal round—he guessed if it came to it, he'd aim for the legs and hope for the best.

The water was turned off, although after a brief hiatus the singing continued, occasionally punctuated or muffled as the guy dried himself.

Freddie felt his nerves building in those couple of minutes, then more so as he heard the snap of an elastic waistband as the guy put on his boxer shorts, then a clunk against the door as he took down his shoulder holster from the hook.

And then there was no time left for nerves because the door swung open and the guy stepped out as if he had somewhere to go and was in a hurry. He was wearing plain white boxers and carrying the shoulder holster, but he saw Freddie and reacted quickly, reaching with the other hand to pull the gun free.

Freddie responded by taking a step toward him, letting him see his own gun.

"Keep still or I'll kill you." There was a flicker of hesitation in response. "I don't wanna kill you. So don't make me. Put the gun on the island there."

Freddie could see how quickly the man's mind was working, and could see that he was judging it right and would come to the correct conclusion. It still took a second or two, and he stood there, taut and threatening, before meeting Freddie's eyes and nodding in defeat.

"On the island."

The guy nodded again and reached out to place the shoulder holster on the kitchen island close to where his laptop still sat, and without it he looked naked, like he didn't know what to do with his hands. Freddie guessed he was in his late twenties, with a physique that suggested he'd trained in the past but had let things slip—he was turning soft at the edges. Freddie knew that feeling.

"You know who I am?" He nodded. The kitchen island had four metal legs on the corners, each bolted into the floor. Freddie pointed and said, "Sit down against the corner of the island there."

The guy couldn't stop himself from glancing at his gun where it lay almost within range, but again, he made the right call in deciding whether or not to reach for it—if it hadn't been holstered, it might have been worth it. Instead, he lowered himself down to the floor and looked up expectantly.

Freddie took the cuffs out of his pocket and threw them to him. The guy didn't catch them, but they landed in his lap and he flinched.

"Cuff yourself to the metal leg."

The guy looked down, only now realizing they *were* handcuffs. He picked them up and when he looked back at Freddie, he had an expression that suggested he thought he was being mocked.

"Are you serious?"

The cuffs were covered in pink fur.

"I'm sure the CIA knows exactly where the local handcuff emporium is, but I'm a civilian—I wouldn't even begin to know where to look. So yeah, they're from an adult store, but they're robust, and I guess they'll also be a little more comfortable. Now, cuff yourself to the island."

Freddie waved the gun at him, and with a shake of the head, the guy clicked one cuff into place around his wrist, then the other around the metal leg. Freddie moved behind him, put the barrel of the silencer into the back of his neck, and checked that both cuffs were secure.

He stepped away then and said, "What's your name?"

"Bennett. James."

Something about the emphasis threw Freddie momentarily.

"Which of those is your first name?"

"Bennett."

In Freddie's experience, people in their line of work tended to keep aliases simple and dull, so Bennett James probably was his real name. Not that it mattered either way to Freddie: he just wanted a name to call him by.

"Okay, Bennett, I'm just gonna take a look around, and then we'll have a talk." He made as if to walk away, but stopped himself with the appearance of an afterthought, and picked up the shoulder holster off the island. "Let's keep this out of temptation's way."

He glanced into the bathroom, then went into the bedroom, which was orderly, the bed made, no clothes lying around, just a cellphone on the bedside cabinet. Freddie slipped the gun out of the holster, smiling when he saw that it was an M9, as he'd hoped. He swapped the magazine for the spare, covering the noise by calling out, "Is this the only phone you have?"

"Cellphone and laptop, that's the only tech I've got with me." The reply covered the second part of the operation, and Freddie slipped the gun back into the holster and tossed it onto the bed—as long as Bennett James didn't have reason to fire his gun a lot in the next few days, the tracker would tell Freddie where he was.

He walked back out, crossed to where he'd left his messenger bag, and slid down onto the floor next to it, so that he was at the same level as his prisoner.

"So, Bennett, what's going on? Why did one of your colleagues try to kill me the other day?"

"You came home early, that's why. You disturbed him. We wanted to make sure you had nothing compromising, that's all."

Freddie shook his head. "No, I don't buy that. You'd have killed me in the surveillance suite if I hadn't come home. What have you done with Jiang Cheng?"

"Why would you even care?" Bennett quickly seemed to sense that was the wrong response. "Look, I don't know. And you must know I wouldn't tell you even if I did, but truthfully, I don't even know what this operation's about."

Freddie thought back to the exchange between Bennett and his boss and reckoned there was a good chance he was being straight, but Freddie still gave him a skeptical look and that elicited another protestation.

"Look, they left me to watch this place; that should tell you how junior I am. They didn't even expect you to come back. They're looking all over Europe for you."

"Why?" That earned a dejected lowering of the head from Bennett. "Who's your boss? Who are you working for?"

"You really are a civilian, aren't you? You're sitting there with a gun, but you've got me trussed up with a sex toy and now you're asking me who I work for. Surely you've been around enough intelligence people in the past to know I'm never gonna tell you that."

"It's not a sex toy. It's an accessory."

"What?"

"Tell me about me. What do you know about my past?"

Bennett looked unyielding again.

Freddie stared down at the gun in his hand, then casually placed it on the floor next to him. "What's that old saying? Might as well be hung for a sheep as a lamb. I killed your colleague the other day. Didn't mean to, didn't want to, never killed anyone before." He didn't mention the other man at Leo's house and wondered if they'd even connect that to him. "You ever killed anyone, Bennett?"

Bennett looked bewildered, as if he feared Freddie might be crazy.

"No. No, I haven't."

"No. But . . . I don't think the police are likely to get involved with the death of your colleague. And the same would apply if I were to kill you. Sure, your colleagues in the CIA—I'm assuming you're CIA, and you haven't denied it—they'd come after me, but it looks like they're coming after me anyway. So I have a free pass to kill you or just shoot you up a bit if I want to. Now, I don't expect you to break whatever special oath you people have, but I do expect you to tell me something. So tell me about me. Or I'll start by shooting you in the ankle and work my way up from there."

Freddie reached for the gun, but before his hand even got there, Bennett cleared his throat.

"What is there to tell? For the last five years you've been a surveillance contractor for Leo Behnke. For the last year you've been working
on a contract for us."

That confirmed one thing—it had been their contract.

"Why didn't you do it in-house?"

For a moment the shutters came down again, before Bennett
seemed to see a way of answering.

"We contract out all the time, different services depending on the
job, and frankly, it's above my paygrade to know why this one was given
to Behnke."

"Back to me. What else?"

Bennett shook his head, the look of someone who thought this was
a waste of time, rather than a man fearing he was being forced to give
away vital secrets.

"Between college and working for Behnke, you worked for
Evanston Electronics, usually seconded to aid agencies, setting up communications systems in the field. You may not have known it, but you
also worked for us on occasion, and for other intelligence agencies."
He looked smug as he delivered that piece of news, and when Freddie
looked slightly taken aback, it emboldened Bennett to take one more
step. "You left because something went wrong in Yemen. Two of your
colleagues were killed in a helicopter crash. You were meant to be in the
chopper too, but you took ill, missed the trip. Left you in a bit of a mess
apparently, broke off your engagement, became a bit of a nomad." He'd
almost been gloating, but as he mentioned the engagement, he seemed
to sense that he'd gone too far and said, "Sorry, I didn't mean to bring
up your personal stuff, but you did ask."

Freddie nodded sadly, thinking of Chloe, and how she'd become
part of an intelligence report. He was also thinking that even if they were
CIA, they still didn't know the full truth about him or about Evanston
Electronics, or even about that incident—the supposed helicopter crash

had been the cover story, the kind of thing that had hardly made the news in a place like Yemen at the time.

"Three colleagues."

"What's that?"

"Three colleagues. Our interpreter, Talal. He was a local, which is probably why you don't count him, and I'm not judging you for that—how could I? But he was our friend and our colleague, and he was twenty-two years old and had just become a father."

"I'm sorry, I'm just going on what was in the report."

"Can I ask you a straight question, Bennett?" He looked curious and Freddie said, "What's likely to happen to me? I mean, seriously, just . . . how do you see this playing out?"

Bennett sighed and shook his head.

"Seriously? You'll remain a target, no matter what you do now. You could try to disappear, but sooner or later you'll make a mistake. And if you go public with what you know, that'll just accelerate the process."

"I don't *know* anything." Bennett didn't answer. "So you're saying I'm a dead man?"

"I'm sorry."

"I don't get it. I think back over this last year, and I just don't get it. What was I watching? What was it you were hoping I would find?"

"I told you, I don't know!" He was angry, but perhaps more because he'd been kept out of the loop than because Freddie had asked about it again. "I probably know less about Seahorse than you do. I know he's a Chinese national, that he teaches some genius IT course—you know, the kind of academic we like—but that's the extent of my expertise. I don't have the first idea what any of this is about. If I did, they wouldn't have left me waiting here for you—no offense."

"None taken. I guess Seahorse is your code name for Cheng?" Bennett looked momentarily concerned by his own slip, but Freddie made a show of seeing no significance in it. "And I guess I shouldn't have taken this job. What would you do now, if you were me?"

"I wish I could offer you something, but in truth, I wouldn't wanna be you. There's no way of this ending well for you."

"Sorry I asked. But I don't want you worrying about me. Whatever happens, it *will* end well."

He picked up the gun and jumped to his feet, ignoring Bennett's flinching reaction. Then he reached down and picked up the messenger bag, slipping the gun inside, a move that made Bennett visibly relax.

"What will you do?"

"Well, Bennett, you told me I need to disappear, so I guess that's what I'll have to do. But I'm not so stupid as to tell you where I'm going. Who knows, maybe I'll stay here in Vienna."

He took the key for the cuffs and put it on the island, out of reach. He went into the bedroom then and brought the cellphone and placed that on the island too, just within reach.

"Okay. I'm sorry about your friend." Bennett looked confused. "Your colleague, the one I killed. It's weird, but I haven't been able to process it properly, you know, take on board that I killed somebody. Doesn't seem real. And yet I guess he was a decent man, probably had a family."

"I don't know. I didn't know him that well. But he was one of us, and we look out for our own."

"That's nice. I like that. I'll say goodbye."

As Freddie headed for the door, Bennett raised his voice. "What, you're just gonna leave me like this?"

"The key's on the island." He turned back, walked over to the drawer and took out a teaspoon, dropping it onto the floor between Bennett's legs. It bounced with a little percussion on the tiles.

"What am I meant to do with that?"

"I don't know. You're in intelligence—consider it an aptitude test." He pointed at the island's countertop. "Or you could probably reach your phone with a bit of effort. You could call your colleagues and have them come and release you."

Bennett couldn't stop himself glancing down at the pink fluffy handcuffs, and Freddie could tell from that look alone that he'd gnaw his own hand off before he'd submit to being found like that by his colleagues.

Chapter Fifteen

Freddie hadn't expected Bennett, as he now knew him, to give away any key information about Cheng or what this last year's surveillance operation had been about. He'd wanted to find out how serious the threat to his own safety might be, but even that had come more as confirmation than revelation. He'd also wanted to reinforce in their minds that he was a civilian, and he'd managed that well enough.

But as it happened, Bennett had given away one vital nugget of information, because he'd called Cheng by a code name, Seahorse, and they only gave code names to assets, not targets. It didn't tell Freddie any more about what they'd been looking for, or what had precipitated the events of the last few days, but it told him that Cheng had been working for the CIA.

He thought about it as he ate breakfast back at the hotel. If Cheng had been a CIA asset, then maybe Drew Clarke would be able to help after all. Whether he'd be able to help enough to get the target off Freddie's back was another thing.

Once he'd eaten, he went up to his room, passing through the lobby which was crowded with a whole group of indistinct-looking people waiting to check out. It was only as the elevator doors were closing and one of the group turned and looked at him that he realized they were the superheroes he'd seen on his arrival at the hotel the other night, reduced back to their civilian clothes.

It was well over an hour since he'd left Bennett, and when he opened the feed he saw him standing there, fully dressed, looking at his laptop as he talked on the phone. It was clear he was being admonished, and when he ended the call he looked for a moment as though he might throw the phone across the room.

Instead, he slipped it into his pocket and disappeared into the bedroom. While he was gone, Freddie studied the view of the kitchen. Apart from the laptop, he could see the handcuffs and a white cloth of some sort on the central island. He brought up the tracker, and smiled when it pinged and gave him the location of the gun inside his own apartment.

A few minutes later, Bennett came back out of the bedroom with his small suitcase. He closed up the laptop and slipped it into the pouch on the front of the case. Then he wrapped the cuffs in the white cloth and took the bundle with him as he left, although Freddie had little doubt he'd dump it before he got to wherever he was going.

Freddie switched over to the archive to see how Bennett had escaped. Sure enough, he'd spent a while fumbling with the teaspoon, trying to use it as a lever to break the chain linking the cuffs. When that didn't work he tried brute force, pulling his hands in a movement that was painful even to observe.

Finally, he came up with the solution, one that also explained the white cloth. Bennett had slipped off his boxer shorts, tearing them to make a longish cotton rope which he used to fish for the key, getting it within a dozen or so attempts.

As Freddie watched him unlock the cuffs, he expected him to reach immediately for his phone, but he didn't. With a touching display of puritanical decorum, he went into the bedroom and came out wearing another pair of boxer shorts, but then he moved slowly around the room, looking up at the light fittings, the sockets, fleetingly looking at the camera but without seeing it. He disappeared into both bathroom and bedroom then and was missing for as long, presumably, as it took him to repeat the search.

Bennett had obviously come to the conclusion that Freddie had been watching him. Freddie had been careful not to reveal any information that he'd picked up from the camera, but the very fact that he'd turned up while Bennett was in the shower suggested either inside information or a piece of spectacularly lucky timing.

So Bennett's instincts were right, but as Freddie finished going through the archive, he noted with a little pride that the search had proved fruitless. He switched back to the empty apartment as it was now, then to the tracker—wherever Bennett James was going, he was probably getting there by train because he was now at the Hauptbahnhof.

Freddie checked the time, unsure what to do with himself. Seeing the date, and realizing that it was Wednesday, he felt even more adrift at the thought of his weekly afternoon spent in the Café Griensteidl as Cheng and Marina Mikhailova played chess.

He wondered if she knew about Cheng's disappearance, and he wondered too if she'd known anything about him. Those weekly conversations had been transmitted by Freddie blind, because it was their tradition that Mikhailova spoke to Cheng in Mandarin and he spoke to her in Russian. It probably wasn't much of a lead, but he really didn't have much else either, so maybe he'd go along to the café as usual, in the hope she'd turn up.

He had some work to do first though. He did some searching and found that Drew Clarke was now stationed at the American Embassy in Athens. It was frustratingly close and yet too far, given that flying was out of the question, even with a different ID and passport. Freddie had no choice but to revert to his old tricks and make Drew come to him.

He thought through the possible scenarios that might make Drew come to Vienna, then hit upon it and smiled to himself as he went to an old ghost email account he'd opened years ago for Khaled Qabbani.

He started to type, surprised at how easily he fell back into writing in Qabbani's florid English. According to the email, Qabbani had some nasty little files pertaining to past mutual acquaintances that he was sure his esteemed friend would like to see. If he was interested, he should meet with Qabbani in Vienna on Friday morning at eleven . . .

Freddie thought about the location—the kind of place that might appeal to the real Qabbani, but the kind of place that would equally pique Drew's interest. He raised his eyes and looked out through the wall of glass and saw it there before him.

Qabbani would be in front of Bruegel's *The Hunters in the Snow* in the Kunsthistorisches Museum at eleven on Friday. He hit send, and within half an hour he'd had a reply from Drew, asking which former acquaintances he might be talking about and what he wanted in exchange.

Freddie wrote back. *Are we not gentlemen? If you wish not to meet, esteemed one, yours is not the only bazaar in town.*

He laughed a little, not least because he could imagine Drew laughing at that phrase, but it worked anyway, and Drew responded immediately to say he'd be there.

Freddie nodded to himself, satisfied, and shut the laptop down, left a little mournful by that brief reminder of a former life. But it was a reminder in more ways than one, because for all those years he'd been doing little more than playing games, and eventually the game had turned against him.

His mind skidded back involuntarily to the back seat of that SUV, to Abdullah pointing the gun at Freddie's face, mimicking a shot and mocking him with a "Pow!"—the word muffled by the scarf that covered his mouth. He remembered Abdullah tossing the gun into the car then, into the well in front of Pete's blood-spattered body, and he remembered the way he'd jumped at the clatter it made as it landed, and he remembered Abdullah's eyes on his and an expression Freddie had been trying to decipher for five years.

Pow! That was why he did this and why he'd left that former life behind, because it had been a game, and he'd lost.

Chapter Sixteen

If it hadn't been for his weekly visits to the Café Griensteidl, Freddie might have forgotten that Vienna was a tourist city. In following Cheng's routine, he'd seen tourists, but never in great numbers, and it always surprised him anew when he saw all those people around the Hofburg and then the horses and carriages in Michaelerplatz, and the tour groups.

The café was full, the usual mix of locals and visitors, but one of the waiters spotted Freddie as he walked in and immediately gestured to his little table, the reserved sign sitting on it. As he sat down, he noticed the reserved sign was also in place on the neighboring table together with the chessboard, which he hoped was a sign that she might still be coming, that she didn't know about Cheng being missing.

He ordered coffee and cake, but was conscious of having no book with him today, so he left the cake untouched for now. Instead, he went onto his phone and checked the tracker. Looking at the direction of travel, unless he was mistaken, Bennett James was headed for Prague.

He'd never been to Prague, but had always wanted to see it. Idly, he thought about going up there to check it out, before reminding himself that his job in the coming days was to stay away from Bennett and his colleagues, not pursue them. He wanted to see Prague someday, but he didn't want it to be the last place he saw.

Both Cheng and Marina Mikhailova usually showed up just after two, so on the hour, Freddie started to eat his cake. Despite the constant background chatter and noise, he heard the door open and saw Mikhailova come in, then saw one of the waiters stop what he was doing and glide over to her.

He could understand why. She was in her sixties, he guessed, but still attractive, an imperious quality that demanded attention. She shrugged her coat off her shoulders, allowing the waiter to take it from her and hang it up, then sat down diagonally across from Freddie.

He looked up from his cake and gave an acknowledging smile, which she returned. He turned away again, and continued to eat while she ordered and then set up the board ready to play. With every piece she placed, he had to fight the urge to tell her it was pointless, that Cheng wouldn't be coming.

Once she'd finished she looked to the door, then took out her phone and checked it, presumably to see if Cheng had sent a message. She frowned, and after a moment's hesitation, she called a number and held the phone to her ear. The frown intensified as she ended the call without success. So she didn't know he was missing.

Freddie finished his cake as a waiter placed her tall glass of tea next to the chessboard. The same waiter whisked away his empty plate and Freddie glanced across then, and checked the time.

"Your friend's running late."

Mikhailova turned and looked at him with a mix of playfulness and mock outrage, as if she couldn't begin to think why he'd taken it upon himself to speak to her when they'd never been formally introduced.

"So it would seem." She looked down at Freddie's table and, as if accepting that the dam of formality had been breached, she said, "And it seems you have forgotten to bring a book."

He nodded, but he'd already prepared for that observation. "I occasionally suffer from ocular migraines. I had one this morning, so . . . reading can be a challenge afterwards."

"I'm sure it can." She smiled, and he saw now that the air of formality was an act, or perhaps just a paper-thin façade that came with being a professor. "I'm always intrigued to see what you're reading. You have rather existential tastes, with odd little forays into eccentricity."

"Well, that's me on a plate." She laughed, and he held out his hand. "It's funny, we've seen each other so often without ever speaking. My name's Freddie."

She leaned over, her handshake slightly limp and detached, as if she were more used to having her hand kissed than shaken, although he guessed that too was probably an act.

"Marina. Marina Mikhailova. And my friend is called Cheng, Jiang Cheng."

I know, he wanted to tell her. *I know everything about Jiang Cheng except what happened to him and why.*

"Then I'm Freddie Robbins."

"And perhaps there's a positive to Cheng being late, in that it's allowed us to finally meet."

She glanced at her watch.

"I've always been impressed by the way you both maintain a conversation, your friend speaking Russian, you speaking Chinese."

"Mandarin, to be precise."

"Oh, sorry, I didn't—"

"Don't worry, most people don't know the difference. Are you Freddie or Mr. Robbins?"

"I prefer Freddie."

"Good, as I prefer Marina, although my students will insist on calling me Professor Mikhailova. That's the reason for the combined language lesson too. I teach Asian History at the university, so it's a nice way of keeping in practice."

"And Chang? Cheng?"

"Cheng. He's just a rather frightening polymath. He learned Russian for fun, and he's very good." She checked her watch again.

"Well, I can't think what might have gone wrong, but it does look like he isn't coming. Do you play chess?"

"Not since I was a boy."

She smiled, and gestured for him to join her.

He shrugged and moved across, but said, "I'm not likely to offer up much of a challenge, and I don't speak Russian."

She was playing white and moved a pawn as she said, "You have me at a disadvantage, Freddie. You know what I do, but I don't know what you do that allows you to spend every Wednesday afternoon reading books in cafés."

He moved one of his own pawns. "Not just Wednesday afternoons. I'm a technology contractor. I go in and sort out high-level problems for businesses, usually after office hours, which is why I'm free during the day."

She stopped mid-move and smiled. "Then it's a shame Cheng isn't here—the two of you will probably get on splendidly."

"How so?"

"He's a professor at the technical university, computer science of some sort, although I understand all of that about as much as you understand Russian." For the third time, she checked her watch, and he could see that she was concerned. "This really isn't like him at all."

"Has he been unwell, or had problems with work that might have held him up?"

"You don't know Cheng. His entire universe is wonderfully ordered."

Freddie nodded, unsure how to respond directly to that. "How do you know each other?" She gave him a mocking look, suggesting the question might be intrusive, but he sensed again that she was simply teasing him. "I mean, you teach very different subjects, and presumably you're at different universities."

"Yes, that's true. An academic mixer between the two universities, a rather foolish attempt to bridge the two cultures of science and the humanities. Although perhaps it worked in this case. As you see, we do have some shared interests."

They'd each moved a few more pieces as they talked, but looking down at the board, Freddie already sensed he was slowly being hemmed in, and worse, he couldn't quite see how she was doing it or where she'd strike. Reluctantly, he moved a knight into what he hoped was an advantageous position.

"You'll think it fanciful, but I imagined you were both spies."

She laughed a little but said, "Not that fanciful. Many academics are involved in that world, although I suspect they'd have more interest in Cheng than they would in me."

"Why?"

She'd been about to move a pawn forward, but stopped and smiled, humoring him. "I can't imagine Asian History being a particularly hot topic for most spymasters, given that it's all in the past, although of course, they might learn some valuable lessons if they did study history a little more. No, what they want are computer wizards. Cheng's being approached all the time."

"But he's never accepted?"

"Not as far as I know. He's the sort of person who only does things he's interested in, so he'd have nothing to gain from working for governments. I just don't think it's his style."

Freddie knew that couldn't be true, but if her assessment of Cheng's character was right, it suggested something specific had lured him in.

"Well, I only thought you were spies because, you know, meeting here to play chess, you speaking Mandarin, him speaking Russian, and you always look so serious in the way you talk to each other."

"Do we?" She laughed. "Usually we're just letting off steam about departmental politics in our respective institutions, although we do sometimes discuss the news or art, or various things that interest us both. Perhaps we only look serious because we're concentrating. And clearly you read too many novels."

She finally moved the pawn, and in so doing, the noose seemed to tighten in some indistinct way. He studied the grim topography of the board as it now stood, then looked at her.

"I've already lost, haven't I?"

She looked down at the pieces herself, then back at him.

"Yes, I think so, but that doesn't mean the game is over. One can learn more on the way to an inevitable defeat than from a fortuitous victory."

"Okay." He looked down again at the opposing armies, no longer hoping to win, but merely to thwart her.

He moved a bishop into a protective position and she smiled.

"Good. That's much better. See?" She let her eyes drift over her own pieces and said casually, "It's intriguing that you thought we were spies, because I was rather suspicious of you for a while."

"That's a first. What, you thought I was a spy?"

She shrugged in response to his bemused tone. "Not a spy as such. A silly word, if you think about it. I did wonder if you were watching Cheng, perhaps for some industrial concern rather than a government. And yes, saying it out loud makes it sound ever sillier, but I remember a few weeks after you first showed up, I spoke about you to Cheng while we were playing chess."

Freddie raised his eyebrows. "While I was here?"

"Of course! I wanted to know if you understood Mandarin or Russian, so I raised my suspicions, and Cheng, who hadn't even noticed you up until that point, just told me that he couldn't imagine you having any reason to follow him at all. You can ask him when you meet— I'm sure he'll remember the conversation. And of course, you remained oblivious, because you *don't* speak Russian or Mandarin and you *weren't* watching him."

Freddie made a show of looking astonished, but he knew that the recording of that conversation over the chessboard would have gone back to people who did speak those languages, that Bennett James's colleagues would have known more than Freddie could have done about how close he'd come to being rumbled.

He managed to extend the game by another ten minutes before Marina finally declared checkmate. He nodded in response and she smiled.

"As it happens, once you knew you'd lost you played pretty well."

"Thanks."

"Another game?"

"Why not?"

They started to set the pieces again.

"Of course, Cheng has nothing to fear."

"I can believe that. Who usually wins out of the two of you?"

"You mean you've never noticed, kept a tally?"

She was playing with him again, but she'd have been genuinely surprised if she knew what he'd really been doing there, because for all his observations, he'd never paid attention to the way the chess games had concluded.

"I might have done if your conversation had been subtitled."

"I don't think that would have helped. The game itself rarely figures in our conversations. But I'd say we're about evenly split. I win a few more than him, but he has so many other skills. Chess is a dalliance for Cheng, whereas it's been a bit of a passion for me. In the past, anyway." They'd finished setting up the board and she reached for a pawn for the first move. "Now, concentrate."

He did, but he still lost.

They left together, and as they stood briefly outside, Freddie said, "Well, thank you, that was really enjoyable, and the last traces of my migraine have gone."

"I'm so glad, and yes, it was fun. Perhaps I'll see you next week. I can introduce you to Cheng."

"I'd like that. Take care, Marina."

She nodded and turned on her heel, heading off in the general direction of the university. Freddie left too, taking a slightly circuitous route back to the hotel, and as he walked, he was simultaneously intrigued and disappointed and saddened.

Marina had told him nothing that might explain Freddie's current situation. But what little she had said only served to portray Cheng as even more of an enigma—a man who'd learned Russian on a whim, who'd had no interest in working for governments, but who'd still managed to acquire a CIA code name. And of course, she'd talked about that puzzle of a man as if he were still alive, while Freddie was pretty certain he was already dead.

Chapter Seventeen

Back at the Madhouse, two guys were sitting on the big rocking chair, one with a guitar, one tapping on a drum. The one with the guitar was singing a reedy ballad Freddie didn't recognize. Enough people were watching them for Freddie to assume it was a planned event, but it was hard to be sure.

Across the lobby, Eva was checking in an Asian couple who were wearing identical outfits in what Freddie thought of as a broadly rockabilly chic. She didn't see Freddie as he slipped into the elevator and headed up to his room.

When he got there, he opened the tracker on his laptop, smiling at the confirmation of his earlier thought, that Bennett had gone to Prague. He used Google Maps to bring up the location and look at it from the street—a fairly anonymous office building in a part of the city that looked busy but not overly touristy.

He spent half an hour searching for details on who'd let the office, and when he finally got there he wondered why he'd bothered. For the last eighteen months it had been rented by a company called Marine Finance AG, based in Liechtenstein. A little more searching revealed what he'd also already expected, that Marine Finance AG wasn't a company that seemed to be openly engaged in very much business—none that was tangible anyway, apart from renting Prague office suites and, no doubt, employing the services of Behnke & Co.

As he sat there, he sensed the sky growing lighter beyond the windows, and looked up to see that once again the sun had emerged late to bathe the buildings before him in a golden light. That was enough to encourage him to shut the laptop down and head up to the rooftop bar.

There was no music on yet, and most of the low tables seemed to be occupied by people working on laptops, using it as an informal office. He ordered a gin and tonic and looked around—it would be pretty hard to sit inside even if he wanted to, but he'd come up here for the view anyway.

He headed out onto the narrow terrace that surrounded the bar on two sides. There were quite a few people here too, sitting looking over the gold-tinged buildings of the inner city.

Then he noticed Eva sitting on her own at the far end, smoking and drinking coffee. He was about to turn the other way, but she seemed to sense his presence and looked right at him and waved.

He waved back and headed over to her.

"Hey, Freddie! How's it going? I saw you sneaking past earlier, when I was checking in the Koreans."

"I wasn't sneaking past. Can I join you, or would you rather be on your own? Is it even allowed for me to join you?"

She responded to the final question with a confused expression, making clear it wasn't that kind of hotel, then gestured to the seat next to her.

"You don't mind me smoking? I'm on my break."

"Not at all. If you don't mind me drinking."

As he sat down, she said, "So what have you been up to—seeing the city, or working?"

"Oh, nothing interesting." He looked out at the view, then turned back to her. "So, do you always come up here for your breaks?"

"Not always. I'm trying not to smoke—Izzy says I should give up— and if I come up here I always feel like smoking, so I try not to. But I like coming up here because it gives me a chance to think. So I'm torn, you know?" He nodded. "Do you smoke, Freddie?"

"No. I was a little bit asthmatic as a kid—not bad, but enough to put me off the idea."

She'd been about to lift the hand-rolled cigarette back to her mouth, but hesitated. "Does it bother you, the smoke?"

"No, not at all." He smiled, thinking that in some way she was one of the sweetest people he'd met in a long time, and that it was probably best not to get too friendly with her, not now. Even so, he said, "What is it that you like to think about when you're up here, or is that too personal?"

She shook her head, curious, almost disbelieving. "You really want to know?"

"Of course, why wouldn't I?"

"Because you're like a successful tech person and I just work in a hotel. You know, normally, if guests show an interest it's only ever because they think they can hit on me."

"You think I'm hitting on you?"

"No!" She looked alarmed. "No, I didn't mean that, I mean . . ."

"Relax, I'm kidding."

"Oh." She shook her head. "Not that it happens all the time or anything."

"I don't see why—you're a beautiful woman."

"So you *are* hitting on me."

He laughed and sipped at his drink, then said, "So are you gonna tell me or not?"

She shrugged theatrically. "Now I've built it up too much. I don't think about anything important. I'm an artist. I finished art school last year, so I think about whether I'll ever make it, you know, ever get my work recognized. I mean, I love working here, but I don't want this to be all I ever amount to."

"What you do is never what you amount to."

"I know. I know you're right. And I'm not saying there's anything wrong with working here, it's just . . ."

"You don't want to be doing it when you're fifty."

"Exactly!" She finished the cigarette then looked out across the city. "I want to look back on these as happy times, but for that to be possible, I need to be looking back from somewhere else. Does that make sense?"

"It does. And I wish you luck."

It was an empty phrase, devoid of any real meaning or emotional heft, and yet she looked touched and said, "Thanks, Freddie, that means a lot." She finished her coffee. "I should go. I don't like to leave Arnold too long—you know how he is."

Freddie nodded, although he really didn't know how Arnold was, or what she meant by it, and once she'd left, he leaned back with his drink and looked out as the orange glow slowly faded on the buildings and darkness seeped into the city. Then he ordered a second drink from one of the bar staff who came out to turn on the heaters that were spaced along the terrace.

It was ridiculous to dwell on the conversation with Eva, because she was just a young recent graduate, the future still to be mapped out ahead of her, a young woman beset by the same doubts and insecurities he imagined most people had when it was all still to play for. He dwelt on it all the same.

He didn't need to give much thought to what his own life amounted to, because it didn't amount to anything. That had almost been the point these last five years, a conscious attempt to remove himself from the world, successfully too, until the world had come calling again in the shape of a man called Phillips.

Instead, he was dwelling on what she'd said about looking back on these as happy times, but only if she were looking back from a different place. But life was more complicated than that, and some of the happiest memories he had were now the worst to recall.

Chapter Eighteen

Freddie ordered food in the bar, because he didn't want to bump into Eva again on the way to the restaurant. And then he moved inside and drank more, sitting in a darkened corner, watching as the bar filled and the music started to pulse.

He'd been thinking too much about Yemen this evening and was hopeful that drink would protect him from the almost inevitable dreams. He could feel his head cloudy and numb with it by the time he headed back down to his room.

Pulling off his clothes, he crashed onto the bed, forgetting to draw the blinds. And the alcohol did indeed hold the dreams at bay, but he wasn't used to drinking that much anymore and woke with a feeling of intense pressure on the inside of his skull, as though his brain had expanded in the night.

Rolling onto his back, he stared at the windows, puzzling for a moment over why the glass wall looked a uniform gray. It was just after ten, so he'd slept, although he didn't feel rested or particularly lucid.

He sat up with a struggle and understood now that there was a dense fog clinging to the city. He loved fog—difficult from a surveillance point of view, but he loved it all the same, perhaps for that very reason, because it hid the world away.

Even so, he was struggling to muster much enthusiasm for the day and wasn't sure what he planned to do with it, or with all the subsequent days. Right now, the fact that a CIA team wanted him dead was just about his only reason for existing.

He stood, sat down again, resentful at the lack of room service, then forced himself up once more. In quick succession, in fear of losing his already faltering momentum, he took painkillers, drank a couple of pints of water, and made himself coffee.

While the coffee cooled a little, he walked over and looked down where the ground was just visible below and he could see shadowy, heavily clothed figures milling about outside the lobby. He would need to buy more clothes, including a winter coat.

He walked back across to where the laptop sat on the desk and opened it up, his eyes smarting against the brightness of the screen. And then he felt sharply sober as he realized the feed in Cheng's apartment had pinged last night and that, understandably, he'd missed it. It seemed impossible, but could it be that Cheng hadn't been killed, and that he'd come back?

Freddie clicked on it, then went over and fetched his coffee. He smiled to himself, remembering now that he'd spent quite a lot of time the previous night thinking about his past hubris and complacency, and while he'd been thinking about those things he'd missed a potentially vital development in the present.

The timer showed just after eight the night before, when the door of Cheng's apartment had opened and the camera in the hall had sparked into life. Freddie hadn't really been expecting to see Cheng walking back in, but the face that actually appeared in the doorway was such a surprise that Freddie froze the image and stared at it for a second, then reached for his coffee and took a sip.

Maybe it wasn't so strange, because they were friends, but he knew for a fact that she'd never been there before. Even so, it seemed after spending the afternoon playing chess with Freddie, Professor Marina Mikhailova had gone to Cheng's apartment.

She closed the door behind her and slipped a key into her purse as she called out, "Hello? Cheng?"

It was the natural response of a concerned friend, and she had a key, but that still didn't quite fit. Marina and Cheng had first met when the surveillance operation was already in place, and Freddie would have known, not only if she'd been to the apartment before, but also if they'd been close enough friends that Cheng might have given her a spare key.

She left the hall, and briefly crossed into shot of the camera overlooking Cheng's desk before disappearing again. About two minutes of dead air followed, long enough to carry out a reasonably thorough check on the rest of the apartment, and then she appeared in front of the camera again. This time she looked directly up into the lens before once more stepping out of shot.

Another thirty seconds passed, and then Freddie laughed with grudging admiration as the image shook and flickered and went dead—she'd found and removed the camera in less time than it had taken Freddie to install it. So much for the pretense of being nothing more than a concerned friend, and so much for just being a history professor who liked chess.

It was another twenty minutes before she appeared once more in the hall and left without facing the camera again. She'd probably guessed there was a camera there too, but it wasn't about being spotted—he could imagine her searching the desk and the area around it, even taking out the drawers to see if anything had been taped inside or underneath them, and she hadn't wanted that search to be filmed.

He moved online to see what he could discover about her, finding she'd been born in London to Russian parents, but that she'd been raised in Washington, DC, where her father was a diplomat. Her mother had been from an aristocratic émigré family, which even in the midst of all these revelations, was the one thing that didn't surprise Freddie at all.

She'd studied at Harvard, married a US diplomat called Chalmers in her late twenties, had a daughter and played homemaker until becoming an academic in her early forties, first at Yale, then in Vienna where she'd been ever since. Her husband had died of throat cancer at the age of fifty-two.

Freddie nodded to himself, impressed that it seemed like a comprehensive biography and yet was possessed of many gaps. His automatic assumption in terms of what he'd seen was that she had to have an intelligence background. She'd even hinted as much, telling him that it was quite common for academics to be approached, but this was more than a casual involvement—Bennett and his colleagues had failed to spot Freddie's camera in his old apartment, but she'd known exactly where to look in Cheng's place.

There were two bigger questions. One was about the exact nature of her relationship with Cheng, whether she'd really befriended him or had just been playing him, and if so, to what end. Whatever the truth of it, she was potentially a much richer source of information for Freddie than he'd assumed the previous afternoon.

The second question, perhaps even more interesting, concerned where that intelligence background lay. In theory, she could be operating on behalf of London, Moscow, or Washington.

He dug into the university website, checking on her teaching schedule. She took a lecture immediately after lunch, and then she was free for an hour before an afternoon tutorial, so that was his window.

He went down for breakfast, finding the restaurant busy even this late in the morning. Pedro greeted him like an old friend and seated him at the same table. The Korean couple were nearby, once again wearing matching outfits—yellow hoodies under pristine denim overalls.

After breakfast he went shopping for clothes, conscious of veering just a little more toward the hipster aesthetic that he'd already adopted by default, and he wasn't sure if that was because he *needed* to blend in at the Madhouse, or because he wanted to.

He stopped for an early lunch at the vegan café, looking out at the patchy fog that had even managed to creep into the covered arcade. Then he took his purchases back to the hotel, loaded up his messenger bag, and headed out again.

In the open, the fog was dense and unyielding, punctuated by the dull egg-yolk glow of car and tram lights. There was a chill in the air, but it was hardly cold enough to warrant the way the other pedestrians he encountered were swaddled in padded coats, hats, scarves, and gloves.

He checked his watch as he headed up the steps and in through the main doors of the University of Vienna—Marina's lecture would just be starting, but he took his time walking through the building, making sure not to stand out.

Unlike the modern campus where Cheng had worked, this was a grand old university, columned and vaulted and ornate, large halls with broad stone staircases and galleried landings, the whole place humming with hushed and ghostly echoes and the occasional bang of a door closing. There were plenty of students walking about or sitting in nooks reading or studying their phones, but the presence of many more seemed to carry about the building on the air.

When he reached the lecture hall he didn't even need to open the door. He heard Marina's voice, unmistakable even though he couldn't catch the words, followed by the laughter of her students.

He made his way to her office, knocked, tried the door. He casually worked the lock and stepped inside. It was lined with bookshelves, which were piled with books and journals and papers at every angle, to the extent that more piles lay on unutilized patches of floor.

It was easy enough to find a shelf of Asian journals that looked slightly dusty and unused. He slipped a matchbox-sized unit behind them, the camera peeking out between two copies. She'd have to do a sweep to find that one.

Satisfied, he went to the large leafy internal courtyard and sat in the colonnaded café drinking a coffee. There were a few students sitting in twos and threes at other tables, wrapped up against the fog, which even here had draped itself across the quadrangle and spilled between the arches.

He could tell when the time had reached the hour because the number of students coming and going suddenly increased. There was a turnover at some of the other café tables too.

His phone vibrated in his pocket and he looked at it and went onto the feed for Marina's office, keeping the sound off. She'd just come in with a female student in tow, but Freddie could tell from Marina's body language that she wanted rid of her. Sure enough, a moment later, the student seemed to thank her with a nod of the head and left.

Marina took some papers out of a drawer and sat down to look at them, but he closed the feed now. She was there and she was alone, and the camera's real purpose was to find out what she did after his visit, not before.

Chapter Nineteen

Marina responded to his knock with a curt, almost abrupt response, her tone like a warning, that this had better be good. He could imagine many a student or even colleagues changing their minds and walking away. But Freddie was neither, and he was pretty certain this would be worthy of the interruption.

He opened the door and stepped inside, and had closed the door again behind him before she looked up from the paper she was studying. Her face was frozen with a look of haughty bemusement he well recognized, but her eyes betrayed the quick thought processes going on behind it.

She'd placed him almost instantaneously, but there was some surprise too, and calculation. Freddie could be wrong, but he sensed she hadn't imagined him to be the person who'd placed the camera in Cheng's apartment. She was probably reassessing that now.

"Freddie, what an unexpected surprise."

"Marina. Or should I call you Professor Mikhailova in this setting?"

"Oh please!" She laughed as though he were teasing her, and gestured to the seat in front of the desk. "What can I do for you? Is it about Cheng?"

"Kind of." He put his messenger bag on the floor next to the chair and sat down. She moved the paper to one side so there was just an expanse of open desk between them. He knew that if he hoped to get anything out of her, he'd have to put at least some of his cards on the table, so he decided to start by being open. "That was my camera you took down in Cheng's apartment last night. So I'm curious, about where you got a key, and exactly what your interest has been in him these last nine months, or maybe even longer."

She smiled, a dismissive edge to it, making him feel that he was out of practice at this kind of thing.

"I would have thought you were the one who had questions to answer, Mr. *Makin*. You see, Freddie, I know quite a bit about you. I never bought the slightly anonymous-looking young man who just happened to sit at the next table to us each week reading his English novels. I guessed you were watching Cheng. What have you done with him, by the way?"

"Nothing. I work as a freelancer providing surveillance services for Behnke & Co. out of Munich. For the last year, my job's been to keep tabs on Cheng for a private client. I had a surveillance suite in the same building, monitoring and sending the feeds from his apartment, and from TU. I followed him to work and around the city, and recorded and transmitted all the conversations you had with him."

"Which, naturally, is why you were always at a neighboring table. Were you wearing a wire?"

"A little simpler than that. Each week I'd attach a limpet under my table, microphone pointed in your direction, then take it away with me when I left."

She didn't seem at all shocked, focusing on details instead. "But you really don't speak Mandarin or Russian?" He shook his head. "Who was the private client?"

She was comfortable with him, conspiratorial, as if they were in this together, but she was playing him too, just as he was attempting to play her.

"Give and take, Marina. What was your interest?"

"It seems we both have a past, Freddie. I won't tell you who I worked for or who I still occasionally work for now. I was asked to make an assessment of Cheng, that's all. But I was telling the truth—we do like each other, we enjoy each other's company, and in fact, I think our afternoons of chess are one of the highlights of my week." She looked momentarily wistful before the smile dropped. "Give and take, you say. So . . . Cheng never told me directly, but a few things he said gave me the impression he was involved in some way with nuclear weapons, which seems odd: he was passionately opposed to them. And I can see from your expression that you didn't know about that." Freddie shook his head. "Then let me repeat, if you haven't done anything with him, who was the private client?"

This was a key moment. She was probably some way from trusting him, but he sensed she was trying to figure out if she could work with him. And if Freddie wanted to keep that hope of collaboration alive, he had to offer her something else.

"I'm hoping to find out soon, but I'm pretty certain we were acting as a CIA proxy. They shut it down on Sunday, killed Leo Behnke, tried to kill me, and I guess they killed Cheng."

He could see it hadn't surprised her, and that she knew far more about this than she was letting on. Perhaps she'd even already known about Cheng's disappearance when she'd turned up at the Griensteidl. For all he knew, she'd gone along specifically to see if Freddie would put in an appearance.

She nodded, a cold acknowledgment of the likely reality, and seemed to change the subject then as she said, "Speaking of proxies, you worked for Evanston Electronics. We—and no, I'm still not going to tell you who I mean by 'we'—we always worked on the assumption that Evanston was a cover operation for one of the intelligence agencies. We were never sure which, but I heard a few rumors that it was actually a front for S8."

He smiled a little, enjoying this, realizing he'd missed it, the gradual surrendering of truths, carried out as warily as if they were prisoner swaps.

"I don't know what that is."

"Then that makes two of us. Your career ended in Yemen, didn't it? Some sort of ambush?"

He glanced at the window, but there was nothing to see beyond the fog. He was impressed, because whomever "we" referred to, Marina knew more about his past than Bennett James had, not only in her speculation about Evanston but in knowing that the final calamity in Yemen had not been a helicopter crash.

"Marina, the only thing you need to know about my career is that it ended five years ago. Since then, I've contracted for Behnke and I've tried to mind my own business and leave everything of that world behind."

"Then you should have opened a coffee shop, or become an academic like me, because it looks like you're right back in it now."

He nodded, accepting the point. "That's why I need to find out what happened to Cheng, and what it is they think I've seen." Marina tilted her head to one side and looked at him questioningly. "It seems something Cheng did, sometime near the end of last week, brought about the decision to close him down. They think I might have seen it, which suggests it was something he did on his computer, and that's why they want me dead. They're searching all over Europe for me, everywhere except here, apparently."

"How secure is your identity?"

Again, it sounded like genuine concern for Freddie's welfare, but she was more likely assessing how safe it was to get involved with him.

"Secure enough for now, which is why they're currently searching in vain. I probably have a few weeks. Of course, every contact I make increases the risk a little more."

Kevin Wignall

"Oh, you don't need to worry about me." She smiled, and he supposed that was as close as she'd come to telling him she wasn't CIA. "I'm not sure how much use I might be though. I told you he'd been approached by governments and wasn't much interested, and that's certainly what he told me, but he was still to all intents and purposes a patriotic citizen of China, so if he worked for anyone it was probably them. He had a girlfriend. I never met her, Chinese tour guide, but I always assumed she was his handler for the Chinese. He only saw her once every two weeks, but then you know that."

Freddie thought back to Wei Jun coming out of the bathroom into the subdued light of the bedroom, slipping off her robe, waiting a moment for Cheng to notice her naked beauty, the same crushing moment each time before crossing the room and sliding into bed with him. If she'd been his handler, she'd fallen for him all the same.

"Yes, I know that. She'll be here this Sunday, if she doesn't know about him being missing. I could try to talk to her."

Marina said, "If she's still alive."

That was a pertinent point. If they'd killed Cheng, killed Behnke, tried to kill Freddie, they might have decided that Wei Jun posed a risk too. He nodded, but then decided if Marina was going to be any sort of ally he'd probably need to trust her—he certainly doubted he'd be able to play her.

"But I think you're wrong about him working for the Chinese. He had a CIA code name."

"Really?" Was she acting, or had that taken her by surprise? She pondered it for a second or two before speaking again. "Now, that doesn't seem like him at all. Perhaps I didn't know him as well as I thought I did."

Freddie had known him intimately this last year, and yet he too wondered how well he'd known him. Everything about Cheng's life, every action, every activity, had been so considered that perhaps in truth it revealed nothing at all about the real man and his beliefs.

"What were you looking for last night?"

Marina smiled, making clear he'd reached the limits of their cooperation. "I didn't find it, anyway. What will you do now?"

"I don't know. I have no idea what I saw, or why they think it's a worthwhile precaution to kill me."

"You must still have contacts?"

He shook his head. "Well, one, and I'll be meeting with him in the next few days, but if you mean from my Evanston days—no, I left all that behind."

For a moment, she looked as if she wouldn't respond, but then said, "Was it very bad, the ambush situation? I couldn't find out much, but someone told me it left you pretty shaken up."

He smiled a little, curious about who might have told her that; curious about the entire hinterland that lay behind the composed and slightly haughty edifice of Marina Mikhailova. But then perhaps she was equally curious about him.

"Ambush is probably the wrong word, but yes, it was bad. There were four of us, and I came out unscathed."

"The others were all killed?" He nodded. "These things happen, not that it ever makes it any easier if you're the one who's caught up in it. Survivor guilt's a terrible thing."

"That's it, though, I didn't survive. I was spared. It was my operation and the person who pulled the trigger didn't shoot me because he wanted me to know that I thought I'd been playing him, but he'd been playing me."

"I see." For a moment she looked uncomfortable, perhaps because the two of them were involved in a similar game right now, but as if wanting to show that she wasn't playing him entirely, she said, "I was involved in something very similar once, with someone who was reasonably close to me. None of us is quite the master of circumstance that we believe ourselves to be." She glanced at her watch. "I would speak to Cheng's girlfriend if you have the opportunity—I just have a feeling she might know more than the rest of us. That could be key. You see, one thing I've always liked about the CIA is that you can usually go above someone else's head and cut a deal, if you get the politics right, but for that you need information."

Freddie laughed. "And isn't that the ultimate irony? I've done nothing but collect information for the last year, and yet I haven't got the first clue what any of this is about." He reached down for his messenger bag and stood. "I won't keep you any longer, but thanks."

"I'm not sure what you're thanking me for, but for what it's worth, I think our interests are mutual in this one. If I'm able to find out anything useful, I will let you know. Perhaps we could meet as usual next Wednesday . . . if you're still alive by then."

She was joking, the kind of gallows humor he'd engaged in himself in the past, until it had stopped being funny, and until he'd no longer had anyone to share it with.

"I hope for your sake I am. To lose one chess partner might be considered unfortunate, but to lose two . . ."

She laughed, and he raised his hand in a wave and left her.

Chapter Twenty

He didn't linger at the university, but made his way back out into the fog, which was a little acrid now with a day's worth of exhaust fumes mingling with it, and walked the short distance back to the hotel. The fog had the advantage of making it difficult for anyone to follow him, but he couldn't imagine Marina doing that anyway.

He wasn't sure he could trust her exactly, but he couldn't see her having any reason to work against him. The truth of it would really depend on what she'd done in the time after he left, and he'd find out about that soon enough.

He found the lobby of the Madhouse transformed into a pop-up clothes store and heaving with people, including waiters walking around with canapés and trays of drinks. Pedro saw him and walked over.

"Hey, Freddie. Prosecco?"

"No, thank you, I had a bit too much to drink last night." He looked at the people mingling, mostly overdressed in a high-maintenance kind of way. "This doesn't look like the normal crowd."

Pedro shrugged with disapproval and then smiled before continuing on his way. Arnold was behind the desk on his own and waved as Freddie walked past. He waved back, but didn't speak. He could see Eva in the back office looking at the computer.

He got back to his room, still thrown by the sight of his glass wall reduced to a uniform gray. It was so eerie that he found himself crossing the room and looking down again, almost as if to reassure himself that the world was still out there.

He went to his laptop and brought up the feed from the camera in Marina's office, moving back through the timeline to the point at which he'd left. She'd sat for a little while, looking deep in thought, and that was the real limitation of surveillance work, because those thoughts were closed to him, just as Cheng's had been.

She reached down, perhaps to a bag or briefcase, and retrieved a cellphone. There was another pause, and when she put in the call she spoke with the same authority he'd noticed himself, the tone of a person who didn't answer to anyone.

He heard his name mentioned and he hoped no one else was listening in on this conversation, because it would reveal to them that he hadn't been bluffing when he'd told Bennett James he might stay in Vienna. Crucially, though, the entire conversation apart from his name was carried out in Russian. So that was who she worked for.

She ended the call, put the phone back, sat for a little while longer. He thought she might go back to the paper she'd been reading earlier, but instead she opened one of the desk drawers and took out a different phone—and now he was really interested.

Marina put in a call and started to speak without any pleasantries. "Yes, frankly it's becoming rather messy out here. I just had a visit from our friend from S8." Freddie hit pause, rewound, watched it again, paused it again, just to let the fact sink in. So she knew exactly who he'd worked for and what Evanston Electronics had really been about. He pressed play again. "His instinct is that this is CIA, which backs our suspicions. They killed Behnke, probably killed Cheng, tried to kill our friend too." He noticed she was avoiding the use of his name on this call. "Of course he's onside, or at least, as much as he's on anyone's side. It's like you said, I think he was burned badly; you can see it in his eyes.

Sad, really. But yes, if he can stay alive I wouldn't bet against him find-ing out what's going on." There was a pause as the person at the other end spoke, and she smiled in response and was still smiling as she said, "You let me worry about that. Try to find out how high this goes, and if there are any rumblings—watching Cheng this last year is one thing, but the events of this week strike me as someone going off script."

The call was ended, again without pleasantries. She put the phone back in the drawer, checked her watch, and went back to reading the paper as if absolutely nothing had changed in her normal routine. Freddie smiled—that was the kind of operative he'd once imagined himself to be.

But that in turn made him think back to the comment she'd made about him being burned, about being able to see it in his eyes. He felt exposed even thinking over it, and had cringed as she'd said it.

He made a mental effort to focus instead on the important things. Who had been on the other end of that call? Just because she'd talked about the CIA in that way didn't mean it hadn't been an American contact. He could almost certainly narrow it down to a US or UK intelligence agency anyway.

But Marina was also working for the Russians. And that in turn made him wonder which of the two was the most important, or if either knew about the other. The important implication was that she'd felt the need to tell both of them about his visit—that would make sense if Cheng's activities had indeed been linked to nuclear weapons.

He shut down the feed and closed the laptop, then walked across and turned the armchair so that he could look out at the fog. Inevitably, he could also see his own faint reflection, hardly someone he recognized with the beard developing nicely and his hair artfully unkempt.

Seeing himself, he didn't think he looked distinct at all from the kind of people who stayed at the Madhouse, or the regulars who were probably right now upstairs in the bar working on laptops, having informal meetings, or just relaxing. And yet Marina had said she could see it in his eyes, the fallout of that last catastrophic job in Yemen.

Maybe she'd just been projecting, seeing what wasn't actually there because of her knowledge of his past. That same knowledge had probably colored her impressions when she'd seen whichever book he was reading each week in the café—had that been the source of her comment about his existential tastes?

He'd have liked to mention Marina to Drew when he saw him the next morning, but it was probably best not to. Drew was someone he could trust, but it wouldn't be wise to confuse things, and depending on which outfit Marina was working for, it might even scare Drew off getting involved.

Because she was obviously a serious player—half the people Freddie had ever worked with hadn't known the truth about who'd employed him, but she did. She knew about S8, which meant she was well connected, probably well respected, and quite possibly very dangerous.

Chapter Twenty-One

One of the reasons Freddie had chosen the Kunsthistorisches Museum for his meeting with Drew was that it was an easy place to watch from afar, to make sure that Drew was alone and that no one else who looked suspicious went in during the half hour before or after.

If Drew had known the identity of the person he was really meeting, that wouldn't have been an issue. But Drew thought he was meeting Khaled Qabbani, and that might induce him to take precautions.

Freddie's own precaution in choosing that location was rendered useless anyway, because the following morning, the fog, if anything, had deepened. As he was leaving the Madhouse, there were three people at reception whose flights had been canceled because of it; one of the three refused to accept that the hotel was full and that he couldn't just stay in his room for another night.

It was colder too, giving Freddie the first opportunity to wear his new military-style overcoat. Wearing it, he felt like he'd finally adapted completely to the Madhouse aesthetic and to the wider city. His old apartment already felt like a strange choice of place to live, for all the reasons he'd first chosen it.

Once inside the museum he strolled around, looking for anyone tagging onto the back of a tour group or walking around solo who might fit the type, but either Drew had come on his own or Freddie no longer knew what he was looking for. Maybe, on reflection, he'd never been that good at looking for it in the first place—if he had been, he wouldn't have let Abdullah play him the way he had.

When he reached the Bruegel room it was just after eleven, and he found Drew sitting on the bench looking up at *The Hunters in the Snow*. Freddie stood in the entrance to the room, maybe only ten feet from the bench, but Drew wasn't even paying attention to the people coming and going and it took him a few seconds for his gaze to drift to his left.

Drew tried to play it deadpan, but couldn't stop himself smiling. He was a big man, a lover of food and drink, less keen on exercise, and his smile made him look like someone who'd been caught doing something he wasn't meant to be doing.

Freddie drifted over and turned to look at the painting, and Drew said, "It's the first time I've seen this in the flesh. I could sit here all day."

"Well, at least your trip hasn't been wasted."

"Oh, it hasn't anyway. See, you're out of the loop: Khaled Qabbani was killed a year ago in Beirut."

Despite being confident that he hadn't spotted anyone suspicious, Freddie glanced around the room again, but Drew was quick to add, "Don't worry, I'm alone."

Freddie turned to face him. "So why did you come if you knew he was dead?"

"I was curious to see who was impersonating him. I swear, I'm *so* bored in Athens!" He laughed, a warmth and affection to his smile now. "Good to see you, Freddie."

"You too." Drew stood, and they shook hands. "There's a coffee shop in here, could be a good place to talk."

"Show the way."

They started to walk, and Freddie said, "So how long have you been in Athens?"

"Two years. Don't get me wrong, it's a great place, and Jen and the kids love it. But . . . you know, I'm a Middle East guy. Oman, Jordan, Yemen." He allowed a brief pause. "Still in the surveillance business?"

"I was, until Sunday. That's what I wanted to talk to you about."

"Well, that's the most intriguing thing I've heard since . . . I don't know, forever."

They talked of Drew's wife and kids until they got to the coffee shop, and while they ordered. Drew took his phone out and showed Freddie pictures of the two girls, and a boy called Ben, a new addition since the last time they'd met.

Then, as Drew worked through a piece of cake, in silence after an initial ecstatic moan, Freddie told him his story, or the bits of it he felt mattered.

"For the last year I've been on a job here, watching a Chinese academic, computer specialist. The company behind the job is called Marine Finance, based in Liechtenstein. I wasn't tasked with getting anything specific, just full surveillance on his apartment, his office, his life. Sunday, I went home early, disturbed someone breaking into my apartment, who pushed past me and ran down into the street, but was then sent back to kill me."

"How do you know he was sent back to kill you?"

"I just do. And he had a gun. But I killed him." Drew raised his eyebrows, a forkful of cake briefly suspended halfway between plate and mouth. "Yeah. Anyway, he was part of a team. They emptied the surveillance suite, the Chinese academic disappeared, they killed Leo Behnke."

Again, he stopped short of telling Drew everything that had happened at Leo's place and wasn't sure why, because he knew he could trust him.

"Who's Leo Behnke?"

"The guy who owns the company I've been working through these last five years." That earned a nod, before Drew looked down at his plate, visibly disappointed to see it empty. He put the fork down and

Freddie continued. "I'm pretty sure they're Company men. If they're not, they're no more than a couple of steps removed." He took his phone out and brought up a picture he'd pulled from the footage of the trader looking up at the camera, a picture he'd retouched to make it impossible for anyone to work out where it had been taken. He handed it over. "That's the guy who's running it, as far as I can tell."

Drew looked at it, his expression inscrutable, then handed it back.

"Lars Oberman." He registered Freddie's confusion. "No, he's American. The Oberman comes from a Swiss great-great-grandfather, like nineteenth-century or something. And I think Lars was just a name his parents liked—I don't know, was Metallica around that long ago? Anyway, he's a real son of a bitch. I thought he'd left, but I saw him in passing at Langley last year. He's a pole-climber, you better believe it."

"So not a good person to have on my case?"

"No. Are you sure he's on your case?" Freddie nodded. "Does he know who you are?"

"No. They know about Evanston, and they have the helicopter crash story from Yemen. Nothing about who I really was."

"Well, that's promising. Still in touch with any of your old crew?"

"You know how it was with us, but I cut those ties anyway."

"Of course. Well, I'll see what I can find out. Who was your target?"

"His name was Jiang Cheng. Like I said, he was an academic here, computer specialist."

But Drew had nodded as soon as he heard the name. "Last night a Chinese guy took a dive off his hotel balcony in Skopje. They haven't released his identity yet, but unofficially we've been told, and that's who it was, Jiang Cheng. The word is that there's an underworld connection—he had gambling debts to some Macedonian crime boss that he couldn't pay."

"No, he didn't. Trust me, I'd have known—Cheng wasn't a gambler. Why were you told?" Drew looked confused by the question. Freddie could feel the beginnings of something like anger or resentment simmering deep within him and wasn't sure why, because he'd known this was the likely outcome. "What, you get informed every time a Chinese national dies in the Balkans? I'll make it easy for you, Drew—I know he was an Agency asset."

"So then you also know that's why I was told. But I have no idea what kind of asset he was."

"Something to do with nuclear weapons."

"Oh. Well, that explains why I had no idea about it. And how did you find out?" He frowned, the hint of an accusation. "You sure you don't have any connection with S8 anymore?"

"Absolutely. And what about your people—you think they believe the story about the link to the underworld, or are they just covering to avoid upsetting the Chinese?"

"Always hard to tell, but I'd say genuine."

"So that might be something for me to work with. If it was unsanctioned, this Oberman and his team are vulnerable."

Drew looked hopeful but unconvinced. "Except, as you well know, there's sanctioned and then there's *sanctioned*. And even if he is vulnerable, that makes your position even more dangerous. In fact, what are you still doing in Vienna?"

"I'll be moving on soon." Even as he said it, Freddie realized he didn't want to move on, that he liked it here, liked it more now than he had a week ago, and he wanted to stay. "They've been looking everywhere else for me, but I guess they'll work it out sooner or later."

Drew checked his watch and said, "I'm having lunch with someone at the embassy, but look, I'll email the Qabbani account if I find anything. And if you need me, likewise, send it through there." He reached into his jacket and took out a pen and a business card, which he looked at before turning it over and writing a number on the back. "This is my cell number. If there's anything urgent you can call me."

"Is it secure?"

"As much as anything is nowadays."

119

Freddie took the card, glancing at it, seeing it was for a pet store in Athens.

"Thanks, I appreciate it, Drew."

"Not at all. You'd do the same for me, I know you would." He picked up his fork and moved it into a different position, then looked up with an uncertain smile. "I bumped into Charlotte Walters earlier in the year."

Freddie nodded. Charlotte had been at Princeton with Drew, but she'd also been Chloe's friend since childhood, one of those six-degrees coincidences the world seemed to be full of.

"How is she?"

"She was, well, she . . ." Drew stopped, picking up on the tense and the fact that Freddie wasn't asking about Charlotte. "Of course—Chloe. Married. She had a baby boy last year."

"Good. I'm pleased."

It had actually been a concern of his in the five years since he'd broken off the engagement. Chloe was the same age as him, and at thirty-three had imagined marriage around the corner, a family shortly afterwards, only to see herself single, faced with the prospect of starting all over again, her thirties racing past.

He thought Drew was about to say something else in relation to Chloe, but instead he said, "You know, Freddie, what happened in Yemen, it wasn't your fault. I know I told you that at the time and you weren't ready to hear it, but I'm telling you again now. It wasn't your fault."

"Tell that to Mel and Pete and Talal."

"If they were here, I would, and they'd agree with me. It was so messed up! Really, what did any of us think we were trying to achieve? You think you were guilty of complacency, of arrogance, and you were, because we all were, including Pete and Mel. Didn't that underpin everything we did out there?"

Freddie smiled. "Is this your attempt to make me feel better, that it was my fault, but it doesn't matter because everyone else was just as incompetent?"

Drew shrugged and moved the fork again. "You know what I mean."

"I do, and I appreciate it. And I really am happy that Chloe found someone."

"And you?" Freddie smiled but didn't answer. "Do you think you would have still been together if it hadn't been for the way the mission ended?"

"You mean, because I slept with Melissa?"

"No! God, no. That's not what I meant." Drew looked embarrassed. "No. I mean, I knew about it, obviously, or I guessed. The night of that party—everyone got so drunk. And afterwards, the two of you were always making subtle jibes at each other, how you weren't each other's type. But, Freddie, it's the kind of thing that goes on in places like that, people cooped up together . . ."

"Did you ever cheat on Jen?"

"No, but—"

"It wasn't just once." Drew looked intrigued. "It happened again, a few days before . . . before she died. And there was no alcohol involved that time, or not much."

Freddie had a brief searing memory of Mel, the soft warmth of her skin, the ease with which their bodies had fallen together, the familiarity of her touch.

"Is that one of the reasons you broke it off with Chloe?"

Freddie shook his head. "I don't think so. I know it sounds phony, but I was still in love with her. And Melissa was crazy about her fiancé."

"You and Mel just had a natural chemistry. Everyone could see it. If Mel hadn't died, it would've meant nothing."

Freddie wasn't sure about that, wasn't sure that he trusted his past self with something of such importance. It was a hypothetical anyway.

"But she did die. They all did."

"And it was a big loss to everyone. I just wish you hadn't . . . I don't know. You made yourself pay such a price, for something . . ."

He gave up, and Freddie could see that the sentiment was genuine. But Drew had never messed up, not to the extent where it had cost lives. Pete had left a wife behind, though no kids. Mel had been due to marry that year, the venue and everything else already arranged. But despite that treachery, it was the loss of Talal that was still the hardest of all to bear—Talal with his young wife and baby.

"If it means anything to you, Drew, I'm in a good place now, and I don't think I would have been if I'd tried to carry on. You know, there was a time in the months afterwards, I really . . . I was in a bad way." And they'd given him pills, so many pills, and it had often seemed so tempting to wash them down and fall away into sleep. But he hadn't, and here he was. "I just found a new way of being, a way to carry on, and I couldn't have done that if I'd stayed in."

"You're right. I'm sure you're right. You know how it is, I'm institutionalized—I can't understand why anyone wouldn't want this insane life." Drew stood and reached out his hand and they shook. "I'll be in touch."

"Likewise. And enjoy your lunch."

"Jen's got me on a diet." He said it as though it were the most outlandish thing in the world, and looking at him, Freddie would have to agree. Drew shrugged and headed off out of the café.

Chapter Twenty-Two

It was out of his way, and felt more so in the fog, but Freddie headed to the vegan café in the covered arcade. He liked being lost in the fog anyway. He was less keen on being alone with his thoughts, because the talk with Drew had brought up a lot of memories, the sweetest of which were also the hardest to dwell upon.

He tried to concentrate instead on his lingering, low-level anger about Cheng, imagining the miserable days that had preceded his fall from a hotel balcony in Skopje, wondering whether he'd been drugged or thrown conscious, able to picture too well the sublime acceptance Cheng would have maintained until the end. But as much as Freddie had been lulled into believing it this last year, he had not *known* Cheng, not really, and his thoughts would not gain purchase there.

Yemen. It all went back to Yemen. He couldn't stop thinking about that day, Talal singing along to the radio and then the roadblock and Pete, still lighthearted, asking Freddie if he recognized the masked gunmen, and the taste of Mel's blood on his face, and Abdullah pointing the gun, his eyes meeting Freddie's—"Pow!"

But even that was better than thinking about Chloe. She was happy now, or at least married, mother to a baby boy, and he'd been telling the truth to Drew—he was pleased for her—but it did little to lessen the self-loathing he still felt at the way he'd cheated on her and then abandoned her. Him leaving had been the best thing for her, he still believed that, and believed it all the more now, knowing the way he'd struggled in the year or so afterwards, but that made it no less shameful an act on his part.

Once again, the fog had crept into the covered arcade and now lingered in pockets. He stepped into the lit world of the café and the waitress looked over from where she was putting plates of food in front of other diners and gave him a regular-customer smile. He smiled back and took a seat and started to read through the menu.

He glanced up as a woman walked past outside, drawn as much by the shift of light and peripheral movement as by the sound of her footsteps. He looked to the window a second time as he was ordering, two students passing by. And he was gazing idly at the window as he waited for the waitress to come back when a man walked slowly into view and stared into the café as if considering coming in.

He was wearing a smart overcoat and plain scarf, his dark hair cut short and neat. He probably wasn't much older than Freddie, but he looked too formal for a place like this. Unsurprisingly, he decided against coming in, and Freddie made a show of hardly noticing him, but in fact he'd recognized him, and had placed him even before he walked on.

Freddie had seen him in the Kunsthistorisches Museum. He'd been with a woman, also smartly dressed, studying one of the paintings on the far side of the Bruegel room. They hadn't looked out of place there, and by the time Freddie and Drew had made for the café they'd already moved on themselves.

So he'd only seen him that once and this was a small city, but it was still too much of a coincidence that the guy had walked down this hidden arcade and looked into this café. Freddie doubted they'd try anything here, but he leaned down casually and released the straps on his bag, and throughout the meal he kept an eye on the window.

Had they tracked him down, and if so, how had they managed it? Yes, they knew he was in Vienna, or had been a couple of days back, but it would have been a big leap to get from there to the Madhouse, to the meeting with Drew—Freddie knew his technology was clean, he knew Oberman didn't know about his past in S8, so there was no trail to follow.

But if they hadn't tracked him down, that left only a scenario he disliked even more, that someone had tipped them off. He trusted Drew completely, but that trust was based on the person Drew had been five years ago, the person Freddie had been, and it had arisen out of being part of the same team, something they'd ceased to be on the day Freddie left Yemen.

Marina was a different proposition. He knew he couldn't trust her, because he knew too little about her and because everything he did know suggested she was dangerous. Yet he wanted to trust her, a scary prospect in itself, because it reminded him of his relationship with Abdullah, someone else with whom he'd felt an instant but misleading connection.

But Freddie thought back to that second phone call she'd made from her office and held on to the hope it offered, because she hadn't sounded like someone who was on the same side as Oberman. Besides, if she had been, Freddie probably would have been in the morgue by now.

After lunch, he headed back out into the cool air, keeping his bag open. He didn't see anyone as he walked the rest of the way along the arcade, but when he stepped out into the denser fog beyond it, he turned left instead of right and walked slowly toward the quieter streets that surrounded a small park nearby.

It was only as he turned left again, moving around the park, the trees looming up to his right, that he became conscious of the footsteps behind him. He reached into his bag, checked the safety, then kept his hand there as he walked on, turning right, the next side of the square, and still the steps followed, keeping pace.

Freddie kept on toward the next corner, fighting his adrenaline to keep his pace constant. And he was nervous, not because he was afraid or because there was any risk of being seen in this fog, but because he'd somehow managed to accept that he would kill this man. What else could he do if he wanted to stay ahead of them? And yet he didn't want to kill anyone else. He hadn't even wanted to kill Phillips or the guy at Leo's house.

After turning the next corner, he walked on then went through the gates and into the park. For a few seconds, the sound of his own footsteps on the graveled path made it hard to hear the man following. He picked it up again, but then as he walked deeper into the gray interior, the city falling away even further, the second set of steps stopped.

Freddie stopped too, suddenly conscious of the cold damp on his skin. He listened, his nerves notching up another level because of the stillness. He heard a noise, astonished that it had carried across the silence, because he was certain it was the sound of a phone vibrating with a message or call. He stared in that direction and, a short while later, the steps started again.

Freddie held his ground, keeping his eyes fixed on the blank gray between them, and it was only when the sound of the steps changed that he realized the guy was walking away from him. Had he lost his nerve when faced with the opaque stillness of the park, or had he been called off?

Freddie retraced his own steps, making his way back to the gate where he stopped and listened, but a car drove past somewhere nearby and by the time silence resumed, he could no longer hear any steps at all. He had been tailed, he was sure of it, and whatever had just happened, his cover was still at least partially blown.

He walked quickly and quietly back the way he'd come, but ironically, given that he'd lost the tail, his nerves had ratcheted up yet another notch. Maybe it was precisely because he'd been denied the confrontation and was left no wiser as to how close they were, how they'd closed in on him, what their next move would be.

He stood still again, this time on a street corner, and only when he was convinced that he'd lost him completely did he start to take a circuitous path back to the hotel. Even then, it was another ten minutes before he reached into the bag and put the safety on, then fastened the catches.

Time was running out for him here, he knew it. His only consolation was that they didn't know he was staying at the Madhouse, and not even Drew or Marina knew about that. But still, just before reaching it, he stepped into a doorway and waited there for a while, listening, watching, until the cold began to eat at him and he was convinced he was alone. Only then, and still reluctantly, he walked the final fifty yards to the hotel.

The hotel lobby, for once, was empty and quiet. Freddie felt a kind of peace settle back over him, just being in here. Arnold was behind the desk, looking bored.

"Hey, Freddie. I like your coat."

"Thanks, Arnold. Quiet in here today."

"Too quiet," he said dramatically, aping a cliché from a thriller or horror movie. "Eva's on her break—you should pop by and say hello."

This was just what he needed, particularly now he knew he wouldn't be able to stay much longer.

"Maybe I will."

He took the elevator up to the top floor and ordered a Laphroaig, looking around as the bartender poured. It was the usual daytime crowd of people using the bar as an office space, a few hotel guests, no one out on the terrace, or almost no one.

He saw Eva sitting in the same spot as last time, wrapped in her coat, smoking. He walked over once he'd been served, slid the door open and stepped out onto the terrace, the cool fog immediately bathing his face. As he closed the door again, she glanced in his direction and her face brightened.

"Arnold said I'd find you up here."

"I *like* your coat."

"Thank you. I just bought it yesterday."

He sat down, and she looked at the glass and said, "What are you drinking?"

"Whisky. Laphroaig. I thought it suited the weather somehow."

"I love the fog."

"Me too." He looked out at it, finding it all the more beautiful knowing that the city's grand architecture was wrapped up beneath that uniform blanket of gray. "Do you have any pictures of your art on your phone? I'd like to see it if you do."

"Really? I do, but they're not very good—the photographs, I mean. See, I paint, but a lot of what I do is about texture, so they're almost three-dimensional. It's hard to capture that with a camera. Maybe I could bring one of the smaller pieces in one day."

"I'd like that."

"You're serious?"

"Of course."

She nodded, accepting the point, took a drag on her cigarette, and said, "You look a bit down today."

"Do I?" The smoke caught on his chest slightly, so he raised his glass and took a sip of the whisky, the peaty warmth sinking through him, fixing him to the world. If he was forlorn, he knew it wasn't because of what had just happened, being compromised—it went back further than that. "I met an old friend earlier, someone I haven't seen in a few years. I guess it's made me . . . I don't know . . ."

"Nostalgic?"

"Maybe. Something like that." He thought it was the wrong word, but perhaps it was right after all. No doubt there was a word in some language or other, one of the Scandinavian tongues, or Russian, maybe even Mandarin, for a distinct nostalgia for sad times past. "Kind of conversation that makes you think, a bit like you when you're sitting out here."

"I know that feeling. Do you have a girlfriend? Or a wife?" He shook his head. "I could introduce you. I know some really beautiful women."

"There really is no end to your talents!" He laughed, and she laughed with him. "What about you and Izzy, how long have you been together?"

"Since college. She was here for a year before me."

"Oh. I don't know why, but I imagined her being quite a bit older."

She cocked her head to one side. "No, I'm twenty-five and she's twenty-seven, but it's weird you say that because she's a really old soul. I hope you get to meet her." But as if sensing that this nascent friendship was illusory, and that soon enough there would be another guest moving into his room, she said, "How long are you staying?"

"I don't know. Maybe another week." It didn't feel like a lie because he wanted to stay, even although he knew he couldn't. "I kind of like the idea of moving here—not to the Madhouse, to Vienna."

"You should."

He nodded and sipped at his drink again. Yes, he thought, he should, but that all depended on Lars Oberman, the guy he still thought of as a trader even now he knew the truth, and he was pretty sure Oberman didn't care about what Freddie or anyone else wanted.

Chapter Twenty-Three

Freddie didn't drink much more and ate lightly, conscious of the traps his thoughts had been constructing for him since seeing Drew. But it was all in vain, and drinking heavily might have been as useful an approach.

He woke on Saturday morning in a terrible state, having fought through confused and jarring dreams, the present merging with one particular part of his past, both tearing at each other throughout the night. He jolted out of sleep for the final time, stumbled from the bed as if trying to flee, and fell to the floor.

He sat there for a minute like a rag doll, his hair matted with sweat, his blood thick and lifeless in his veins, and then he clambered up again and sat on the edge of the bed. A sliver of brightness glowed around the edges of the blinds, but Freddie could also see against it the beginnings of the aura, a jagged dancing arc of light to the left of his field of vision.

He went to the bathroom, took some painkillers, then crashed back onto the bed. He closed his eyes, although the aura remained even in the dark, beyond his left eyelid. He made a conscious effort to slow his breathing, to relax.

As he had done so often before, he tried to remind himself in a measured way of the facts of that day in Yemen, but it didn't work. Too many of last night's dreams had featured Chloe, who hadn't even been in Yemen, and who couldn't be reduced to the sequential facts of a debrief. He couldn't even remember how it had felt to be in love with her, and yet he had been once, more than he had ever loved anyone.

And even as he thought about how much he'd loved her, one of last night's dreams skittered back out of the darkness, the fragments assembling themselves. He knew why he'd suddenly recalled it, because predictably, it had involved Chloe walking in to find him and Mel in bed together—a dream that felt tawdry even in its lack of originality.

He lay there for an hour or more, the headache part of the migraine never quite materializing, and he was grateful that he didn't fall asleep again. When he eventually leaned over and pressed the button to open the blinds, he screwed up his eyes, because the fog had gone and there was a dazzlingly clear blue sky in its place.

He went down for a late breakfast, reminded that it was Saturday when he noticed someone he didn't recognize behind the reception desk. Arnold and Eva weren't around, and nor was Pedro in the restaurant. There were still plenty of people eating though, and he felt better for being surrounded by them and for having something in his stomach.

Only as he headed back up in the elevator did he notice his phone had pinged a couple of times this morning and he'd missed it. Immediately, he thought of the man yesterday, who'd tailed him and almost willfully lost him. He waited until he was back in his room, then opened the laptop to see what it was.

The first was the feed from his own apartment, but when he checked in, it was dead. He brought up the archive from the time the ping had come through and saw three men walk into shot.

Two of them, including Jimmy Fernandez, had been among the guys who'd put Phillips in the body bag—Oberman's foot soldiers. He had to assume they were a kill team and they'd been sent there for him, confirming all his fears about the tail yesterday.

But almost more disturbing than that was the third guy, tall and built like a marine, wearing frameless glasses and carrying a briefcase. Without speaking to the other two he opened up the briefcase on the island, unpacked the equipment inside, and almost immediately started a sweep. Within ten minutes he'd found the camera unit and taken it down.

The second ping was from inside Cheng's apartment. This time the same guy was on his own, and again there was only a brief run of footage before he located the final camera in the hallway and took it out of action.

Freddie stared at the blank screen for a few seconds, then almost idly switched across to the tracker on Bennett's gun, but that too had gone blank. He felt uneasy all of a sudden, this abrupt blindness leaving him vulnerable.

He needed to get out of the city, there was no question about it. But no matter how they'd homed in on him or who might have tipped them off that he'd remained in Vienna, he was still pretty confident that they wouldn't know to come looking for him here—it was just too unlikely a place, and that could prove a crucial advantage.

Because he needed to stay here long enough to meet Wei Jun when she arrived in the morning, if she arrived at all. Once he'd seen her, he could move on, but even as he clung to that thought he was conscious that it was pointless moving on if he didn't know what he was running away from.

In the absence of any live feeds to study, he went back to the footage he still had of Cheng in his apartment, and in particular the footage of him sitting at his computer. He worked through it more slowly now, in the light of the few additional things he'd learned about him, looking for clues as to what might have earned Cheng that dive from a hotel balcony.

But there was nothing obvious. Freddie hardly expected him to have been looking at pages detailing the technical specifications of nuclear weapons or websites campaigning for nuclear disarmament, but he'd hoped to find something that might have triggered alarm bells among Oberman and his team.

Instead it was the usual cross section of random subjects that he was used to seeing in Cheng's browsing sessions. There were a few Chinese cultural sites that he kept in his favorites, a lengthy academic article in English about the predictability of tsunamis and the mathematical models used to understand them, a handful of pages of company reports and articles about investing in stock markets, a handful of pages on marine biology, the web address for one of which he copied into an email sent to someone in China, a few pages on the staff section of the TU website. After that he'd settled down to watch an episode of *The Big Bang Theory*.

Freddie was distracted, thinking about the person who still seemed so alive in front of him there, the person with an endless curiosity and an equally endless appetite for American sitcoms. It was difficult to reconcile the footage with the fact that Cheng was now dead.

And then an alarming truth struck home and Freddie went back through to the point at which Cheng had been looking at marine biology, and in particular the page for which he'd sent the link to someone in China. Naturally, Freddie couldn't read the email it was attached to, but the article itself was in English, and about a rare seahorse being spotted off the coast of Southern California.

Could that be it? Had sending that page cost Cheng his life? And had it been an innocent coincidence—it was possible Cheng hadn't even known that his CIA handle was Seahorse—or had it been a coded attempt to discuss something with a contact in his home country?

It seemed tenuous somehow. And yet it was more of a link than anything else he could see or remember about Cheng's activities in the days before Oberman and his team moved in.

He had to speak to Wei Jun, even though part of Oberman's team was back in the city, and time was probably running short for Freddie. Twenty-four hours, long enough to speak to Wei Jun and find out what she knew about her boyfriend, and then he would leave. It would be enough. It had to be enough.

Chapter Twenty-Four

Sunday morning once again saw the sky a cloudless blue. His original idea had been to wait until Jun got to Cheng's apartment, but Oberman's tech specialist had forced a rethink on that. Not only did Freddie no longer have any cameras in place, but for all he knew, the tech guy had substituted them with his own, which could make turning up at Cheng's apartment a calamitous decision.

Fortunately, he knew that Jun generally arrived a little before eleven, he knew the U-Bahn station she came in on, the route she took from there to Cheng's apartment. It would be harder to explain what he had to tell her in the street, but it would be safer for Freddie, maybe for both of them.

He found a café on the first street she walked along after leaving the U-Bahn. It was already busy, with people sitting outside in the sun, albeit wrapped up against the crisp edge to the morning air. Freddie took a table just inside, looking out through the window, invisible.

He'd been there about twenty minutes when Wei Jun walked past, pulling along the usual small suitcase, but this time with an extra bag on top of it. She looked composed and content, with something about her expression that reminded him of Cheng. And clearly, she had no idea what she was walking toward.

He waited another minute, wanting to be sure she wasn't already being followed. Then he left, looking first one way as he stepped out of the café, making sure no one was trailing her from a distance, then turning in the direction she was walking. He couldn't see her, but he was confident of catching her.

He set off along the street, turned the corner, still no sign, but before he reached the next corner he could already hear the sound of the suitcase wheels on the paving stones. He saw her as he rounded the corner, and picked up his pace until he was only twenty yards behind her.

At some level he didn't want to stop her, didn't want to destroy that composure and contentment. She was still, in her own mind, heading toward something happy, and it wasn't Freddie who'd destroyed that happiness, but that's how it would seem to her.

But she was nearing the next corner, and would soon be in sight of Cheng's building, so he had no choice but to act now.

"Jun!"

She stopped and turned, confused, perhaps not sure that she'd heard her own name called out. She looked ready to accept she'd been mistaken, so Freddie raised his hand in a wave and called again. "Jun!"

She smiled uncertainly. Maybe she thought it was someone who knew her, one of the local tour guides or someone from one of the places she regularly visited. The smile became even more fragile as he got closer and she failed to identify the face.

She was beautiful, slender and with flawless skin and big eyes, and younger than Cheng, he thought, maybe only thirty. Even as he walked the final steps toward her, he remembered her naked, and felt oddly exposed in thinking of it.

"Jun, hi. My name's Freddie." She smiled again, being polite but wanting to know what all this was about. "He isn't there—Cheng, he's gone. I'm sorry."

"I don't understand. I'm sorry, Mr. . . . ?"

"Freddie. Just Freddie."

"You're a friend of Cheng's?"

"No. Look, it's difficult to explain here on the street. There's a café not far from here we could go to. I can tell you everything."

She started shaking her head even before he'd finished, and he felt stupid for not realizing how it would sound to her, a strange man stopping her in the street, asking her to accompany him to an unknown location.

"No, I'm sorry, but I have to go. I can't come with you."

She started to walk away from him, flustered, even afraid.

"He's dead."

She stopped and turned, her face aghast at the brutality of the statement, although still looking skeptical, as if she feared he might be a crank who'd say anything to stop her.

"What are you talking about?"

Freddie looked around, making sure that even on this quiet street there were no other pedestrians, no open windows from which people might be listening.

"Okay, there's no easy way of saying this. For the last year, I've been paid to watch Cheng, surveillance. I had cameras set up in his apartment, his office at TU, even the lecture hall. I monitored everything he said and did, and I sent it to my clients." He saw his comments sinking in, saw the growing horror in her expression, but also that she was beginning to believe him, for now at least. "I'm sorry."

"You were watching us?" He nodded regretfully, and yet he had felt no regret at all until that very moment. "How can I be sure you're telling the truth?"

He took his phone out, pulled up the archive, and brought up footage of Cheng in the kitchen, then held it out to her.

"This was taken last Sunday, in the hours before he disappeared."

Reluctantly, she took the phone from him and looked at it, holding her other hand over it to block out the light. But then she raised that hand to her mouth and looked in danger of dropping the phone. He eased it from her grip, stopped the feed, slipped the phone back into his pocket.

"I'm sorry. I was just doing my job. If it hadn't been me, it would've been someone else."

She lowered her head, and when she looked up, there were tears running down her cheeks, but then she surprised him by saying quietly, "He knew. He told me many times that he thought the apartment was bugged, that he was being listened to, watched. He said a friend in Hamburg warned him. I still thought he was being paranoid, but now you tell me he was right."

Freddie thought back over a year of footage, amazed that Cheng had believed he was being watched and yet had never once searched for cameras or bugs, had never once changed his behavior the way some people did when they suspected they might be under surveillance.

"Who was the friend in Hamburg, do you know?"

She shook her head, looking lost, as if such details could hardly matter now, even if she'd known the answers.

"You said he's dead. Did you kill him?"

"No. The people who employed me killed him. They tried to kill me too and they're still trying."

"Who?"

"I don't know who they are exactly, but I think they're linked with the CIA."

Despite the initial tears, she looked stoic, never in danger of collapsing with grief, and yet he could see behind her eyes the devastation, as if he'd taken everything from her, hollowed her out. It seemed out of all proportion to the almost formal nature of the relationship he remembered watching, a relationship which had seemed like something from an earlier age.

"What happened?"

He nodded, accepting it was a legitimate question, but said, "It's best we don't talk here on the street. I can understand you're suspicious:

you don't know me, and I've just given you the worst news, but there's a café we can go to not far from here, in the open, lots of people around."

She seemed to accept it now, and looked around as if asking which way they should go. He pointed the way they'd been walking.

"But we turn right."

She turned without another word and started walking, taking a right up ahead, not even looking in the direction she should have taken, where Cheng should have been waiting for her, a building she'd never need visit again.

Chapter Twenty-Five

Freddie walked alongside her, pointing casually to show her the way, and he thought she might still be wary, making sure he wasn't directing her into quiet streets, but she appeared to have lost all interest in her own safety and tagged along without comment.

As they got closer to where they were headed, Freddie said, "You have an extra bag." She looked at him, confused. "Normally you just have the case, but you have an extra bag."

Her eyes fixed on him, the look of someone having to remind herself that this stranger knew so much about her.

"I have an extra day off. I'm staying until Tuesday. I was."

He pointed. "It's just over there." The café was in a cobbled irregular square that surrounded a small church. It was open, but it was on the side that was still in the shade, so all the outside tables were empty.

They sat down, and a waitress came out right away and smiled and asked in English what she could get for them.

He looked at Jun and said, "What would you like to drink?"

She appeared not to hear him and stared blankly for a second before snapping out of it.

"I beg your pardon?"

"What would you like?"

She looked up at the waitress and smiled faintly. "Lemon tea?"

"One lemon tea."

"Thank you." Her words were so lost that the waitress looked a little concerned.

Freddie made an effort to look understanding and said, "Actually, I'll have the same, thanks."

"Two lemon teas. Anything to eat?" Freddie shook his head, but she'd anticipated the response and was already walking away again.

Once they were alone, Jun stared at him and went back to the point where they'd left off in the street.

"What happened?"

"I think they took him last Sunday. I don't know where they took him to begin with. He fell from a hotel balcony in Skopje on Thursday." He thought she might respond, gasp, or express some shock, but he saw now that her lips were pursed, that she was trying hard to keep her composure. "They haven't released his name yet, but a contact of mine told me it was Cheng."

She cleared her throat and relaxed her mouth just enough to say tightly, "Where is Skopje? I've heard of it, but . . ."

"Macedonia. In the Balkans. They're making up some story about him having gambling debts, but it's just a story—they murdered him, because of some work he was doing for them."

He saw a flicker of recognition in her eyes that filled him with hope, and he knew it was callous to feel hopeful in this situation, but he couldn't quite locate the emotion that was appropriate, for now at least.

"You saw them take him?" He shook his head and her tone was accusatory as she pressed him. "But you watched everything. How did you not see this, the most important thing, if I'm to believe you?"

"I went home early, with a headache. There was a man breaking into my apartment. He tried to kill me. At the same time, someone had gone to the place with all the surveillance equipment and turned it off. After that they must have gone for Cheng."

Long seconds crept past before she responded. "I feared this would happen."

"Why? Did you know what he was doing?" She didn't answer, didn't look as if she'd even heard. "Did you know he was working for the Americans?"

Her eyes looked moist with more tears ready to fall, but as the waitress appeared and headed across to them with a tray, Jun smiled and started to speak.

"Perhaps you think you knew him, watching him for all that time. Perhaps you think you knew both of us, because you watched everything."

The waitress put the teas on the table and Freddie nodded his thanks. She smiled back, sympathetically, maybe thinking there was some domestic drama going on here, and left them. Jun appeared not to notice she'd even been there, and barely paused.

"But you saw nothing. He was so full of love, so caring, so special."

Freddie nodded, but in truth he *had* seen those things in Cheng. What he hadn't seen was passion or desire or boredom or slovenliness or anger or frustration. Cheng had been living the way Freddie had aspired to live—in a measured way, attachments shed away, attachments to the past most of all—and yet now that he thought of it, Freddie pitied Cheng for the tidiness of his life.

"I was just doing a job," he said. "You feel like you get to know people, because you get to know their routine, their habits, the things they like and don't like, but you don't really know them. I was just doing a job, recording his life and turning it into data." His words seemed to pacify her, so he returned gently to the more pressing concern. "The thing is, Jun, I need to know him now. I need to know what I've been watching, what got him killed, and why they want to kill me. I'm sad that they killed him, even though I didn't really know him, and if I can find out why and do something about it, then that's a good thing. But my main concern is that I stop them before they get me."

"Who do you work for?"

"No one, not for a long time. That's why I have nowhere else to turn."

She looked down at her tea, then picked it up and tried to sip it, but found it too hot.

He waited, but again she didn't seem inclined to speak, so he said, "I'm sure I know the answer already, but I assume he didn't have gambling debts?"

She shook her head and smiled at some memory. "He didn't have any interest in money, in gambling or the financial world. He was approached once and asked to design a system for gambling, and he was always being approached by financial companies, but it wasn't a world that interested him at all."

"Did you know he was working for the Americans?"

Frustratingly, that was met with a brick wall again, and at first he thought she might not reply, but finally she said, "Why don't you tell me what you know, and I'll tell you what I know."

"That's the problem. I don't know very much at all." He thought back to what Marina had said to him and decided to gamble on that. "I suspect it could relate to nuclear weapons, even though Cheng disagreed with them. I know he was working for the Americans, so I'm guessing he was helping them with their weapons systems, but that doesn't explain why they killed him."

Jun tried her tea again and managed to sip it this time. Freddie followed suit, although her tolerance to heat was apparently greater than his because he still found it too hot.

"What will you do, with the people who did it?"

"I'm not gonna kill them or anything. I don't have the skills or the ability to do anything like that. I can try to ruin their lives."

"And do you have the skills for that?"

Yes, he did—ruining other people's lives had once been his job, until he'd become the biter bit.

"I'll be able to put them out of business, as long as I know enough."

And as long as it hadn't all been sanctioned at the highest levels.

She stared at him. She was more beautiful in person than she had been at a distance or through the filter of the camera lens. And Freddie felt for her and wanted to make her life better, even though he was no more equipped to offer that kind of assistance than he had been five years ago. What could he possibly give to Jun that would replace what she'd lost?

She said, "I don't understand computers, so this might not sound very technical."

He nodded, absurdly grateful that she'd decided to help.

Jun looked to one side, visibly putting her thoughts in order before she continued. "Cheng is a genius. It's a simple fact. He developed a program which can be added to a system and sit there for years without doing anything, almost impossible to detect, because until it's activated it's as if it isn't there at all. When it's activated, it creates a delay between a command and the fulfillment, anything from seconds to minutes—I don't know, perhaps even longer. But the operator believes the command has been fulfilled immediately, and will believe it until real events tell him the truth." She paused, looking at him to make sure he was still following. "If one country can infect another country's nuclear systems with Cheng's program, it gives a big advantage if ever there's a nuclear confrontation. For a period of time, the host country will believe it's fired its missiles, and the other country will know that they've been triggered, but have not yet fired. It provides a window of opportunity in which they can act."

Freddie nodded, and although his tea was still too hot, he took a sip. No wonder Drew hadn't known about this—it had the feel of something that was above almost every paygrade.

"He sold it to the Americans?"

"He didn't sell it. I told you he had no interest in money. He helped the Americans to embed his program on the launch systems for China's nuclear weapons."

"Did you ever talk about this in the apartment?"

"No. I told you he was paranoid. He would tell me when we walked. Were you following us?"

"Sometimes, but it's tough for a one-man operation to record people on the move. And the client wasn't interested in you." He thought of the way she'd just explained Cheng's program. "Are you Chinese intelligence?"

"Do you mean was I pretending to be in love with him? No, I wasn't. We were in love, and maybe you didn't think that, watching us, but that's because you didn't know us." He once again thought of her coming out of the bathroom, slipping off her robe—he'd never doubted that she was in love with Cheng. "But I'm a Chinese citizen working in Europe, so of course, I have a connection, a contact with the Ministry of State Security, and of course, one of the things I talked to them about was Cheng. I never told them what I've told you, only what they needed to know."

He wondered why the Chinese had never had Cheng under surveillance, given that the Americans had, and the Russians too to some extent. Then it struck him, that they hadn't been watching him because they'd had no reason to, because Cheng had been working for them too, which also backed up Marina's comment about how much he'd disliked nuclear weapons.

"He was working for the Chinese as well, wasn't he? Helping them to imbed his program in the US systems?"

She nodded, a faint sad smile, tinged with something that looked like pride. "He would have worked with the Russians too, but he reasoned it wouldn't be necessary. He was a patriot, he loved China, but he hated nuclear weapons, hated the danger they posed. He believed China would be destroyed if ever there was a nuclear war. He hoped his program would buy time, time in which people might step back from catastrophe. He even hoped to create a patch that he could upload without them knowing, that wouldn't just delay the command but make it invalid, but even without that . . ." She lowered her head. "He was an idealist."

"So America would have infiltrated the Chinese and Russian systems with his program. China would have tackled America, maybe India, all the likely flashpoints covered between the two of them. I'm not sure it will ever make a difference, even if it's never detected, but I can't fault his ambition."

"Does it help you? To know?"

"I doubt it." In some respects, it had been the worst possible revelation. Infiltrating the launch systems of another power's nuclear weapons was about as high-end as intelligence work got, almost the opposite end of the spectrum to the nonsense they'd been engaged in back in Yemen. "Had he started work on the patch?"

She shook her head. "That was just a dream. He believed the main work was already done. Is that why they killed him? Because they didn't need him anymore?"

"When did he deliver the program?"

If the answer was two weeks ago, then Freddie might as well just give himself up. If it was at the beginning of the surveillance period, then maybe there was a window, because something specific had happened recently to change the situation.

"Just over two years ago."

"Sorry?" He had heard her, but the answer didn't make any sense at all.

"Just over two years ago, to both the Americans and the Chinese."

"But that doesn't make any sense."

They'd waited over a year to put him under surveillance, over two years to kill him. Freddie tried to think how the events of the last week might still be linked to Cheng's program, but he just couldn't see the connection.

Jun said, "It must be why they killed him."

She'd bought into it, his pacifist idealism, a work of global sabotage she believed so important that it had cost Cheng his life.

"No, Jun, it can't be why they killed him." She looked ready to respond to a challenge, as if Freddie were criticizing Cheng's character. "That's why I asked about the additional patch he wanted to make, the one that would completely invalidate the commands, because something changed in the last week or two, something that made them do this. They think I saw it happening too, which is why they want to kill me."

He didn't bother to spell it out, but something must have happened a year ago too, something that triggered Oberman to launch a surveillance operation against Cheng more than a year after he'd delivered the only thing they'd ever need from him.

She shook her head. "I'm sure he hadn't started work on the patch. He would have told me. I don't know what else I can say. There is nothing else."

"When Cheng dealt with the Americans, who did he deal with? What was the name of the person?"

She looked doubtful, saying, "He never told me that, but . . . my contact, at the Ministry, she often asked me if he'd mentioned a certain name. I wrote it down somewhere."

"Was it Lars Oberman?"

"No, not a European name, an American name. I'll call her today. I have to call, to tell her what happened . . ."

"Tell her he's missing. Don't tell her you know what's happened to him."

She nodded but said, "I can ask her what that name was. I can tell her Cheng has written something on a note, but it's not clear."

He'd experienced this before from citizens of countries with an intrusive state security apparatus—they always seemed remarkably adept at navigating the system.

"That's good. Lars Oberman is the man who had him killed. But if the man your contact mentioned is the person Cheng dealt with, that might give me something to work with."

What he was actually hoping was that she'd come back with a name that Freddie could give to Drew Clark, the name of someone who'd pull rank over Oberman. It was an outside chance, but still the best he'd had until now.

"I can do that." She lowered her head again. "I don't even know where I'll stay tonight. I have nowhere to go."

"Do you have money?"

"Of course."

"Book into a hotel. Don't tell me where, just check in somewhere." He looked at his watch. "Let's meet again at five. Will that be enough time to speak to your contact?"

"Yes. She's here, in Europe."

"Okay. If you can bear to do it, I'd also like to bring my laptop, so that you can look properly at the footage I have, the websites Cheng visited, to see if there are any clues there."

"If it will help."

It was clear that she'd rather do anything else than look at that footage, but that she'd do whatever it took to avenge Cheng's death. In some way that was difficult to pinpoint, it made him feel like less of a person.

"Good. We could meet here again if you like."

She glanced quickly around, at the café, the wall of the church, the irregular cobbled square, the entry points, taking it all in with such a swift calculation that he wondered again if she might be in intelligence, and the "contact" was really just her superior.

Sure enough, having carried out the rapid survey, she said, "No. There are some small gardens in front of the Rathaus. Do you know it?"

"I know it."

"We can meet on one of the benches there."

"Okay. Five o'clock?" She nodded. Her sorrow and her insistence on how little Freddie had known Cheng had all seemed completely genuine, and yet he was wondering now, was she more than she seemed, did she know more than she'd said, did she have an agenda of her own? "I'm really sorry about everything that's happened. You have no reason to help me."

She smiled, as if to suggest he hadn't understood anything at all. "I'm not helping you. If I can find the name of the person who worked with Cheng, and if you can use that to hurt the man who killed him, I'll be happy." She looked at him coldly—not with hatred, but with no emotion at all. "I don't wish to be rude, but I don't care what happens to you."

"I understand, and it's not rude at all."

She stood up, taking him by surprise, and said, "I can't promise you anything, except that I'll be there at five o'clock, in the Rathaus gardens."

She turned and walked away, the case rattling awkwardly over the cobbles behind her, not the way they'd come in, but into a street that sloped away from the narrow side of the square. She remained in sight for a long time, patiently tugging the case over the small uneven obstacles of the cobbles, and just before she disappeared from view, she turned to make sure he was still sitting there.

At some level, the two of them were alike, because he really only cared about her to the extent that she could help him—and this name, if she could get it, might prove to be his first real break. But still she intrigued him, because she was beautiful and confusing, and perhaps even more of a mystery than Cheng had been.

Chapter Twenty-Six

Freddie became dispirited as he walked back to the hotel. He wasn't sure what he'd hoped to gain from the meeting with Jun, and she hadn't actually told him very much, but he could feel this situation slipping away from him in some way, if it had ever been within his grasp in the first place.

That seemed to be summed up by what he was now left clinging to: the hope that she'd provide a name that Freddie might be able to use to outmaneuver Lars Oberman. Wasn't that what Marina had said about the CIA, that it was the kind of organization in which there was always someone more senior to turn to?

Jun had also agreed to look at the footage of Cheng's web-browsing, but that seemed an even less promising avenue to explore because Freddie had seen enough to know there was almost certainly nothing of note. That meant he'd be causing her even more distress for no reason at all.

So it was no wonder that his spirits had fallen, but he still smiled when he reached the Madhouse and the doors slid open to reveal a game of table tennis taking place in the middle of the lobby. Arnold and Eva were playing, while a twenty-something man with a backpack stood watching.

Arnold was facing him and said, "Hey, Freddie!"

Eva turned, looking delighted to see him. "Hi, Freddie!" The ball went whizzing over her shoulder and Freddie reached out and caught it. She turned back to face Arnold. "That's unfair! You distracted me. We play the point again."

Freddie threw the ball back to the table, where it bounced and Arnold caught it.

"This is . . . interesting."

Arnold said, "Once a week, every Sunday afternoon, unless it's really busy."

"It's cool, isn't it?"

Freddie nodded and said, "But you've reminded me, I should probably extend my stay."

Even as he said it, he knew he couldn't stay. He'd been waiting for Jun and now he'd seen her, and there were no more reasons for being in Vienna and several for leaving.

"Oh, Eva and me did that on Friday. We just blocked you in for another week. Hope that's okay?"

"Sure," Freddie said, even though he doubted he'd be here for more than another day or two. He liked that they'd done it without being asked, almost as if they enjoyed having him around—maybe he was reading too much into it, but it was a long time since he'd come close to feeling like he belonged anywhere, and he realized how much he'd missed that.

Eva held up her paddle and said, "Do you want to play?" Freddie started to shake his head but then she turned to the guy with the backpack. "I'm sorry, were you waiting for a game?"

"No. I'm waiting to check in."

She glanced at Freddie with a smile. "Oops."

Freddie left them to it and took the elevator up to his room. He checked the charge in his camera and used it to focus on people coming and going on the street far below—he wanted to be able to check the

Rathaus gardens and the area around it from a distance, just to be sure he wasn't walking into anything.

He still couldn't shake the idea that Jun might be Chinese intelligence. And it was true what she'd said, that most Chinese nationals working in Europe probably had some involvement with the Ministry of State Security, but something about the way she'd studied the square around the café had put him on edge, making him wonder if that was the real Wei Jun and the devoted girlfriend act had been just that.

She wouldn't even need to do very much to make life difficult for him. She knew that the CIA team responsible for killing Cheng also wanted Freddie, so letting it slip on the wires that he'd be in a certain location at a certain time would be nothing short of an invitation to the men currently living in Freddie's apartment.

At four o'clock he checked the Qabbani email account, and was surprised to see that two messages had arrived earlier that day from Drew. He opened the first, looked at the text, and felt his blood sour even further.

> My friend, this isn't good. I made a few inquiries about what Lars Oberman is up to nowadays, and was told in no uncertain terms that it wasn't a good idea for me to be asking about Oberman at all. I foresee an appraisal for yours truly—because one of them was very suspicious, asking why I wanted to know. I'll still keep trying, but my advice to you is to go now and to go far.

It suggested that, far from being involved in rogue activities, Oberman was so high up the greasy pole that he was untouchable, even by his own colleagues. In turn, that meant the name Jun had for Freddie, if she had it at all, was unlikely to be of much use.

The second message was shorter and should have offered some reassurance, yet didn't, because Freddie sensed the tide was still moving relentlessly against him, and it seemed Drew sensed it too.

> PS You were tailed after leaving me the other day. A misunderstanding, but nothing to do with Oberman, and he lost you anyway. But I meant what I said—get out of Vienna.

Yes, he would get out of Vienna, but Freddie still set off to meet Jun with half an hour to spare. He took a tram past the gardens, looking casually for any signs of activity that might be suspicious. He got off at the university and walked back on the other side of the broad street, looking more at the cafés now and other places where a watcher might sit.

Still seeing nothing, he crossed over and skirted around the gardens, joining the tourists who strolled in front of the Rathaus, staring up at its vast neo-Gothic façade. The camera gave him an extra layer of invisibility, and by training the lens at an apparently confused assortment of targets, it allowed him to study the gardens as he walked alongside them.

It was still just before five when he drifted into the gardens and sat down on a bench that gave him a good view over the whole area. He'd been there only a few seconds when a young mother with a baby in a stroller came and sat alongside him. He smiled at her and glanced down at the baby, who was asleep. The woman smiled back, but then took out her phone and studied it.

Freddie continued to look casually through the camera now and then, occasionally firing off a shot. He checked the time and saw it was just after five, only a few minutes, but he began to wonder if she'd come, and that automatically made his nerves twitch and he scanned the area for anyone who might be watching him in turn.

The baby girl in the stroller began to stir and the mother put her phone away and started to talk to her. The baby smiled and chuckled, then grinned broadly at Freddie. He smiled back and the mother smiled at him too, then unclipped the harness and took the baby out.

The baby burbled, trying to reach for Freddie's camera, and the mother laughed and apologized. Freddie shook his head and pandered to the baby, making her giggle, even as his own thoughts were racing, unsure what he was even meant to do now.

The young mother's phone rang and she answered, happy and carefree. She ended the call and put her daughter back into the stroller with a minimum of fuss, then stood and said goodbye to Freddie. He bid her goodbye in return and waved to the baby, but her attention was already elsewhere.

He checked the time again, nearly ten past the hour. He raised the camera, took a random shot, but then as he lowered it, he spotted her, walking in at the far end of the gardens. Jun was looking about for him, so he stood and started along the paths toward her.

She saw him, and looked briefly at the maze of paths between them before seeing the route to reach him and turning right. Freddie was still looking around, taking in the people, most of them tourists.

When they were finally on the same path, heading toward each other, she smiled, perhaps briefly forgetting why she was here or who he was, what he'd done. She seemed amused by her confusion with the paths, by her late arrival, but with that smile she looked so beautiful, and he thought of her naked again, and maybe Cheng had loved her, but it had always seemed as if he hadn't actually noticed how attractive she was.

Freddie smiled back, but then someone cut across his path and bumped into Jun before clumsily moving around her and off again, offering no apology. The guy was big and Jun was slight so she stumbled sideways a step before righting herself.

The smile stayed in place for a moment, but fell away then and she looked confused and Freddie picked up his pace. He was about to call something after the guy, telling him to watch where he was going, but even from behind, he could see now that it was Jimmy Fernandez.

Jun took another step, but it was unsteady. Fernandez had done something to her, that collision. She smiled awkwardly, then made for a bench off to her right. An elderly couple were sitting on it, looking like American tourists, but she almost fell toward it and slumped down so abruptly that the old woman looked alarmed.

Freddie called to them, saying, "Someone just bumped into her. She's hurt. I'll try to stop him."

Jun didn't look hurt, except for the awkward and confused expression on her face, but the elderly lady could see it too.

"Oh my goodness!"

Freddie was right, they were American, and he was vaguely conscious as he broke into a run that they were eagerly trying to help Jun now.

He looked ahead to where Fernandez was still walking away at a fast but steady pace. Fernandez didn't look back, but seemed to sense he was being followed and with a barely perceptible shift moved up into a jog, and then a run.

He was fast, and Freddie had to hold the camera and the bag to stop them bouncing about as he chased, but he still kept him within sight as Fernandez ran out of the gardens and toward the university. But then, quite suddenly, he lost him. Freddie stopped, scanning the people ahead of him. Too late, he saw Fernandez climb into a black BMW that pulled away smoothly into the city traffic.

He turned and walked back, seeing there was a small crowd around Jun now, including two police officers. Jun lay on the floor and a female police officer seemed to be trying to revive her. The male colleague was talking to the elderly couple and they pointed at Freddie as he approached.

Freddie looked down at Jun's face, disturbed by the glassiness of her open eyes, staring blankly up into the sky above her. Her skin looked waxy, and there was no question in Freddie's mind that she was dead, that the beautiful timid smile she'd given him would be the last thing she'd ever do—the wastefulness of it was overwhelming.

And looking down at her, his mind lurched back to Yemen. How could it do anything else? That final operation had foundered on his failure to see that Abdullah wasn't just a pawn, but someone who had his own agenda, someone who'd anticipated what the Western intelligence agencies were trying to do and had used it for his own ends.

Freddie had misread that situation and now he had misread this one. Oberman's kill team stationed in his apartment had not been tipped off about Freddie's continuing presence in the city. Nor had they come for him—they'd come for Wei Jun. And whether she'd been an intelligence officer or not, she'd probably intended to help him, but any help she might have offered was lost.

"You saw someone attack her?"

Freddie pulled his attention from the futile attempts to save Jun and nodded as he looked at the police officer who'd asked the question. "A man, he bumped into her, really hard, and it knocked her sideways, and then she collapsed next to that lady."

Freddie noticed some of the other bystanders listening in.

The police officer looked confused, and said, "But he didn't hit her?"

"He collided with her. It didn't look hard enough to hurt her." He shrugged, showing his own confusion. "Maybe he did something to her? I don't know. She tried to walk on, then I saw her stagger."

"Could you describe the man?"

Yes, I could show you footage of him in my apartment.

"He had his back to me the whole time. I just saw it was a man, quite stocky . . ."

Two teenage boys with skateboards stepped forward and one said, "We saw him. We can describe him."

"You saw the attack also?"

The other boy said, "Yeah, he bumped into her, but he lifted his hand like this and hit her on the back of the neck." He demonstrated in slow motion, using his friend as a double for Jun.

The officer moved in to talk to the boys in more detail and Freddie edged around him, not making any show of walking away, but looking back to where the female officer now sat on her haunches and shook her head with a look of sadness and bafflement.

The elderly couple were still sitting on the bench, looking down at the scene as though in the front row.

But now the old man took his jacket off and gave it to the officer and said in English, "Use this to cover her up. Poor girl deserves some dignity."

"Thank you," said the officer. She carefully draped the jacket over Jun's face and upper body, with a care and tenderness that left Freddie feeling inadequate. These three people were treating the stranger before them with dignity in death, with a humanity that Freddie had himself misplaced somewhere and never fully recovered.

Once again, he was thinking of Yemen, those moments afterwards, the stillness and the quiet within the SUV, Talal and Pete dead in the front, Mel's head slumped against him, as if she'd fallen asleep on a long car journey, his realization that he had been spared but that he had to get out of there, that he had to drive that SUV and reach safety. The shame of his escape.

The police officer didn't speak to him again, and even when more arrived, there were other witnesses, better witnesses. No one thought it was really anything to do with him, and in some way, that felt about right.

He stayed until the ambulance came, and then he put the camera into his messenger bag, bulky alongside the laptop and the gun, and walked into the old city, not sure where he was walking, but only wanting to think. He wanted to think about himself, and what his plan should be now, but even more than that, he wanted to think about what had just happened, because he couldn't shake the feeling that in some way it had been his fault.

True, it hadn't been his fault that they'd targeted Cheng, nor even that they'd targeted Jun, but if he'd been slightly more observant, slightly less concerned about his own safety, surely he would have seen that Oberman's team had come back for her, not him. Would it have made a difference, had he warned her, and would she have even listened to his warning? He had no way of knowing.

All he really knew was that Oberman had viewed Jun as being a risk for the same reason Freddie was, because he thought they'd seen too much, that they both had an insight into whatever Cheng had done in his final weeks to earn his own death sentence. Yet Freddie was convinced that Oberman was wrong about both of them.

Jun had died for nothing, and after all the death Freddie had seen, he wasn't sure why that bothered him so much, but somewhere deep within he could feel a shift taking place on the back of that feeling. Until now he'd essentially wanted little more than to stay alive, but increasingly, he knew he also wanted Lars Oberman dead.

Chapter Twenty-Seven

He walked slowly but far, thinking only to put some space between himself and his former apartment. Because he was acutely conscious of the gun in his messenger bag, and even though nothing had changed directly for him, he felt an overwhelming urge to confront them, to kill them, the two men who'd holed up in his apartment and murdered Wei Jun.

He tried to tell himself he was angry about her death and about how needless it had been, but in truth he hadn't known her at all, certainly not enough to be moved to vengeance. The real source of his anger was more personal, the fact that he'd badly miscalculated again and that they seemed to be winning.

He wanted to turn that on its head, to confront them, but he also knew it would undoubtedly be a mistake to do so, because he was no soldier. The impulse was still strong, an almost physical desire to distance himself from the person he'd become—passive, watching, doing nothing—and so he walked, because there was nothing else he could do. He walked until darkness had descended, and then he stepped into a small bar that was empty except for a few young guys sitting around playing cards and drinking beer.

He drank a few beers himself, trying to keep it slow, not wanting to get drunk when his thoughts were already in fragments. If Drew was right, then the name Jun had hoped to provide for him might not have been much use anyway, but either way, now he was left with nothing.

Perhaps the only hope was to disappear, to follow Drew's advice to go now and go far. That was what Freddie always seemed to do—he fled, he pulled the body of his friend from the car and left it in the dirt, and he fled.

By the time he left the bar, the city was quieter, a Sunday-night calm, and a patchy fog was clinging to the buildings. He'd crossed the Danube canal before finding the bar and guessed he was still close enough to the river to account for the fog.

He looked around, trying to get his bearings, not even sure he could face going back to the hotel, then walked in what he presumed was more or less the right direction. There weren't many other people about, which suited him, and when he turned onto one street and saw a group up ahead and heard their raised and raucous voices, his first instinct was to change direction and head back the other way.

Instead he stopped, edging into a doorway, and watched, wanting to see what was going on before he committed to setting off again. It was three or four young guys, but he was certain he could hear a female voice too. They were all moving about, agitated, excited in a dangerous way, and as one of them made an odd little sideways jump, Freddie saw the girl beyond them.

Once again, he almost turned and walked away, because a glance was all it took—the floppy purple Mohawk—it was Eva, from the Madhouse. They were hassling her, he thought, and she sounded angry, but with an edge of fear in her voice.

One of them reached out and grabbed at her breast and she knocked his hand away and slapped him, and the other three laughed, but quickly closed in on her, pushing her toward the wall. She shouted, loud enough that they looked uncertain, backed off a little, and then quite suddenly they were running toward Freddie and he wasn't sure why at first, but then he saw that they'd snatched her small backpack.

Freddie was hidden in the doorway, lost in shadow, but he could see them, their faces triumphant, like this was just a game they'd won. They were young, dark-haired, with features that could be Eastern European or Middle Eastern. And they were running in such a haphazard fashion that he kept getting glimpses of Eva still standing some way behind them.

They'd almost reached the doorway. The one at the front saw him there and, even in his exuberance, he gave Freddie a warning look, letting him know this was none of his business, which it wasn't. But that look, it scooped up all of Freddie's anger and self-loathing, all the things he'd been carrying deep within himself for five years, and brought it spilling to the surface.

The first ran past, then the next two, running side by side, and then the one with the stolen backpack following up the rear. But he didn't run past. Freddie stepped out and swung his fist hard into his throat, clotheslining him. The guy almost flipped over and crashed to the ground, the bag skidding away from him.

Freddie stepped in and kicked him in the groin, and wanted to keep kicking him, his own adrenaline racing, but he knew his limitations, and could hear some hurried words and the other three stamping to a halt a short distance away. Freddie slipped open the catch on the messenger bag and reached inside.

The downed guy was crying and groaning and holding himself. The others were running back now, warily, but the one who'd stared a warning reached into his jacket and Freddie saw the flash of a blade. Freddie held his ground, facing them, and then they saw the gun and stopped.

The knife was put away again, and the guy put his palms up to Freddie, trying to show in his expression now that he meant no harm. Freddie didn't speak, didn't flinch, and as the downed guy crawled toward them, the other two pulled him up while visibly trying to keep their distance.

The one who'd had the knife was still looking at Freddie, even as the other three stumbled away up the street like two friends helping a drunk. The guy didn't look like Abdullah, and Abdullah himself was long dead, but the look he'd first given Freddie a few moments ago had reminded him of that day, and it felt like exorcising a ghost somehow as he smiled and raised the gun a little and said, "Pow."

The guy looked even more alarmed, and took a few backward steps, before turning and running after his friends. Freddie nodded to himself, then slipped the gun back into the messenger bag and leaned down to pick up Eva's backpack.

He turned and saw Eva standing along the street, far enough away that she probably hadn't seen the gun, and probably hadn't seen enough to know what had gone on, apart from some sort of standoff.

He walked toward her and she started to thank him, her voice shaky, but as he got closer, she ground to a halt and did a double take before saying, "Freddie?"

"Hi."

He held out the backpack and she took it off him, her hand trembling, her face full of confusion.

"What are you doing here?"

He looked around, up at the fog where it seemed suspended around the lights.

"I don't even know where 'here' is. I had some bad news earlier, just work stuff, and I went for a walk to clear my head and had some beers. I thought I was kind of going in the right direction for the hotel." She shook her head and pointed back the way he'd come, and he could see her hand was still shaking. "I'm sorry, are you okay?"

"I'm fine. Assholes. This is normally a really safe neighborhood. And I don't want you to think it's because they were immigrants—there are lots of immigrants here, but they were . . ." She shrugged. "Thanks so much, Freddie. Did they hurt you?"

"No, I think I hurt one of them, but he deserved it. Do you live near here? I can walk you the rest of the way, but I don't think they'll come back."

"I'll be fine. But you . . . you could come anyway. You can meet Izzy. And you can have a drink. It's the least I can do." He wasn't sure he wanted to meet anyone right now, wasn't sure he wanted to get any more acquainted with Eva than he was at present, but she saw his reluctance and was quick to counter it. "Please, I'd really like you to come."

"Okay."

She smiled. "It's not far. This way." They started walking. "Was it very bad, the news you had?"

"Like I said, just work stuff, but stressful. I wanted to clear my head, but I've no idea how far I walked or where I've ended up."

"This is the Karmeliter Quarter. The Prater park is just over in that direction." She pointed. "Can I ask you something, Freddie?"

"Sure."

"You won't be offended?"

"I doubt it."

She nodded, but still looked unsure of herself. "Are you in trouble?"

He smiled at her. "What makes you ask that?"

"I don't know. Just a feeling."

"I thought you told me I had lots of good energy."

"You do, but sometimes that can get you into trouble. You're not like our other guests."

"How so?" He was actually thinking about the businessman who'd checked in on the same day as him—now, he *really* hadn't been like the other guests.

"Maybe I didn't say it right. I like our guests, a lot of them anyway, but they're all kind of the same, and you're not. Arnold thinks so too. That's why I asked if you were in trouble, because it's like you're carrying something heavy a lot of the time, you know, like something you know about and no one else does."

He smiled again, not wanting to dismiss her, but wanting to throw a protective wall around the area she was inadvertently probing. "My life isn't as interesting as you think. Sure, I've got some problems, but nothing as serious as a lot of people are dealing with."

"Okay. I just had a terrible feeling when I realized it was you just now." He thought she was going to say that she feared he'd been following her, but she took him by surprise. "I had a terrible feeling you might . . . I don't know, be thinking about doing something stupid, something . . ."

He looked at her. "Eva, I've had a bad day, and yes, there are things in my life that I wish were different, but I would never, ever contemplate killing myself. No matter how bad things got, I have too many reasons to stay alive."

She smiled, so reassured that he wondered quite how suicidal he'd seemed.

"I didn't mean to suggest . . ."

"Not at all. And it's kind of you to think of me at all."

She pointed at a door and said, "You're going to love our apartment."

"And I can see your art."

"Yes!" She was beaming, as if she'd already forgotten the attack in the street and her analysis of Freddie's mental or emotional state. And as he followed her inside, he was determined to keep the mood like that for as long as he was here.

Chapter Twenty-Eight

She opened the door to let him into a surprisingly grand hallway, high-ceilinged, the sort of place that might have belonged to a lawyer or banker a hundred years ago. But that aside, the whole place had the feel of something that now belonged to young artists.

There were paintings and random objects hanging all over the walls, odd assortments of furniture, most of it upcycled and brightly colored, sculptures and various artifacts from various Eastern religions, including both Buddha and Shiva statues, and candles everywhere, many of them lit.

There was a pervading smell too, that took Freddie back to college and the rooms of people who'd had similar tastes. Was it incense, or jasmine, or a mixture of different scents? Whatever it was, he immediately felt relaxed.

They walked into a large living room, big sofas covered with throws, and patterned sheets attached to the ceiling and hanging down in billows so that it almost resembled the inside of a tent.

A young woman was sitting there reading, engrossed. She had short blond hair and was dressed all in black, and as she looked up Freddie almost took a step back because she was one of the most beautiful people he'd ever seen.

She smiled, put the book aside, and rose from the sofa in one grace-ful motion. She came over, kissed Eva, and then looked at her with concern.

"I'm fine. Some guys were hassling me on the street, tried to steal my bag. Freddie was passing. He stopped them."

"Freddie from the hotel?" She looked at him with bemused aston-ishment, and even as he was feeling flattered by the fact Eva had spoken about him, she held out her hand and took hold of his rather than shaking it. "I had a feeling we would meet. Hello, Freddie. I'm Izzy."

"I've heard a lot about you."

"Will you have some wine?"

"I really should be going. I have a busy couple of days ahead." She smiled at him, an expression that was at once quizzical and calming, and he realized she was waiting for him to actually answer the question. "Sure, thanks."

"Good." She gestured at the paintings. "Most of these are Eva's."

She left the room as Eva said, "Only some of them. Let me show you."

But she only needed to point out one for him to be able to spot all the others. They were an unusual mix of abstract and figurative, vibrant colors, and the texture she'd talked about, deep terrains of paint. It made him wonder how often he'd checked into a hotel in the past, or been served in a restaurant, and not realized he was being served by someone talented, because these paintings were as beguiling as Eva herself.

They turned at the sound of glasses clinking, and Izzy came in carrying a bottle and corkscrew in one hand, three wine glasses in the other. She carried them with the easy confidence of someone who'd probably worked in a bar or restaurant herself.

"I hope red is okay?"

"Red's fine, thanks."

She nodded, and as she uncorked the wine, she said, "What do you think?"

"The paintings? I think they're amazing. I mean, I'm no expert, but they're so beautiful." He turned to Eva. "And I understand what you mean, about capturing the texture in a photograph. You need to see them in the flesh."

He thought of Drew, who'd used the same expression about the Bruegel, seeing it in the flesh for the first time.

"I'm pleased you like them. And I need people to see them. I need to get a gallery to back me, but . . . it's difficult."

"You could open your own."

She laughed, thinking he was joking, which in itself suggested he didn't know much at all about the art market or how tough it was. Sometimes he felt he didn't know much about anything. For the last year, he'd been dedicated to studying Jiang Cheng and it seemed he hadn't even learned very much about him.

They sat down as Izzy poured, then raised their glasses and drank.

"Are you an artist, Izzy?"

"I studied art, but I'm a theater set designer. I've had a few successes, but my dream is to design for the opera."

Eva leaned over and leafed through a large book on the coffee table. "These are some of Izzy's designs." She handed it to Freddie. "This was for a production in Graz last year."

Even as he looked at it, Izzy said, "That's really just an idea book. Naturally, I make more detailed drawings, models too, but it gives you a snapshot, maybe."

He looked at the drawing, a three-dimensional rendering of the set for a production of Wedekind's *Spring Awakening*. He turned through some of the other pages, drawings that were part creative, part architectural.

As he put the book back, he shook his head and smiled. "I don't like being around this much talent."

Izzy laughed, then said, "But you are . . . an IT specialist?" Did she sound doubtful? Before meeting her, he'd imagined Izzy as a spiritual earth-mother type, not the stunning metropolitan in front of him now, but she still seemed to have something uncanny about her, something that tied in with the things Eva had said.

"It's complicated, but yeah, I work with computers, information. So I guess that makes me an IT specialist."

In truth, his original job had been as creative as theirs. It was just that, in the end, Abdullah had rewritten the script and Freddie had been the last to know about it.

As if tuning into that thought, Eva said, "It's been such a crazy day today. Not just those guys hassling me on the street. A tourist died on the Rathausplatz." She turned to Freddie. "You know the gardens in front of the Rathaus, the city hall?"

"What happened?"

"We're not sure. One of the guests told us, and then Arnold found out. They think maybe she just died of a heart attack or something, but she wasn't old. She just collapsed on a bench there in the gardens and died. I think she was Chinese."

Freddie wondered what they'd used. From what the skateboarders had said, Fernandez had almost certainly punctured her skin with something, but that had never been Freddie's field and there had probably been developments in the last five years anyway, because there were always developments in the technology of death.

Hearing about it again, and knowing the truth of it, only reinforced his sense of the wastefulness of her death. Jun hadn't been in a position to harm Oberman, and it was true Oberman couldn't have known that, but her murder still seemed wanton.

They planned the same for Freddie, of course, but he was determined not to let that happen, a determination that kept growing even as his options appeared to be drying up. He wasn't a soldier, but he was more than the civilian they took him for. And maybe his career had ended with a disaster, but he'd once been a master in his own small field. He just had to exploit the gap between who he'd been and who Oberman thought he was.

"Freddie had a bad day too."

"Oh?"

"Not a bad day. I had some bad news, about work, and in the end it meant I had a good day." Izzy looked questioningly. "I went for a walk, got lost, and that's why I'm here."

Again, he thought she might say something about the coincidence of happening along at that precise moment, but that was a paranoia from his world, not theirs.

"I think you were always meant to come here at some point. I just sense it."

"Me too," said Eva. She looked at Izzy. "Didn't I tell you?"

"Yes. Eva told me you have lots of good energy, and I see that, but I think bad things have happened to you, maybe a long time ago, but you've been thinking about them recently."

Freddie sipped at his wine and smiled. He didn't want to be rude to them, and it was tempting to let himself be swept up in this little world of theirs, an environment that felt warm and comforting and full of an unquestioning love, but it was a step too far to believe that this was any more than educated guesswork.

It was much the same as Eva's palm-reading, trading in vagaries. He was sure most people could think of something bad that had happened to them at some time in their lives, and that most people on their own in a strange city would be prone to dwell on the past and think about the wrong turns they'd taken in life. There was no magical insight, and no special powers at play.

Even so, he said, "I lost some friends a few years ago, in an accident, and it's true, I have been thinking about it the last day or two, but only because I'm thinking about bigger questions, changing my life, doing something different."

"You mean giving up your job?"

"Kind of. I work for myself, but . . ." His words fell away, and a terrible sense of urgency swept in on the silence. Confronting Oberman's men in his apartment would have been a mistake, but he still had to confront them, on his own terms, in his own way. Freddie looked at his watch. "I really need to go. I've got a lot to do over the next few days."

Eva looked at him, alarmed, maybe still fearful about his state of mind, then at Izzy, as if asking her to do something.

"It isn't so late, Freddie. Couldn't you stay a little bit longer?" She picked up the bottle and leaned over and he allowed her to top up his glass, then watched as she emptied the rest of the wine into their own glasses. "What kind of accident was it, that killed your friends?"

"A helicopter. We were installing communications systems for an aid agency in Yemen. I should have been there too, but I was ill. The helicopter crashed and the three of them were killed."

"That's terrible. And you feel guilty?"

"It's natural, don't you think?" Tuning in to the way Izzy and Eva thought, he added, "You might disagree, but I think the best course is to accept that it's a natural feeling, to acknowledge it, to carry it and not let it carry you."

"I agree," said Eva. "That's beautiful. You know, I had a boyfriend . . ." She saw Freddie's reaction. "When I was younger, you know how it is. But he committed suicide, and for a long time I felt guilty, and sometimes still do. What you said, it's the correct way."

And now he felt cheap, because he'd been making it up, a little random hippy philosophy so that he didn't have to talk about what had really happened in his life. But Eva was relating it to a traumatic experience of her own, an experience that also put her worries that he might be suicidal into different relief.

There was a beautiful atmosphere in this apartment, and these were beautiful people, and any other time he could have happily relaxed, sinking into this sofa, drinking wine with them, but he didn't belong here, not yet, maybe not ever.

He looked at his watch again and took a gulp of his wine. "I have to go."

Eva said, "Where?"

"To the Madhouse, of course." He finished the wine and put the glass on the table. "You can't know how glad I am that I came here."

Izzy put her own glass down and leaned forward, saying, "Freddie, why don't you stay tonight? You probably won't get a taxi, and it's quite a walk. We don't have a spare room . . ."

"We do, but we use it as a studio."

"But you can sleep on the sofa."

There was such an eagerness there, one still wrapped up with a fear that it wasn't safe for him to leave, and a little part of him acknowledged that maybe it wasn't all hokum, that maybe they could sense something. But that changed nothing. He had to leave.

Chapter Twenty-Nine

Out on the street, the fog had deepened, but didn't look in danger of reaching the density of earlier in the week. He opened up his phone, checked the map, and set off walking, but not toward the hotel.

He still carried the sweet smell of Eva and Izzy's apartment, the velvet-berried taste of the wine, the warmth of their welcome, and he was happy to keep those things as he walked, but he also knew that he'd have to put them away and forget about them. He had too much to do in the days ahead.

In the chill of the shrouded and quiet streets, those more pressing needs slowly began to eat away at the pleasant sensations of where he'd just been. He had so much to do, but everything was still jumbled and incomplete, because of course, he didn't actually know for sure what he could do to counter Oberman.

What he needed was someone to talk to, someone who could give him a perspective, someone who knew something of this world. And he knew that he was taking a risk, one that he might end up ruing for the next five years, or forever, but his instincts drew him to her all the same. Going back into his phone, he put in a call.

She answered immediately, but in such a casually offhand way that it threw him.

"Marina? It's Freddie Makin. I'm sorry about the hour, but I need to talk to you."

There was a brief but weighted pause. "Can it wait?"

"No." He tried to pin down the unusual tone in her voice. "You weren't in bed?"

But she laughed now, and sounded haughty and faintly mocking again as she said, "I'm not *so* old, Freddie. Do you have a pen? I'll give you the address."

"I have it already."

"Of course you do."

"I'm on my way. I'll be there in ten minutes."

"Then I'll be expecting you."

She ended the call without saying anything more, and he checked the map again and took a left up ahead. The streets were empty and eerily still, so quiet that the noise of some sort of machinery carried faintly from a long way off.

She buzzed him up without speaking when he reached her building, a place that had a similar old-world charm and faded grandeur to the one Eva and Izzy lived in. When he reached Marina's apartment he found the door ajar, so he knocked lightly and walked in.

Again, in the basics, this place was similar to the one he'd just left, but the banker or lawyer of an earlier age wouldn't have felt so out of place here. It was classically and expensively furnished.

From somewhere unseen, she called, "Go on through to the living room. Make yourself at home."

He walked into a large room on his right, bookshelves from floor to ceiling, and the walls between them crammed full of art, most of it oriental. He studied a couple of them, feeling this room represented a life he could envy just as much as Eva and Izzy's. It seemed every place he stepped into lately spoke to him of lives richer than his.

He heard her come in and turned to see her carrying a small tray. She was wearing an oriental dressing gown, but with normal clothes beneath it. And she didn't look like someone who was being kept from her bed.

"I thought coffee and brandy, given the hour. You're not one of those people who can't handle caffeine late at night?"

"Not at all."

She put the tray on a small table and gestured for him to sit in one of the armchairs.

"Do you take milk or sugar?"

"No, this is fine, thanks. And thanks for agreeing to see me."

She sat opposite him and smiled. "You didn't give me a great deal of choice." She raised her glass. "Good health."

Freddie nodded, and sipped at his brandy, but then said, "I met with Wei Jun this morning. She told me a certain amount, but she was hoping to get a name for me, from her government contact, someone who might have dealt with Cheng. I arranged to meet her again at five, in the gardens in front of the Rathaus."

Marina put her glass back on the table.

"She was the tourist who died there today?" He nodded. "I assume you didn't kill her. Do you know who did?"

"One of the same team who killed Cheng. I knew they were back in the city. I thought they'd found out I was still here, but obviously they'd come for Jun. Either her government contact wasn't secure or she spoke to someone else—she gave herself away somehow. He bumped into her right in front of me. I'm guessing he poisoned her."

Marina nodded and looked deep in thought for a moment, as if analyzing what she'd heard, deciding how it affected her, if at all, and then she appeared to come to some sort of decision.

"Cheng dealt with someone called Lars Oberman. CIA."

Why had she told him that? Was it another step toward openness between them or was she just feeding him facts she suspected he already knew as a way of putting him at ease? His intuition told him it was the former, but he was still cautious in choosing the words of his response.

"I know, and that's whose team killed him. But I suggested that name to Jun and it didn't seem familiar to her. She said there was an American-sounding name, but it could have been a false lead anyway. I have no way of knowing. All I know is that my only lead is dead, and my contact in the CIA tells me Oberman is untouchable, and wants me dead too."

"I assume you have no dealings with S8 anymore?" Freddie shook his head, not bothering to continue with the charade of denying he'd been a part of it. "Then I can offer you sympathy, good coffee, and excellent brandy, but I'm not sure what else I can do to help. Do you have anything in mind?"

"The opposite of our chess game, I guess. I don't think defensive moves will be enough. I have to go after Oberman in some way, destabilize him, but that could be almost impossible. You were right about the nuclear weapons—it looks like that's what this is all about."

She remained impassive for a few seconds, then reached down for her coffee and took a sip, and only as she placed the cup back on the saucer did she speak again. "I was always curious about how much Cheng shared with Jun. Did she know very much?"

"Enough. Enough to describe Cheng's program to a layman like me." He smiled a little, grudgingly. "You know all about it, don't you? Did Cheng tell you?"

"Goodness no, Cheng and I never discussed anything like that. But yes, naturally we knew about it, and, as it happens, I believe we've already detected and disabled it on our own systems."

"And by 'we,' of course, you mean the University of Vienna?"

She laughed, but then grew serious again. "The one thing that's really puzzled me these last few days is the timing. Why now?"

"That's puzzling me too. Jun told me the program was created two years ago, but my surveillance operation only started a year ago, and then this all happens in the last two weeks. Jun talked about a new patch he wanted to create, but she didn't think he was working on it before he died."

"I have a hunch, and you should hope I'm right, because it could dramatically improve your chances of survival. So, I think we both accept that if this does concern nuclear weapons systems and they think you saw something sensitive, they'll keep committing resources until you're eliminated. But the timing is wrong. We also both know that most of what goes on in this shadow-world of ours is never about the big things—it's always something peripheral, something destined to be rendered irrelevant by history."

"But I have no idea what else it could be. Unless Cheng was writing a sitcom and plagiarizing *The Big Bang Theory*."

She smiled as if at an undergraduate and said, "I have no idea what you're talking about, although I presume it was an attempt at humor. The thing is, Freddie, you saw something, because you were forwarding everything to them and they believe you saw it, so it was there—you just have to drill down, through any material you still have, through your memories, every little thing, and find out what changed for Oberman in this last year and in this last fortnight."

Even as he thought back over the remaining footage he had of Cheng, of his apparently random web-browsing habits, and even as he remembered how lacking in promise that footage was, Freddie still felt an edge of adrenaline. Because at every level, he knew Marina was right, that the timing was wrong for this to be about Cheng's nuclear program, and that it was never about the big things—Freddie's whole career with S8 had ultimately supported that truth.

"You're right. I guess I knew it all along, but when you have no one to bounce ideas off . . ." She nodded her understanding. "I'd intended to have Jun look through them with me, but I'll go back through the tapes."

She nodded again, but her eyes were fixed on him, and finally she said, "Did you . . . have any sort of plan in mind before coming here?

I mean, if it had been about the nuclear weapons, what could you have done, apart from try to disappear?"

He smiled. "I'm done with disappearing. I didn't realize it, but that's what I've done these last five years, disappeared behind a bank of monitors, or behind an existential novel in a café. No, I'm done with that." She still looked curious, and he was aware he hadn't answered the question. "I'm not sure what I would have done. Probably reverted to my old tricks. Use what information I have to spread a little discord in his operation, maybe get some of his guys called back to Langley, bait Oberman into the open. Maybe try to kill him."

She laughed, and at first he thought she was laughing at him, because Freddie was no killer, but then he realized that she was laughing with him. At least, he *hoped* she was laughing with him.

Chapter Thirty

It took him thirty minutes to get back to the hotel, but he preferred to walk, giving himself time to think of practical things he could do to gain some breathing space and unsettle Oberman. There was a danger in taking that line of action, but he knew from experience that most people were likely to make mistakes when they sensed they were losing control.

When he reached the Madhouse, the door didn't slide open: it was the first time he'd ever come back after the doors were locked at 1 a.m. He stood there for a few seconds, looking at his faint reflection in the glass, still very much the *appearance* of someone who belonged in a hotel like this. A night porter he didn't recognize came and opened the door.

As soon as he got to his room, he emailed Drew through the Qabbani account with a simple message—*I'm going after Oberman. I just wanted you to know. If it comes back to you, tell them it's me.*

Next he transferred his pictures from the camera to the laptop. He expanded them and searched the faces of the people he'd captured on the Rathausplatz, disappointed not to see Fernandez or anyone else familiar.

Then he held his breath as he saw that his final random shot had captured Jun, just as she'd entered the gardens, before he'd actually seen her. He expanded it and felt a small wave of sorrow as he looked at her face, serene and beautiful and only minutes away from death.

Supporting evidence from the Rathausplatz would have been better, but instead, he went back to the final footage he had from his own apartment, and used it to cut pictures of the two-man team, one of whom he knew was called Jimmy Fernandez. Constructing fake dossiers and manipulating the news had been an everyday part of his former life and it felt oddly satisfying to find himself doing it again.

Once he was done, he created a new Gmail account in the name of "Friend of China," and used it to email the information to a few key people at the Chinese Embassies in Vienna and Washington, telling them that a CIA cell had killed both Cheng and Jun, giving them the address of his old apartment where they'd been staying and the location of their base in Prague.

He used the same account to email much the same message to the Federal Police in Vienna. Then he sent the picture of the two-man team to the Orion News Agency in Istanbul and the Qatar News Network in Doha, using a proxy account from his S8 days, informing them that these were the two Americans the Austrian authorities were seeking in relation to the death of two Chinese nationals.

It was a scattergun approach, because he had no idea how the Chinese or the Federal Police would act on it, or if they'd act at all, although he'd disseminated enough fake stories through Orion and QNN in his time to know that he could rely on them. And he also knew that any activity or chatter on the wires would be enough in itself to unsettle Oberman and his team, making them fear an imminent attack from some quarter or other.

He pushed away from the desk now, got up, and walked around the room, thinking he probably needed another line of attack. Freddie's manipulation of the news might rattle Oberman, but in real terms it might only knock two people out of his team and Freddie felt he needed much more than that to tilt the field in his favor.

Years ago, he'd known a German intelligence officer, and Freddie thought of emailing him now with the possible link between the CIA unit stationed in Prague and the death of Leo Behnke. The only trouble was that Freddie couldn't remember the contact's surname. He was called Tom, and as Freddie walked, he silently worked through the alphabet, trying to get the second name to shake itself loose.

It didn't work, but as he paced about, he glanced up at the shelves above the sofa, an automatic reflex he had nowadays, searching for signs of tampering, for a camera, a telltale wire. That in turn made him think of Cheng, and how lacking in suspicion he'd seemed, even after the warning from his friend in Hamburg.

Freddie stopped walking, but still stared at the shelf, as if the answer lay there. Hamburg. A friend in Hamburg had warned Cheng. But hadn't Sonja also told him that Leo had sent the surveillance material to a contractor in Hamburg for translation, to someone who *did* speak Mandarin?

Freddie went back to the laptop, checked the time for the first Railjet to Munich in the morning and booked himself a ticket. He felt bad about it, because Sonja had needed him, had pleaded with him, and he'd offered nothing more than reassurance, but he needed her now.

It could easily turn out to be nothing more than coincidence, but if the two contacts in Hamburg were the same person, it could equally prove to be the breakthrough that Freddie needed. The translator in Hamburg had told Leo there was nothing of interest in Cheng's recorded conversations, but what if the translator was also the person who'd warned Cheng that he was being watched? If that were the case, he'd have had every reason to lie to Leo on behalf of his friend Cheng, and it was possible those transcripts really did contain the information Freddie was looking for.

He shut everything down then and set his alarm, determined to sleep for a few hours. And when sleep wouldn't come, he let his mind drift back to Eva and Izzy, and the familiar scent and warmth that filled their apartment. He thought of Eva's art and Izzy's set designs, and the velvet smoothness of the wine, letting those memories flood in over everything else.

It worked, in that he fell asleep, but he didn't feel much rested when the alarm woke him a few hours later and he jumped from the bed, agitated, fragments of dreams falling away. Nor had he been dreaming of Eva and Izzy.

The bathroom light was on, and even though he knew he'd simply forgotten to turn it off, he was nervous as he pushed the door open, half expecting to see Talal's face reflected in the mirror, or Melissa soaking in the bath. The room was empty, of course, but he knew he couldn't keep going on like this, that it was eating him away.

Chapter Thirty-One

He dozed on and off throughout the four-hour train journey, and felt sluggish as he stepped out into the cold gray of morning in Munich. He stopped and had an espresso, scanning the station as he stood at the counter, reassured by the normality of everything around him.

He left then and took a taxi directly to Sonja's apartment building, reckoning that the Behnke & Co. office was probably permanently closed now. He had to hope she was still alive, and that she'd help him. Not that he'd helped her when she needed it, and although so little time had elapsed since he'd last been here, he already found it hard to excuse the way he'd abandoned her like that.

There was no response when he got to Sonja's apartment and pressed the buzzer. He listened, but there was no noise anywhere. He knocked on the door and heard a chain sliding free, but it was behind him, and he turned as an elderly lady opened her door and looked out.

"Good morning," he said in German.

She nodded in response, and said, "She's gone to visit her mother."

"I see. Do you know when she'll be back?"

The woman had been standing cautiously, as if ready to jump back and slam the door, but something about Freddie seemed to reassure her and she opened the door fully and stepped out. She was smartly dressed, her gray hair short and neat.

"I don't think it will be soon. The police were here, and I saw in the newspaper, the boss of her company was murdered. I think it must have upset her very badly."

"Yes, naturally." He made a point of looking concerned, then of being unsure what to do for the best. "Does her mother live in Munich?"

"Dresden." She smiled and gestured toward Sonja's door, her words heavy with implied meaning as she added, "You see, she wasn't *from* Bavaria."

"I see. Yes, I see." He frowned. "I need to get in touch with her, but . . . I only have her office number, not her cellphone."

"She kept herself to herself. I don't have a contact number, no spare key." Freddie nodded, seeing it had been a wasted trip, and that by refusing to help Sonja earlier he'd lost his connection to the potential contact in Hamburg. "I told the electricians the same, but they had a key. Nice young men. Foreign, maybe Polish, but nice." Freddie nodded again, realizing it might not just have been a wasted trip but a foolish one as well. "They fixed the smoke alarm out here too, though they weren't required to. I offered them coffee, as Fräulein Edel was away. They were most polite."

He was conscious as she spoke of the smoke alarm in the ceiling above them, certain that the "electricians" had probably fitted it with a camera, but he resisted the urge to look up at it. He just thanked the lady for her time and made his way out, certain now that he'd made a terrible mistake in coming here.

He could only hope they didn't have any operatives left in the city. The chances of that were good, but he knew from experience that, with the right access, a unit like Oberman's would only need their target to twitch the thread once before they started closing him down.

He found a taxi and headed back to the railway station, but stopped short of getting there, went into a store, and bought a hoodie. He put it on under his coat and pulled the hood up, then made his way into the station, keeping his head down, conscious of the cameras.

He sat like that on the platform too, next to an Arabic-looking man who was drinking coffee from a Styrofoam cup. Freddie was still conscious of the other people around him too, but stubbornly, his mind crept back to Yemen, to drinking tea with Abdullah, the Tuesday before it had all fallen apart.

Freddie had worked hard to get to that point, and it had finally looked as though the work would pay off. The drinking of tea had been an opportunity to agree the final details of the meeting Abdullah had arranged with two of the Hashid tribal chiefs.

And then, at the very end of the discussion, Abdullah had posed the casual question, "How many of you will be there?" Freddie told him three of them, plus their translator. "That's good. It's good to show that you're serious, committed."

And something in Abdullah's eyes at that point should have told Freddie the truth. If Mel or Pete had been there with him, perhaps they'd have seen it. Afterwards, he'd replayed that little ceremonial tea-drinking time and again, and retrospectively he always saw the look, the fleeting expression that should have told Freddie he was being played. But he'd missed it when it had counted most.

It felt important all over again somehow. Oberman's team had probably been scratching their heads trying to get a lead on Freddie, and he'd just handed it to them by allowing himself to be filmed outside Sonja's apartment. Worse, if it hadn't been for the old neighbor, he wouldn't have even known he'd given them a lead. After five years of self-recrimination, right now it felt as though he'd learned nothing at all.

Chapter Thirty-Two

He hadn't brought his laptop, but wished he had, because going through the surviving Cheng footage on his phone was hardly practical, and so he had another long journey ahead of him with nothing much to do.

What he did have in his messenger bag was the gun, which had seemed overly cautious early this morning but seemed less so now. And he spent most of the journey back to Vienna looking out of the window and wondering how close they might be to finding him, how close he'd come to getting caught right there at Sonja's apartment.

Finally, after Salzburg, he went to his phone and checked the German-language news websites. He'd only scrolled through a couple when he stopped and smiled with a slight resurgence of professional pride, because there were the pictures of Fernandez and his colleague, and a story explaining that the police wanted to talk with them in connection with the disappearance of an academic and the death of a Chinese tour guide.

He tried to imagine how it had gained traction, and his instinct was that Orion News and QNN had done his job for him, just as they had so often in the past. But it was equally possible the Chinese had decided to exploit the situation, and probably didn't much care about the truth behind it.

At the same time, Freddie wondered why Oberman hadn't used the same trick on him. They'd apparently been searching for him across Europe, and yet they hadn't tried to frame Freddie for the disappearance of Cheng or the murder of Jun.

It would have been the easiest way to get him detained, and the fact they'd chosen not to employ that tactic suggested some grounds for hope. Oberman might well be untouchable, as Drew had suggested, but it seemed this particular part of his operations—the surveillance and murder of Cheng, the employment and subsequent pursuit of Freddie—wasn't fully sanctioned by the top brass at Langley. That probably also answered the question of why they hadn't done the surveillance in-house to begin with, because Oberman didn't want his superiors to know about it.

Of course, the operation being unsanctioned also meant that Oberman and his team could pretty much do what they liked, as long as it never got back to Langley. Even worse, the longer things went on, the more imperative it would become to eliminate the risk that Freddie posed.

Freddie kept that in mind as he left the train in Vienna. His carriage was at the back and he followed the other departing passengers along the platform, remaining casual but slowly scanning the people ahead of him, the people on neighboring platforms, looking for anything or anyone that didn't fit.

Taking the escalator from the platforms into the station mall, he was even more on edge. The place was bustling, a mixture of people rushing for trains or killing time, shopping and window-shopping, such a variety of behaviors that it was hard to spot anything that stood out.

And yet he could almost feel it in the air, that something was amiss. He saw someone up ahead standing against a storefront, and any other time Freddie might have thought nothing of it, but something about the man standing there looked familiar—he was wearing dark casual clothes, aviator sunglasses, his hair cropped short, and maybe it was the look that was familiar rather than the man himself.

Freddie stopped where a broad staircase and escalators descended onto the next level. He leaned on the railing to one side, able to look down at the people moving between floors, a little of the floor below, the whole of the section he was on.

The store opposite sold electrical goods, and a handful of TVs were showing the same channel. Bizarrely, it seemed to be documentary footage of the German army rolling into various towns and taking them over, infantry marching, happy townsfolk waving Nazi flags.

Freddie glanced back in the direction he'd just come from, and saw a couple of men standing there—even without recognizing them, they all had that same workmanlike approach to civilian attire—pretending to engage in conversation while one of them casually kept an eye on Freddie's location.

Freddie looked down the stairs, but it was still clear below as far as he could see. Turning again, he noticed that the one who'd been against the storefront had also been joined by a partner, Jimmy Fernandez. Now that he saw them together, even at a distance, he knew that he *had* recognized the first guy, even with the aviators—he was the one who'd moved into Freddie's apartment along with Fernandez.

They started walking toward him, their pace relaxed, not drawing attention. Freddie looked back down the stairs and another two had appeared at the bottom there too—Oberman must have had most of his team in this station right now. It was like playing chess with Marina, that same sense of becoming hemmed in, not knowing how it had happened.

As big as the mall was, there were no other easy exits. Freddie had a choice: take the stairs, rush the two guys down there and hope to knock them off balance, or duck into one of the stores, maybe even ask them to call the police. Neither option appealed to him.

His heart was pumping hard, adrenaline coursing, his body firing up, ready to act, even as his mind skipped through the limited options, undecided. He looked about again, taking in the six men, four blocking his escape, two closing in.

He looked at the store opposite. A sales assistant had just walked onto the shop floor and spotted the Nazi soldiers parading proudly across half a dozen screens. The assistant moved quickly back to the counter and all the TVs jumped through a couple of channels—a children's cartoon, sport—before landing on the news and a picture of the Rathausplatz.

Freddie stared at it, desperately hoping it was what he thought it was. He turned to check on Fernandez and his friend, maybe only thirty yards away. He looked at the other people milling around, deciding who was most likely to intervene—a couple of ruddy and heavyset young men wearing the distinctive green and white soccer shirts of Rapid Wien looking in the window of the clothes store behind him. He looked at the TVs again, a newscaster now, and then he almost whooped when the screens filled with the pictures of the two men.

Fernandez was almost on him.

Freddie pointed at him and shouted, "Hey!"

Fernandez looked briefly startled in response before laughing and making some joke to his colleague. Freddie turned to the two young sports fans who were staring at him now. He walked urgently across to them, pulling one by the arm, pointing at the approaching men and at the screens.

"That's them! Call the police. Help me stop them!"

The one he'd grabbed went to push him away, but the other glanced quickly between the men on the screens and the men in the mall.

"He's right! I saw it earlier." He turned to Freddie. "They killed a tourist?"

"Yeah, that's them!"

The other's hostility to Freddie fell away and he stared at the approaching men curiously even as he took his phone out.

Freddie looked back again, and a confused Fernandez glanced up at the screens himself and almost staggered backward—it was clear they didn't know they'd made the news.

Fernandez said something urgently to his colleague, but the pictures disappeared, the shot went back onto the newscaster, and Fernandez's colleague was more concerned about the first Rapid Wien fan, who was approaching them with intent and shouting to other people to call the police.

Fernandez and his friend started to back away a little, unsure how to play what was already beginning to look like a volatile situation, bystanders becoming interested, shouting questions and accusations. Fernandez turned and looked ready to run, but the sports fan's blood was up now and he lunged forward and threw himself on Fernandez, knocking him to the floor.

Even as Fernandez fought back, more people rushed in, helping to pin him down, while others grabbed his colleague, knocking off his sunglasses in the process. Freddie was tempted to look back to see what the rest of Oberman's team was doing, but he ran into the melee instead and, in the confusion, continued past it, running until he was almost out of the station and a few police officers came jogging in the opposite direction, increasing their pace as the shouting became audible.

Freddie's heart was tearing along so quickly that it was hard for him to slow down and adopt a casual pace. And he was conscious of how scarily close he'd just come to being taken down. He wasn't out of it yet either, despite the massive stroke of luck provided by those TV screens.

Freddie had given them a thread to follow by showing his face at Sonja's apartment. They'd probably intercepted CCTV feeds from the station in Munich, and might even be following live footage of him this very moment—the thought produced an impulse to look up in search of the cameras, but he fought it and just kept walking, out into the darkening afternoon and the busy streets.

It looked like it had been a fine day in Vienna, although the sky was once again developing a misty edge. He moved off the major streets as soon as he could, but the whole area was busy and when he looked back for the first time he was certain he could see one of them following him, maybe one of the men who'd been behind him.

Freddie opened his bag, slipped his hand inside, and carefully released the safety on the gun. He was conscious too that he was heading almost directly toward the Madhouse; he would need to go back there, but not now. Seeing a turning to the left onto a much quieter street, he took it, then crossed the road and turned right onto another street that was empty of people.

Almost immediately he slipped into a doorway that was some sort of service entrance. He looked up, but there was no camera and he pulled the gun from his bag and stood with it by his side.

He waited a long minute, beginning to think he might have been mistaken, that the guy he'd seen hadn't been one of Oberman's. An old woman turned onto the street on the other side of the road and looked across at him vaguely before going on her way—she was so short that she was almost invisible behind most of the parked cars.

And then he heard an approaching voice, the words inaudible but the accent clearly American. He didn't even try to hear what the man was saying, but listened instead to the increasing volume, using it to calculate how close he was.

Freddie still smiled though, when he heard him say tetchily, "I'm on him! Gimme a break." And then the guy reached the corner and muttered "Dammit!" under his breath and started to run. He almost ran straight past the entrance to the service door, but looked at the last second, over his shoulder, saw Freddie, tried to stop himself and reach for his gun at the same time. Too late.

Freddie barreled into him, knocking him face down onto the floor. The guy put his hands down to stop himself, but Freddie was on top of him even as he landed, a knee in his back, the gun pressed against the nape of his neck.

Freddie could hear a tinny voice in the guy's earpiece and then he spoke back, winded and hurt, "He's got me. Get someone . . ."

Freddie pressed the gun harder and the words dried in the guy's throat. He was breathing hard, and Freddie took a second or two to catch his own breath before he eased some of his weight from the downed man's back.

"Very carefully. Reach in and pull out your gun and move it across the ground in front of you."

The guy nodded, but as he moved his hand awkwardly and slid it under his own body, Freddie could hear an admonishing voice in the earpiece, desperate and yelling, probably telling him that under no circumstances should he give up his firearm. It was easy, thought Freddie, to give advice like that through an earpiece, and he had no doubt it was one of the suits, maybe Bennett James, maybe Oberman himself, acting brave from a distance.

Once the gun was out on the ground in front of him, Freddie said, "Okay, bring your hand back and spread it out to the side."

The guy moved both arms at the same time, putting himself in a cruciform posture. Freddie leaned forward, once again pressing the gun harder into the prone man's neck to reinforce the foolishness of trying anything, then picked up the gun and slipped it into his bag.

He leaned forward a second time, and said, "Tell Oberman I'll be in touch."

The guy nodded, but Freddie had been speaking to the person in his earpiece, hoping it *was* Oberman, rather than to the man beneath him. Freddie stood, and in one fluid movement put the barrel of the silencer into the back of the guy's knee and pulled the trigger.

191

The clack sounded as if the bullet had gone straight through and cracked the paving stone beneath, the guy let out a short deep scream, followed by a pained cry as he understood what had happened to him. Freddie glanced up the street, but the elderly lady was nowhere to be seen.

"Count yourself lucky. You would've killed me."

Muffled, into the paving, the injured man responded defiantly, "We still will."

"No. You won't."

Freddie turned and walked quickly away, checking as he reached the junction that no backup was coming. That was most likely three of Oberman's team who'd be pulled from operations, and maybe that wouldn't be enough on its own, but it could be enough to unsettle him. Perhaps now he'd also be rethinking his assertion that Freddie was just a civilian.

Chapter Thirty-Three

He made his way into the inner city and found a touristy bar where he sat inside and drank a couple of glasses of wine. He was thinking about how close he might have come to getting caught or killed, how foolish he'd been to think he could just go to Munich and see Sonja again as if nothing had changed.

But in the end, it had worked out okay, so far at least. He'd escaped the net they'd cast at the station, and Oberman had taken casualties, one with an actual injury, two others with the potentially more damaging attention of the police to deal with. He still had a way to go, but it was a start.

Once it was dark he walked back to the Madhouse. Arnold was checking in a couple, but called out as Freddie crossed the lobby.

"Hey, Freddie!"

Freddie raised his hand and said, "How's it going, Arnold?"

The couple turned around and looked at him as if he were part of the establishment. He pressed the button for the elevator and when it arrived and the doors opened, Eva was standing there. Her face lit up.

"Freddie!"

"Hello."

He stepped into the elevator and she hugged him, then stood back and smiled.

"Where have you been?"

"I had to go out of town for work." He put his finger on the button to hold the door. "Were you on your way down?"

"Yeah, I was just finishing my break, but I'll ride back up with you." He took his finger off the button and pressed for the fifth floor. "Was it a tough day? You look tired."

I have two guns in my bag and I kneecapped someone earlier today, though I didn't kill him.

"It was an early start, that's all. I wanted to say, though, thanks for the hospitality last night."

They reached his floor and the doors opened and both of them drifted out, Eva apparently forgetting that she had a job to do.

"No way. I wanted to thank you. What you did, beating up those guys . . ."

"I didn't beat them up."

"You scared them off, and you got my bag back." She smiled and watched in silence as he put his keycard into the panel and opened his door. He pushed the door open and she said, "Can I come in?"

"Sure." He gestured for her to go in ahead of him as he slipped the card into the panel on the wall and the lights came on.

"Oh, I love this room! I forgot you were in 520. Such a great view." He had to agree with her on that point. The grand buildings before him were floodlit and cloaked in a thin haze. "Izzy really liked you, by the way. I knew she would."

"I liked her too. You make a really nice couple, and your apartment, it has a beautiful atmosphere." She nodded, smiling, still just young enough to be absolutely confident of these things without being told. "Sit down. I could make you a coffee or . . ."

"No, I can't stay. I don't like to leave Arnold." But she sat on the long sofa and Freddie placed his bag on the bed and sat on the armchair facing her. As if breaking bad news to him, she said, "I think I'm leaving."

"Vienna?"

"No! No, never. Here, the Madhouse. I love it here, but I think I have to leave."

"How long have you been here?"

"A year." It shouldn't have surprised him, but it did, because in his mind he associated the place entirely with its people, with Eva and Arnold and Pedro, as though they had always been here and the place wouldn't be the same without them. But it would, just as any institution survived and thrived with a constant turnover of personnel; including the one he'd worked for himself, where most of the current employees had probably never even heard his name, let alone remembered him. "Arnold and me started on the same day. But Arnold's a natural."

"What will you do?"

She shrugged. "I need to get serious about my art."

"It looked pretty serious to me. You just need to get serious about selling it."

"That's what I mean, I guess. You know, I think meeting you is one of the reasons I started thinking about it more."

He was flattered, but also mystified. One thing Freddie knew for sure was that there was nothing exceptional about Freddie Makin, certainly not enough to inspire someone so immensely talented into changing her life.

"I'm glad. And I'm glad I met you too."

She nodded, but stared at him, her expression hard to pin down.

"You would tell me if you were in trouble?"

"Of course. I'm not in trouble. I just have a lot of work on right now—difficult, taxing work."

She looked reassured and smiled brightly. "I should go. I'll miss Arnold. I might even come back for a drink every now and then, but I have to leave, I think."

"Not until I do, I hope."

"Deal." She jumped up and leaned over to hug him again, then headed for the door. "As long as you don't stay till Christmas!"

And then she was gone. He sat for a little while, still wearing his coat, wishing his life were different, as he seemed to whenever he was around Eva. If he came through this, that's what he would do—make his life different, make it right.

Slowly, he got to his feet and took off his coat. He booted up the laptop and made himself a coffee, then drew the blinds, even though he was convinced there was no surveillance outfit in the world that could spy on him in this room. It was more a psychological need for privacy—the knowledge that in the next few hours he needed to find the truth hidden in the last twenty-four hours of Cheng's life before it had all come crashing down.

Once again, when he brought the feed up, he fast-forwarded through long sections: Cheng in the kitchen, the bathroom, on the treadmill, things he knew well enough to know they concealed nothing unexpected. And it was strange, because he'd watched all these simple routines and intimacies without emotion over the last year and yet now he felt a little embarrassed to be lingering over them.

Perhaps it had been talking to Jun that had produced this new-found sense of squeamishness. Or perhaps at a distance, and knowing that Cheng was dead, he saw beyond the screen to the human he'd somehow managed to overlook.

As before, he concentrated on Cheng's web-browsing. The Chinese sites weren't much use, but then Oberman knew Freddie didn't speak Mandarin, so he also knew Freddie would have struggled to find anything complex hidden within those pages.

He paid a little more attention to the company profiles and the pages about investing in the stock market, but again, could see nothing that stood out as suspicious. Finally, he looked at the marine biology websites, and in particular the page about the seahorse that Cheng had forwarded to a contact in China, but as much as he read over it, there was nothing to suggest hidden or coded meanings.

As a last resort, he even looked at some of the mathematical pages Cheng had studied, but again, they might as well have been in Mandarin for all the sense that Freddie could make of them. It seemed that if Freddie was meant to have seen something dangerous enough to threaten his own life, it hadn't been within the final twenty-four hours.

Frustrated, he clicked over onto the news websites and read the latest on Jun. The most recent update said the police were questioning someone in relation to the unexplained death of a Chinese tour guide on the Rathausplatz. The bulletins were still linking her death to the disappearance and subsequent death of Jiang Cheng. But, with a possible indication that Oberman's people had stepped up their own information game, it was also being suggested that Cheng's case might be related to gambling debts.

He nodded to himself, remembering Jun's earnest assurance that Cheng hadn't been a gambler. Given the man he'd been, gambling was probably the least plausible explanation for his death, even less so than a program for disabling nuclear weapons. Cheng hadn't been a gambler, and hadn't been interested in money, that's what she'd told him—that companies had tried to recruit him, but that the financial world just hadn't interested him . . .

Freddie closed the news feed and went back to the frozen footage from Cheng's apartment, scrolling back through time, his heart beating faster, full of hope and fear and astonishment. If he was right, it had been there in front of him the whole time—Cheng hadn't been interested in the stock markets, so why had he been studying company reports and articles about investing?

Now that Freddie looked again, he saw that there were three or four company reports that Cheng had looked at, but one in particular— Waldstrom Inc.—that he'd gone back to several times. Freddie made a note of the names, then moved back to Google and searched.

Waldstrom was a big software and tech services company, financially sound, profitable, and yet in the last year its share price had been volatile compared with the wider market—not huge rises and falls, but a little more than he'd expect for such a safe and steady company. Freddie turned to the other companies on his list and saw a similar, if less marked, pattern—a little more volatility in the stock prices than seemed justified by the underlying position of the companies involved, or the wider state of the stock market.

Freddie checked one more thing, digging deeper into the Waldstrom share price to see when the increased volatility had started. He knew the answer in advance, but it was still satisfying to see it had been just over a year ago, more or less around the time he'd been employed to put Jiang Cheng under full surveillance.

The real irony was that, in his head, Freddie still thought of Lars Oberman as the trader, with his slicked-back blond hair and sharp suit, but that superficial judgment had been much closer to the truth than he'd realized. He saw it all now, why they'd wanted to be sure Cheng wasn't onto them, why the surveillance operation and the events of recent weeks hadn't been sanctioned.

Oberman had been gifted a program for interfering with the launch codes of nuclear weapons, creating an unobtrusive lag between the launch command and the execution of that command, a delay of which the person pressing the button would be completely oblivious. If Marina was to be believed, that program, and Cheng's purpose, had already been cracked by at least one of the affected parties, but if Freddie's instincts were right, Oberman had spotted a much more attractive application.

He'd used it to game the stock market, to cause a fractional delay between buy or sell orders and their execution, a delay in which a fleet-footed investor could pre-empt what was about to happen and profit accordingly. Freddie had to admit to himself that he even had a grudging respect for people who would think to use the program in that way.

The trouble was, in the end, Cheng had worked out what they were up to. Maybe they'd spoken to him about adapting the program for other purposes, and something in those exchanges had encouraged Oberman to be cautious and Cheng to be curious.

Freddie wanted to speak to Marina again, more to bounce the idea off her rather than because he needed her help, but he felt sure he was right. Cheng had given a program to the CIA in the hope of averting a future nuclear war, the idealistic pacifist's ultimate dream, and the person he'd entrusted that program to had used it to make himself rich.

The next question for Freddie was what to do about it. Oberman wanted him dead because he feared Freddie had seen the truth of what he was doing. And now Freddie had seen it and couldn't undo it. Nor was he sure that he had anything much to bargain with.

Oberman didn't know about the footage of Cheng that was still stored in the cloud, but if he was technologically savvy enough to have used Cheng's program in this way, he surely had to have allowed for the possibility of it being there. In the past, it might have been plausible to tell Oberman there was a disk Freddie would hand over in exchange for guarantees, but those days were long gone—any acknowledgment at all of a digital footprint would just make Oberman all the more determined to send Freddie the way of Cheng and Jun.

So, Freddie had to find out about the money, where Oberman was keeping it, how legitimate Marine Finance was, and who knew about it. He had to find a way of undermining the one thing Oberman had been so desperate to protect. And to do that he needed more time.

That only raised the issue of his first priority, to continue slipping the net Oberman was trying to close around him but also to continue hitting his team wherever he could, never allowing Oberman to believe he was completely in control. Freddie didn't know much, but he knew all too well how disturbing it felt to realize someone else was dictating events.

Chapter Thirty-Four

Time and again in the night he woke from dreams, thinking Mel was in the room, not as he'd known her but as he would now always remember her, her face blood-smeared, a hole in her forehead that looked too big and too fractured for the round that had caused it. On two occasions he woke from an all-too-real dream in which he thought he'd already woken and seen her sitting on the sofa where Eva had been.

When he eventually gave up and climbed out of bed, it had only just turned seven, but he knew no more sleep would come, or at least not the kind he wanted. He showered and went down for breakfast, restored as much by Pedro's easy and good-humored welcome as by the food, and as he sat there, the early mist started to lift to show the beginnings of a clear sky and another fine day.

He went back up to his room and checked the news, then checked the Qabbani account where he found an email from Drew.

Call me. As soon as you can.

Freddie took the card for the pet store and called the number Drew had written on the back. Drew answered almost immediately, but warily.

"Hello?"

"You asked me to call."

"Wow, that was quick."

Freddie glanced back at the email and saw that it had come in only ten minutes ago. "I must have checked in just after you sent it. What's so urgent?"

"What's so urgent is I just had a call from Oberman. For one thing, he finally seems to have worked out that Evanston was a front for S8. And from there, well, I guess it wouldn't take Sherlock Holmes to make the link between us, but I'm still a bit concerned by how quickly they did it—you know, my role in Yemen wasn't exactly public knowledge either."

"Is it likely to be a problem? For you, I mean?"

"No, I don't think so." He didn't sound sure. "Anyway, Oberman wants me to set up a meet with you."

"I bet he does. I've had two of his guys arrested and put another in the hospital."

"And killed one."

One that they knew of. Freddie thought back to the blood-mashed face, remembered the sickening crunch of the iron splitting that face open.

Drew's voice was a welcome interference. "What's your endgame, Freddie?"

"To put him out of business, I guess. I won't tell you yet, but I know what his game is, and it's nothing to do with nuclear weapons, and I'll bet it's nothing the Company knows about either. I just need more time."

"Honestly, I don't know how much more time you'll have. The more of his people you take out, the more ruthless he'll get in tracking you down."

"And the fewer people he'll have left to do it. That's how mistakes get made; we both know that."

"I wouldn't bank on it, not with Oberman." He paused, but Freddie waited for him to speak again. "So I guess you don't want to meet him?"

"Do you honestly think it would be a smart idea for me to agree?"

"No, I think it'd be suicidal, unless you had your own team to take in there with you." There was another pause, and even over the distance of a phone connection, Freddie recognized it—Freddie had called so quickly that Drew was still trying to think of a way to help his friend out of what he clearly thought was an impossible situation. Freddie didn't think there was anything impossible about it, but he mistrusted his own judgment, and trusted Drew's too much to question it aloud. "I don't know what to suggest, Freddie, really I don't."

Freddie knew one thing, he had to give Drew something, a line he could take back to Oberman that would protect his own position. And Freddie wouldn't meet, but he could at least try to knock a couple more of Oberman's men out of the field.

"Okay, don't respond to him yet. He wouldn't expect it so soon anyway. I'll call you back in a couple of hours and I'll give you my response then. At the very least, it should be enough to cover your back."

"Freddie, I don't care about that."

"No, I know, but I do. Give me an hour or two and I'll get back to you."

He ended the call and went online to check if the Hotel Danzig had availability. Looking at the website, it was slightly grander than it appeared from the outside—either that or they had a really good photographer.

He moved the guns into his equipment case, packed a change of clothes and essentials into the messenger bag, and headed out, waving to Arnold as he walked through reception.

"Hey, Freddie! Have a good day."

"You too, Arnold, see you later."

And Freddie smiled, because if questions were asked in the days ahead, he doubted anyone at the Madhouse would even notice he hadn't been in his room for twenty-four hours.

Freddie set off across the city, and it was only when he reached the Danzig that he realized it took up almost one entire side of the small street on which it was set. Another smaller hotel took up the rest, separated from the Danzig by a narrow alley.

He stepped into the lobby, which again was spacious, with marble floors and pillars and luxurious pot plants and an ornate ceiling. It had the air of a business hotel that was keen to ape the style of the grander hotels in the city. There was a young man in a suit standing behind the reception desk.

"Good morning, sir."

"Good morning. I don't have a reservation, but I was wondering if you had a room, just for tonight."

"Of course, I'll check."

"Preferably facing out onto the street."

The receptionist nodded and stared at the computer before frowning. "Unfortunately, looking onto the street we have only a suite on the top floor. But with that you also get a balcony terrace."

"How much is that?"

He looked at the screen again. "For tonight, that would be . . . 450 euros."

Again, it gave the lie to the grand veneer that a suite here was the price of a double in the hotels it superficially resembled.

"Okay, I'll take it."

Freddie reached into his jacket and took out a credit card and passport, placing them on the desk. This was a gamble, because it was his last fake identity, but he had no idea what would go down in the next twenty-four hours in this hotel, and he didn't want to use his own identity or the one he was using at the Madhouse.

The receptionist smiled, looked at the passport, and put a form on the desk. "Thank you, Mr. Heston. If you could just fill in your details and sign at the bottom. Would you like me to take payment for the room now?"

"Sure, why not."

Once the formalities were completed, the receptionist turned to a wall of pigeonholes behind him and took out a key with a red tassel on it.

"You're in Room 520."

Freddie smiled at the coincidence and said, "Good, that's a lucky number for me."

"I'm pleased," said the receptionist with the air of someone who responded in the same way to every nonsensical comment his guests made. "You'll find the elevators just over there. And I wish you a pleasant stay at the Hotel Danzig."

"Thank you."

Freddie picked up his equipment case and made his way to the elevators, checking the access to the stairs, making sure there was no other exit. He did the same when he got out on the fifth floor, walking the length of the corridor in both directions before finally making for his suite.

It opened into a living room, ornately decorated in a way that most people could tolerate only in a hotel room. The bedroom next door was much the same—a bed with a canopy, baroque furniture, and it was from here that French doors opened onto the balcony terrace.

He slid them open and stepped out. There were a couple of plants in large classically styled pots, a round table with two chairs to the left, empty space to the right, although a little shadowing on the tiled floor suggested a couple of sun loungers had been there through the summer months.

He leaned back against the balustrade, looking in through the French doors. He was conscious that the move he was planning was a big step outside his normal area of expertise.

And now he was here, he wasn't even sure he could pull it off. The idea was to give Drew some cover and at the same time take out another couple of Oberman's people, but there were so many variables.

What if Oberman sent more than two? What if he didn't send any but came up with some other way of getting Freddie out of the picture? Even if Oberman sent only two, Freddie couldn't let a few lucky breaks distract him from the truth—that he was out of practice, and inexperienced in this sort of fieldwork anyway.

He walked back out into the corridor and checked for a fire escape, but found a door to the roof instead. There were service stairs too, and there had to be a service entrance because he'd seen only the lobby doors on the front of the building, so if more than two came he could cut his losses and escape before they got up here.

He looked at a slightly grotesque table with a vase on it, placed in the corridor just beyond the entrance to the elevators. He could slip one of his few remaining camera units in behind one of the legs, which would at least give him a bit more notice of how they were gearing up to come into the room.

That just left the question of how he could handle two of them, most likely both armed . . . A flashback came in on the back of that thought. For some reason it had seemed smart at the time, that neither he nor Mel had been armed that day in Sana'a. And Talal had never carried a weapon. So they'd driven into an ambush with only one gun in the car and Pete had been the first to die. One thing Freddie could be sure of, the guys coming here to look for him wouldn't be so stupid.

He stepped back into his living room, imagining their progress after working the lock. They'd be vigilant in this first room, and there weren't too many hiding places here. They'd get more jittery as they moved through the suite, particularly stepping into the bedroom, with the door to the bathroom in front of them on one side, the walk-in closet to the left of the bed, the French doors open onto the balcony.

He could almost feel their nerves at this point, and no matter how practiced they were, they *would* be feeling nervous standing on the threshold to the bedroom. They'd focus on those three danger points— bathroom, closet, balcony—silently deciding who'd sweep which area.

But that also meant he couldn't actually be in any of those three areas, because they'd be at their most vigilant by then, ready for an attack.

There was an ottoman at the bottom of the bed, and a heavy brocade bedspread reaching almost to the floor on either side, but when Freddie lifted it he saw that the bed was raised high off the floor. It would be a risk, because it would leave him in a prone position, but it would also provide him with the optimum potential for surprise.

He stood there, thinking, and as he played through the possibilities in advance, the risks, the many variables which could lead to even the most considered plan falling apart, he realized he was also committed to something else. He didn't want to kill anyone else, but he certainly planned to shoot someone, and if it meant killing them, he had accepted that course too.

Chapter Thirty-Five

Once he had everything ready, he ordered lunch from room service. It was the only thing he'd missed at the Madhouse, but as nice as this hotel was, and this suite, the businesslike calm of the place seemed to remind him of everything he wanted to leave behind, whereas the Madhouse, for no reason that was clear, made him think of a different and hopeful future.

After eating, he called Drew, who picked up on the first ring.

"Freddie, what have you got?"

"It's like I said, Drew, I don't want to meet. You can tell Oberman I said we've got nothing to discuss. But then comes the important bit, and I'm trusting your acting skills here. With regret in your voice, because we go back a long way, you tell him that I'm hiding out in the Hotel Danzig. Say you don't know for sure, but I'm probably using the alias James Heston. And tell him you think I'm planning to move on later tonight."

"I'm not sure that's such a smart option."

"No, well, I'm out of smart options. This is what I have—starve him of support, expose his operation."

There was a long silence, but finally Drew said, "I just wish I could do something to help. But the stuff Oberman's involved with, you're talking about a clearance level in the stratosphere."

"For the stuff he's officially involved with. Trust me, the interests he's trying to protect right now are firmly lodged in the gutter."

"All the more reason to be careful. And bear in mind, now that they know about your S8 connection they could get even more dangerous."

"I don't see why."

"Really? Because no one knows what S8 does, and that'll freak them out and make their responses harder to predict. If they knew what I know, that you're just a bunch of flakes and weirdos . . ."

Freddie laughed. "Past tense—I'm an ex-weirdo."

"You got that right. I'll make the call now, but you take care."

"Thanks, Drew."

Freddie ended the call. Then he unmade the bed to make it look slept in and put the room service tray on it, giving the appearance of a late and lazy breakfast, not that of someone who'd planned a trap or been tipped off. He turned on the bathroom light and left the door ajar, and opened the door to the walk-in closet just enough to make it suspicious.

He checked again that the unit he'd installed in the corridor was working, then went out onto the balcony terrace and positioned a chair and put his camera on the table nearby. He guessed he'd have a little while, so he made himself a coffee and took it outside and shifted his seat so he was facing the sun.

Sitting there, he looked down at the street and the few people coming and going, at cars driving through or parking up or pulling away. He tried not to think of his plan, or overthink it, tried not to dwell on the stupidity of trying to outgun these people.

But probably only an hour after Drew had made the call, a black BMW SUV pulled into the street and did a slow drive-by. It turned at the bottom, but came back around a few minutes later and this time it parked, taking so long about it that Freddie guessed the driver wasn't overly familiar with the car.

He grabbed his camera and trained it on them: two men, although it was hard to see them clearly. Then they lowered their windows and the driver became visible. Freddie tried to remember where he'd seen him before and then it came to him—he'd been the removal man who'd carried Cheng's desktop computer out to the truck.

So this was it, but the fact they'd lowered the windows suggested they weren't planning on going anywhere anytime soon. Freddie wondered if they were waiting for more people to arrive, or if they were just playing it safe, waiting for Freddie to show his face rather than trying to take him in the hotel, maybe waiting for it to get dark. For all he knew, it was the beginnings of the nerves Drew had suggested might be induced by Freddie's S8 past.

It meant all his planning for an attack within the room had been pointless, but he was glad of that in a way, glad that it wouldn't now be put to the test and found wanting. He knew something else too: whatever they were waiting for, he wouldn't give them time to let it happen.

He walked back into the room, emptied the change of clothes from the messenger bag and put the guns inside it. He went out to the balcony again, checked through the camera that they were still in the car. If anything, they looked even more bedded down, and there appeared to be cigarette smoke coming from the passenger side.

Freddie grabbed his bag and left, heading down the service stairs, passing two bemused housekeeping staff and then someone with a room service tray who tried to tell him he shouldn't be there. Freddie nodded and smiled, but didn't give him chance to pursue the matter.

After one false turn at the bottom he found his way to the service door and out into a wide alley at the back of the hotel. He ran along it until he reached the narrower alley that separated the Danzig from its neighbor. At the end of that alley he stopped and looked out—he was maybe only twenty yards behind the BMW, but on the wrong side of the street and still too far to get to them quickly without being seen.

He took out the gun with the silencer, held it ready beside his leg, and waited. He could still see smoke rising from the passenger window on the other side of the SUV. A car turned onto the street and he thought about using it as cover, but then he saw a UPS truck pulling onto the street after the car.

As long as it really was a UPS truck and not just more of Oberman's team arriving, it would allow him both the time and the cover he needed. But it stopped first in the middle of the road, before even reaching the spot where Freddie stood.

The driver jumped out and walked into the neighboring hotel with a small package. Freddie waited. Smoke once again drifted from the SUV. Freddie didn't want the guy to finish that cigarette, fearing it might be the point at which they decided to get out of the car and head on in to the hotel, in which case he would have managed to blow two opportunities at once.

Seconds crept by, another waft of smoke rose up. Freddie pitied the smoker's colleague having to put up with that. Finally, the UPS driver came back out and climbed into the truck. He put it into gear and moved slowly along the street, and Freddie left the alley and crossed the road behind him, moving quickly to the far side of the SUV.

The UPS truck stopped outside the Danzig, probably distracting them for an extra second. The smoker's arm was resting in the open window, but he must have seen or sensed Freddie's approach because he tossed the cigarette and pulled his arm back in and said something urgent.

Freddie was on them, even as the guy retrieved his gun from his shoulder holster. The other was slower, maybe not getting yet where the threat was coming from. Freddie shot the driver in the thigh, getting a stifled yell in response. Then he smashed the smoker hard in the face, grabbed his gun hand, and yanked it toward him, pulling backward swiftly until it produced a loud popping crack and the guy screamed and his gun fell to the ground.

Freddie pulled the door open and the smoker almost fell out, his arm still hooked painfully through the open window. He cried out again, struggling to free the damaged arm, and Freddie could see now that he hadn't broken it, but had managed to badly dislocate the shoulder.

He slammed the door against the man's body, managing to catch his head again for good measure, and kicked the gun away. And as the smoker fell out and dropped limply to the ground, Freddie trained the gun on the driver who'd finally thought to reach for his own firearm.

"I don't want to kill you, but I will if you try it." The driver froze, hand poised. The guy on the floor was moaning and trying to crawl clear of the SUV and away from Freddie. "Okay, put the gun on the passenger seat, slowly." The driver did as he was told, and kept glancing down at his leg which was becoming worryingly sleek with blood. "Cellphone, do the same."

Even as he did it, the smoker somehow managed to get to his feet and started running like a drunk along the street. He stumbled to the ground after a few steps before struggling to get up again.

Freddie kept his aim on the driver even as he reached in and grabbed the gun and phone, dropping them into his messenger bag. He crouched down then and picked up the smoker's gun from the ground, doing the same with that.

Then he looked back in and pointed the gun at the injured leg. "You need to use your belt as a tourniquet or you're gonna bleed out in minutes. You get me?" The driver nodded, staring down at his leg in shock. "Do it now, and then get to a hospital."

Freddie set off along the street after the smoker, who was already close to the far end, looking constantly in danger of falling again. There was more traffic out there on the wide street that intersected this one, and by the time Freddie got there, the guy was trying to weave across, a couple of drivers blasting their horns at him. The guy didn't seem to hear them, and yet he did seem to sense Freddie and turned to look at him.

And the fear that Freddie saw there was astonishing. He could only assume that Oberman had driven home to them Freddie's S8 past, and their imaginations had filled in the void of knowledge—if only they'd spoken to Drew Clarke, they'd have known how little they had to fear.

And this guy had even less to fear because Freddie could hardly pursue him into the busy heart of the city. But the guy winced with pain and darted off as if trying to avoid a line of fire. And then there was another horn blast and a flash of color, a tram traveling fast, and the running man was struck and flew into the air as if he'd been snapped backward by a bungee cord.

Freddie stared in horror and he wasn't alone, as the tram screeched to a halt and cars braked—people stood for long seconds, staring at the crumpled heap where it had landed in the road.

Freddie slipped his gun back into the messenger bag and ran toward him now, and despite everything, despite knowing it was impossible, he was hoping the guy wasn't dead. Other people got there first and there was a small crowd crouching around the smoker, one of whom seemed to know what she was doing.

Someone was crying, a few people shouted, others were talking rapidly into their phones. The man on the ground was the still center of it all, his limbs at contradictory angles. There was a pool of blood around his head and Freddie wondered if that injury was the result of the impact or if he'd done it with the car door.

Another woman ran at speed into the group, dropping a bag to the floor as she said, "Let me through—I'm a doctor."

"I'm a nurse," said the other who'd already taken control, and said something that seemed unbelievable. "He's alive. He's alive."

A few people gasped at those words and Freddie was one of them. He stared in disbelief, thinking not only of the beating he'd given him, but of the explosive collision of body and fast-moving tram, and he felt tears in his eyes and willed this man to stay alive, more than he'd ever willed it of anyone, this man who had been sent to kill him.

Chapter Thirty-Six

He stayed for longer than he should have, maybe fifteen minutes, until he'd seen the injured man lifted into the ambulance; until he'd over-heard the doctor talking to the paramedics about the severity of the injuries, saying what everyone else there was undoubtedly thinking, that he was lucky to be alive.

And then Freddie walked back to the hotel, dropping the driver's cellphone into a drain on the way. The alarm on a parked car was sound-ing, shrill and irritating even against the ambulance siren in the back-ground. It was the car that had been in front of the BMW and Freddie could see now that the back wing had been dented, but that the driver of the SUV had apparently made good his escape.

The hotel receptionist was on the phone and staring at the com-puter as he spoke. Freddie nodded and smiled, but it seemed to go unseen. He took the elevator to the fifth floor, removed the camera he'd hidden behind the table leg in the corridor, then went into his room and repacked his things.

By the time he got back to reception, the phone call had finished. Freddie put the key on the desk.

"I've had a call from work. I have to be in Prague. So I'll be check-ing out. And could I have a taxi to the main railway station?"

"Of course." The receptionist arranged the taxi even as he went back to the computer, then said, "So it's just the room service lunch to pay. You took nothing from the minibar?"

"No."

"And I can charge it to the same card?"

"Sure."

"That's great. I hope you enjoyed your stay with us, Mr. Heston."

Freddie smiled. "Well, I was only here for a few hours, but it's a nice hotel. I'll definitely stay again next time I'm in Vienna."

"Thank you, and we hope you'll stay longer next time." He gave a little laugh and Freddie offered a laugh in response, because the guy was trying.

He printed a receipt and handed it to Freddie, who made a show of looking at it before saying, "Oh, I doubt anyone will call, but if they do, would you let them know I'm already on my way to Prague?"

"Of course, Mr. Heston. And have a pleasant journey. Your taxi should be here any moment."

Freddie walked out, looking along the street. The damaged car had stopped wailing, and there was nothing beyond the end of the street to suggest the accident that had just taken place.

A moment later, a taxi turned onto the street and pulled to a stop in front of him.

The driver jumped out, but Freddie held up the equipment case and said, "Just this—I'll take it in the car with me."

He got in and the driver put on his seatbelt and looked in the rear-view. "So, Hauptbahnhof?"

"No, actually, Westbahnhof, please."

The driver nodded and set off. Freddie looked out at the traffic and tried to focus on the fact that the events of the last hour had been a success. He'd left two of Oberman's people badly injured, which meant two more couldn't be called upon to track him down, and he hadn't killed anyone.

Yet it didn't feel like a success. He felt sick, and now that he thought about the way he'd approached the car, shot the driver, messed up the passenger, his mind skipped back and linked it with Abdullah all those years ago. True, Freddie hadn't killed the men in the BMW today, but the violence he'd done, it wasn't him, wasn't who he'd been or who he wanted to be, and he didn't even know how he'd slipped into this course of action.

At the Westbahnhof he paid the driver and found a café where he sat for an hour drinking coffee, trying to empty his thoughts, trying to find his way back to the mindful moment, a state he'd so desired and admired in the year he'd watched Cheng. But it wasn't to be found, and the more he stilled his thoughts about the problems he faced in the present, the more it seemed to allow the past to come flowing back around him.

He thought of taking another taxi, but walked instead, trying to take pleasure out of the golden hour as the sun fell and illuminated the stone of the city's grand buildings. It wasn't working, but when he was a few minutes from the hotel he spotted a familiar flash of purple ahead of him, heading in the same direction, and his spirits lifted immediately.

"Eva!"

She looked puzzled in response to hearing her name, then spotted him and looked touchingly pleased to see him. She waited and hugged him as he reached her and smiled, then looked down at the equipment case.

"Is that your work?"

He nodded, but the inner voice once again imagined telling her the more startling truth.

But I now have four guns in my messenger bag and I shot someone, and chased a man into the path of—

"What are you doing?"

She shrugged. "On my way to the Madhouse. I start in twenty minutes."

"Then we can walk together."

They set off and Eva started telling him about a job Izzy had been offered, working at a theater in the city, small but really influential. He enjoyed listening to her, enjoyed asking questions, wrapping himself once more in their world.

His attention wasn't entirely on her though, and perhaps his past would always make him incapable of that level of commitment to any social situation. He was still looking around as they walked, casually taking in the other people, the cars, a subtle but constant registering of patterns, and more importantly, of anomalies.

That was how he listened and talked, and that was how, just a hundred yards before they turned up toward the Madhouse, with its neon sign already visible, he spotted someone ahead, beyond the turning, standing at a tram stop.

The man was looking about him in a natural way, but when his gaze reached Freddie there was a brief snag before his head continued to turn. A moment later, he looked back a second time, but his eyes met Freddie's, and now that he knew he'd spotted him, the guy held his gaze too.

It was the guy with the frameless glasses, the same one who'd taken down his cameras, and it looked like he'd worked out where Freddie had really been hiding, or at least he'd had a pretty strong hunch that had paid off.

Freddie felt an instant and aggressive fear as he realized that being seen with Eva was the worst possible development. He already knew enough about the way they operated to know they'd be more than happy to use her as a way of getting to him. He couldn't allow that to happen, and he was angry too, that this guy had managed to expose his own complacency, just as Abdullah had five years ago.

"Listen, Eva, I'm gonna carry on walking along here. I just want you to casually say goodbye and head up to the hotel, don't hug me or anything like that, okay?"

He could see out the corner of his eye that she did a double take and looked up at him. "What are you talking about? Why? Is something wrong?"

"No, everything's fine. But there's a guy up ahead I need to speak to, a competitor, and he's a real jerk, a gossip . . ."

"Are you embarrassed for him to see me with you?"

"Absolutely not!" He risked turning and giving her a smile. "Why on earth would I be embarrassed—you're one of the best people I know." She looked flattered but mildly skeptical. "I'm serious. But humor me, just this once."

"Okay." Her tone became teasingly offhand then. "See you later, Freddie."

"Not if I see you first."

She laughed now and turned away and he faced forward again, but the guy had gone. He could understand that. The guy probably knew he couldn't attack Freddie out here in a busy street, but perhaps also feared that Freddie wouldn't be bound by the same rules.

Freddie scanned the crowds, and then thanks to the guy's height and physique, he spotted him, walking away from him. Freddie kept his eye on him as he waited for the crossing light to turn green, then ran across the road and for another fifty yards until he'd closed most of the distance between them.

The guy glanced behind once, but more frequently he looked to his right and at his watch, becoming almost agitated enough that it rubbed off on Freddie and he started to wonder if the man he was pursuing had called in for backup. Not that there could be many people left from the original team to call upon.

And then Freddie saw what it was all about. The guy looked back one more time and jumped onto a tram. Freddie picked up his pace, but was too late and the tram pulled away. As it eased past him, building speed, the guy looked out with a mocking smile and wagged his finger at Freddie where he stood.

There was such arrogance in that gesture that Freddie was almost tempted to chase after the tram and catch the guy at the next stop, but he was no longer sure of the point. Whatever Oberman's men thought him capable of, and in spite of what he'd already done today, he was even less likely than they were to shoot someone in a busy public street, and considerably less likely to kill someone.

But he still had a problem, because this guy's hunch about where Freddie was staying had been proved right. It wouldn't take much more checking to find out that Eva worked at the Madhouse, and that there was someone fitting Freddie's description staying there. He cursed under his breath, because he'd stayed too long, and because he feared this guy was better at this than he was.

Yes, Freddie had stayed too long, and the worst of that was that he might have put Eva in danger as a result. They wouldn't care what his relationship with her was, only that he seemed to like her, and any attempts to downplay how they'd looked on the street would count for nothing, because they'd looked happy with each other like they were friends. Freddie knew how that worked—he'd used other people's happiness against them often enough in the past, and had stripped people of it too.

He crossed the road and headed into the inner city. More than anything, he wanted to go back to his room at the Madhouse, to collect his stuff and get out of there. But it was too late for that.

He kept thinking of Eva, that final laugh of hers, and he knew in his bones that they'd target her. And that meant the time for playing games was over and the men he'd already hurt had suffered needlessly.

He walked into the bar in the Park Hyatt, found a quiet corner, and ordered a gin and tonic. When it came, he sat for a while trying to think of another way forward, but there was only one that he could see, and whatever happened to him it was the path he would have to take, because he wouldn't let it happen again—he wouldn't let other people be hurt by his failures.

There weren't many good reasons for Freddie agreeing to meet Oberman, and he didn't have time to think of better ones. So he'd play the cards he had and take his chances.

He put in a call to the number he'd copied from the inside of his arm all those days ago. It rang for a while before someone picked up.

"Oberman."

"I'll meet with you."

There was the briefest pause and then a self-satisfied laugh. "What a surprise. I wonder is that because we now know about your girlfriend?"

"Give me a break. She's a girl who works in the hotel where I was staying. And credit to your man, he tracked me down. If he'd done it two days ago when I was still staying there, you might actually have caught me."

Oberman produced another truncated laugh, almost to himself, and said, "Maybe you've moved on from the hotel, but if the girl really was just someone who works there, I don't think we'd be having this conversation. You don't need to worry, though, we don't go after innocent civilians."

"You thought I was an innocent civilian when you sent Phillips back to kill me."

"True. Although it turned out you were neither. Now, I know why I'd like to meet, but I wonder what your plan might be."

"The same as it is for most people. I don't care about what happened to Cheng, or to Leo. I care about what happens to me. I wanna make a deal."

"I'm not sure you have anything I need."

"Do you think I'm stupid, Lars?"

"Excuse me?"

"Simple question. Do you think I'm stupid? See, I obviously think I do have something you need. Otherwise I'd be crazy to meet you—I might as well just put a gun to my head and pull the trigger."

"Well, Freddie, I think maybe you are crazy, and I do think you're actually doing this to protect the steampunk freak we saw you with. But hey, I don't care why, as long as we get our face-to-face. Let me think it over and I'll get back to you."

"No, this phone won't be switched on. I'll call you back."

"As you wish. How about you call me in the morning, and I'll give you a time and place?"

"Sure. But if you try anything in the meantime, the deal's off, and so are the gloves. You hear me?"

"Loud and clear. I'll await your call."

Freddie switched off the phone. He knew in his head what the deal would be. He'd claim that he'd left instructions, should anything happen to him, to release information about Oberman's manipulation of the stock market. In exchange for his silence, he'd want a million-dollar payment from Marine Finance AG. That would be more or less it, and that was probably the kind of deal Oberman imagined Freddie had in mind.

But it would never come to discussing deals, because Oberman had only one intention, to kill Freddie. And he surely knew that Freddie wanted him dead in return. That's how the meeting would really go— no deal, and at least one of them dead.

Chapter Thirty-Seven

It was dark by the time he reached Marina's building. He didn't even know if he'd find her in, but she buzzed him up without comment and he once again found the door open. The smell of cooking pulled him inward.

He closed the door behind him and found her in the kitchen.

She turned and raised her eyebrows, then looked down at the equipment case. "You're not planning on staying, I hope?"

He smiled and shook his head. "It's my surveillance kit."

"Do you want the one back that you left in my office?"

"So you found it? I turned it off, later on the day I called in."

She smiled, looking unfazed by the fact that he'd eavesdropped on her phone calls.

"And do you want it back or not?"

He only had three units left, but even so, he said, "No, I don't think so. I'm getting out of that business anyway."

"I'm a good cook, but I eat quite lightly—you learn to at my age. This is a beef stew, an old family recipe, served with good bread and better wine. You'll join me." He was about to object, but she pointed. "Plates are in the cupboard there, cutlery in the drawer to your left, napkins in the drawer next to that. As you see, I eat in the kitchen if

I'm being informal, but then, you've hardly come dressed for dinner anyway."

He put the case down by the wall, and carefully placed the messenger bag next to it. He fetched a plate, cutlery, and a cloth napkin monogrammed with Cyrillic letters, and placed them opposite hers on the heavy wooden table.

"You'll find a glass in the cupboard there, and you can pour the wine. It's already open."

Again, he followed her instructions as she put a plate of thickly cut bread on the table. She gestured for him to sit and then he watched as she brought the stew to the table and served it onto the two plates before sitting down herself.

"Thank you. Seriously, you can't know the day I've had, and how much I appreciate this."

"I'd try it first."

He smiled, but the stew was as comforting and restorative as the aroma had suggested from the threshold of the apartment.

They ate in silence for a few minutes, and then she took a sip of wine and said, "So what have you been up to since we last met? Any progress?"

"Of a sort. I managed to put two of his men under suspicion for Jun's murder, and possibly got them arrested, though I guess they're probably out by now."

"I imagine so, but I also imagine they would have sent them back stateside."

"I shot another in the back of the knee, then this morning I shot another in the thigh, and a third . . ." He shook his head, remembering that explosive thud, the hopeless clatter of his body crashing broken onto the road surface, the nurse calling out—*he's alive*. Freddie took a drink and Marina immediately topped it up again. "I'd already hurt him, but he ran from me . . . he got hit by a tram. It was just . . . I've seen some horrible things, but . . ."

"I heard about it on the news. He survived, I believe." Freddie nodded, although he didn't know if the man had died since or how bad his injuries were. "And I note you've tried to avoid killing people. That's wise. An injured officer raises questions that need to be answered; a dead one only creates an organizational thirst for revenge."

He smiled, admiring her calculating professionalism. "I'm not a killer. That's how simple it is. I wanted to weaken his team, not kill people. Although it's all a bit pointless now. I'll be meeting Oberman at some point tomorrow, ostensibly to cut a deal, but I *will* try to kill him, if he doesn't get me first."

She looked genuinely perplexed.

"I don't understand. You seem to be doing an adequate job of undermining him. Why would you throw away the advantage now?"

"Long story, but it's the way it has to be. One of his men saw me talking to a friend, and if I don't meet with him I think they'll go after her."

She raised her eyebrows. "So. Freddie Makin has friends."

"Actually, it's just someone who works at the hotel where I've been staying, but the guy saw us laughing in the street, and you know what these people are like."

"I do indeed. Perhaps we both do if we're being honest with ourselves."

She was right, in that Freddie had only recognized the risk to Eva in the first place because he'd never been averse to exploiting innocent contacts in his time with S8.

"So that's how it is. I have enough in my life to feel guilty about. I'll call him in the morning, he'll tell me where the meet is, and that's that."

"Did you at least find out what he's been up to?"

"I think so."

"Can you share?"

Could he share? And had he already shared too much with Marina? On paper, there was nothing to trust about her and plenty to mistrust.

All he had to go on to prove otherwise was his own fallible instinct, but he desperately wanted it to be right this time. Could he share?

"I don't see why not."

She nodded, but pointed at his plate. "Then I'd like to hear it, but eat first."

They continued to eat in near silence, and when they'd finished, she cleared the plates and the dish away and asked him to pour more wine. Then she came and sat back down and gave him an expression that, once again, she probably used a great deal with her students, telling them she was waiting to hear what they had to say.

"Okay. A little over a year ago, it seems Oberman found an alternative use for Cheng's program. I don't know if maybe he needed some input from Cheng or if he was just paranoid, but he put Cheng under surveillance, fearing that he'd work out what was going on. Oberman couldn't use company men to do the surveillance because he was doing it to protect his own private enterprise. That's where I came into it. What happened two weeks ago is that Cheng worked out what was going on. You were right, it was there in the footage I still have access to, and the funny thing is, I never would have noticed it if Oberman hadn't come after me."

"Yes. From what I gather, Lars Oberman has done very well within the CIA, admirably in a way, particularly given his lack of . . . finesse."

"But it seems he did miss a true vocation. From what I can gather, he's been using Cheng's program to game the stock market. People make buy or sell orders, but with an adapted version of Cheng's program in place, there's a fractional lag between them making the instruction and the execution of the order, a lag that Oberman can exploit. The red flag must have come when he saw that Cheng was studying the share price of one particular business, a company that's completely sound, but one that's seen incredible share-price volatility over the last year."

"So it's all been about nothing more than making money?"

"Probably massive amounts of money, but yes."

She frowned, and the unshakable persona appeared momentarily cast aside.

"Cheng was such an idealist. An innocent, really, like a child with all-consuming obsessions. I can only imagine how upset he would have been, that something he'd created to protect life had been used for something so . . . shallow."

Freddie thought back to Cheng in those final days, a time when his suspicions had obviously already been aroused. If he'd been upset, it had never been apparent to Freddie, but then hadn't that been part of what he'd enjoyed about watching Cheng—that he had always been completely present and somehow completely absent all at the same time.

She poured the last of the wine into their glasses. "And you're determined to meet him tomorrow?" He nodded. "But you don't know where yet?"

"No. I guess somewhere in Vienna."

She frowned and said, "I wish there were something I could do to help."

He smiled. "You're the second person to say that to me today. I know this probably seems crazy to you, but I'm not planning to get killed tomorrow. Sure, it's a possibility, just like it was every day in my old job, and I'll put some things in place in case that happens. But I have every intention of walking out of that meeting alive."

She didn't respond and they drank in silence, and then as they came to the end of their glasses, she stood and said, "I'll make some coffee and we'll have brandy in the living room."

"I've kept you too long already."

"Well, perhaps you should have thought about that before calling uninvited." She smiled. "You're not keeping me from anything. And you know, as happy and fulfilled as my life is—and it *is*—I do enjoy speaking to someone who's walked a little of the path that I've walked, or at least along similar byways."

He didn't argue the point. With good food in his stomach, and the warmth of her kitchen, he was happy to stay. He wasn't sure why he'd come here at all, except that he'd needed to be somewhere that wasn't the Madhouse, but this contentment felt like reason enough.

He watched her make the coffee. Then he fetched the brandy and more glasses under her instructions, and carried them through to the living room where they sat as they had a couple of nights before. Again, they sat in silence for a while, but then she looked at him as she nursed her glass.

"It's intriguing, I think, but when I look at you I can see that you've been burned, and I wonder if that's because I already know a little about you, or because it's actually there and visible. An interesting philosophical question."

It made him think of Eva and Izzy again, and all their talk of energy and seeing the bad things that had happened to him. Marina was more matter of fact, but perhaps they were only different sides of the same coin.

He looked at the clock, thinking that Eva would soon be heading home, but he chased the thought away and said, "Were you never burned yourself, on those byways you say we walked in common?"

She smiled at his teasing, but shook her head. "No, not directly, and perhaps I've oversold my own role. I know S8 has routinely been involved in some particularly hazardous situations. Either way, I've been lucky."

"Or good."

"Yes, I'm very good." He noticed she'd used the present tense, and he wondered if it was a slip or if she was still active. "But we also know that's not always enough. I was speaking to someone just yesterday—and no, I'm not telling you who—and he told me you had a very good reputation."

"I'll give you that, I did have a good reputation, until five years ago. If I'd stayed in, I doubt very much it's what people would have talked about when my name was mentioned, and I doubt many people would have been thrilled to find themselves assigned with me."

"You're almost certainly being too hard on yourself." She looked at the clock too—and he wondered why, or if she was simply curious to know the time—then back to him. "I said I never got burned, but once, just once, I made a terrible error of judgment, a lapse of concentration, and a very good asset was exposed as a result. He spent years in prison and died of kidney failure. I thought so many times over what I might have done differently, but you know the old saying, to err is human . . ."

"And did he forgive you, the man they sent to prison?"

"No, not least because we'd become very close. He did write to me once, and there was little sign of forgiveness in it. But then, he was also quite a way removed from being divine. I'm glad of that, I think. His rambling accusations actually helped me see that I'd simply made a genuine mistake in very trying circumstances." He nodded, and she allowed a pause before speaking again. "Have you ever spoken to anyone about the ambush?"

"Not really, not properly. I wouldn't really call it an ambush either."

"What happened?" She put her glass down and stood. "No, wait. I'll get more brandy."

She left the room and Freddie smiled because she seemed to have no doubt that he'd share a story that was about as classified as it was possible to get, a story he'd never even come close to sharing with anyone outside of S8 in the five years since it had happened. It was more remarkable that she should imagine him sharing it when she was so fiercely protective of her own secrets.

And yet for all those reasons and more, he wanted to tell Marina Mikhailova the truth about what had happened in Yemen. Above all, he wanted to tell her because he was conscious that this might be the last chance he'd have to tell anyone, and really, what did any of it matter now, except at a personal level where the damage was already done?

Chapter Thirty-Eight

"It was still all about Al-Qaeda back then. Only five years ago, but how quickly things change. AQAP was the big danger—Al-Qaeda in the Arabian Peninsula. That's what we were doing in Yemen, before we cut our losses, as we always seem to." He sipped his brandy. "How much do you really know about S8?"

"I know that you're a smoke-and-mirrors outfit. You specialize in getting other players to carry out your actions, often in such a way that they might even think they're working against Western interests. That means playing all sides against each other, often getting embedded in very unconventional ways, and often involving deep, very deep, long-term cover."

Freddie nodded, reckoning that was a pretty accurate summation. But he also wondered if her final comment had been an attempt at fishing—did she suspect him of still being part of S8 now? If so, he was about to remove all doubt.

"This case wasn't even that complicated by our standards, or didn't seem to be. This was around the time of the Yemeni Revolution, so things were so chaotic down there, we were having a field day. The particular deal I was working on was an attempt to get some of the Hashid tribes supporting the Houthis to attack Al-Qaeda. I'm sure I don't need to spell out that I shouldn't be telling you any of this, but I certainly can't tell you about the bait we used or the backstory or who we were claiming to represent. Suffice to say it was audacious and I was ever so slightly pleased with myself for pulling it all together. My main contact was a super-connected guy called Abdullah, about my own age and smart—smarter than me, as it transpired. He arranged a meet with two of the most influential tribal chiefs, but it meant us going into a neighborhood of Sana'a that was usually pretty much out of bounds. Do you know Sana'a?"

"No, I don't know Yemen at all."

"The thing is, for any number of stupid reasons, we went in there more or less unarmed."

"Explain. Why would you do that?"

"It was part of our cover: we were civilians, Evanston Electronics, so normally we'd have a security detail, but we couldn't take them this time because it was so sensitive. And I guess we were sloppy, complacent, believing our own hype."

"That doesn't sound stupid at all, and none of us is immune to complacency."

He accepted the point and said, "Okay, maybe not so stupid, but only one of our team, Pete, had a gun. He was in the passenger seat of the SUV. Then there was Talal, our driver and translator. I was in the back with Melissa." Even as Freddie spoke, the heat and dust came back to him and he automatically sipped his brandy again as if to wash it away. "Talal was listening to the radio and started singing along to some song. We were laughing with him, because he couldn't sing, but he knew it and he didn't care. We got to the roadblock, a few guys with guns. Talal spoke to them and then Abdullah came out. He had a scarf over his face, but I could tell, just looking at his eyes, something was wrong. No preliminaries—he shot Pete in the head, then hit Talal in the chest. I remember Mel turned to me, like she was pleading for me to do something, because it was my operation, and this was my contact shooting people. You know, they'd counted on me, trusted me. But then there's another bang. You know how it is. It's like you're deaf and only another gunshot can restore your hearing. So yeah, there's another bang and her forehead caves in and her blood's everywhere, all over my face, just everywhere. I can taste it. I can taste it even now."

He sipped at the brandy again.

"Suddenly, it goes completely silent, like I really am deaf. And I turn, thinking I'm next, thinking I'll look him in the eyes if it's the last thing I do, and he points the gun at me, and pretends to fire, and says, 'Pow,' like a . . . like he's taunting me. Then he tosses the gun onto the floor in front of Pete and he just turns and walks away, no fear. And they're gone. Just like that, they're gone."

"So he spared you, because he wanted you to know that he'd won."

Freddie nodded. "But then I'm left just sitting there in the back of this SUV with three dead people. Three friends. And the roadblock's gone and Abdullah and his men, but people are starting to come out into the street, showing an interest, and like I said, this is a really dangerous neighborhood. I knew I had to get out of there, and I panicked. I was in shock, I guess. Scared. And I guess anybody would have been. But I don't think I'll ever quite forgive myself for what I did next."

She reached for the bottle and opened it, adding more to both their glasses. He nodded his thanks.

"I got out of the car and walked around to the driver's side. There were a lot of people on the street by this stage, getting curious, approaching, and not looking too friendly. I pulled the door open, and I saw Talal slumped there, his shirt soaked with blood, flies already landing on it. And I just . . ." The words stuck in his throat as he remembered it, saw it—Talal's confused expression, the red flowering of blood across his shirt, the flies—and Freddie had to drink again. He clenched his jaw, let it pass. "I just, I pulled him out, into the dirt. I should have put him in the back, I know I should, but I was looking at all those hostile faces. You know, he wasn't just our translator, he was our friend, but I just left him there in the dirt, and I got in that car and reversed, and then drove away and I didn't look back, not once."

"Don't you think most people would have done the same in that moment? A dangerous situation, the deadweight of a body, and you would have had to carry him back around to where you'd been sitting. I think most people would have done what you did."

Freddie nodded, accepting the point while also knowing that it concealed a lie. "If Pete had been in the driver's seat, I'd have thought of his wife and I'd have lifted him out and put him in the back. Mel was due to get married later that year and . . . well, there's no way I would have left her. No. No way." He could feel the tears building in his eyes and resented them. "You know, Talal was our friend, but he was an Arab, a local, and I left him, and I'm ashamed, so ashamed of that. He was twenty-two, he had a wife, they'd just had a baby girl. Five minutes earlier, I'd been laughing at him singing. What kind of friend was I?"

Marina showed a look of understanding now and said, "Was his body ever found?"

"Not his body, no. The next day his head was left outside the TV station. His head. That was all."

"And Abdullah?"

Freddie smiled, still unable to conceal his bitterness. "I so wanted to know. I so wanted to catch him so that I could ask him to his face. Two weeks later he was killed in a drone strike that hit a wedding. He wasn't even the target. I quit the next day. I think S8 ceased operations in Yemen a few weeks later."

"I understand." She looked down at her brandy. "One of the snippets I heard about you made me curious, that you were engaged to be married, but that you called it off when you left S8. But I understand it now. You felt responsible for what happened to your colleagues, and you felt you should have been killed too. You denied yourself the happiness you felt you'd denied their partners."

He thought of Melissa naked, her skin glistening with sweat, the rumpled sheets.

"Kind of, maybe subconsciously, but that makes it sound much nobler than it was. Truth is, it was a few months before I called it off with Chloe, a few months in which I was mixing my drinks with six different colors of prescription meds, a few months in which I never quite managed to leave Yemen, not mentally. Truthfully, the way I was back then, it would have been an act of cruelty to stay with her."

Marina nodded, but said, "I still stick by what I said. You're being far too hard on yourself. And I know I said earlier that you look like someone who's been burned, but you haven't struck me this week as someone who's carrying this kind of weight around."

He thought back over the last week or so, since a migraine had saved his life and he'd killed a man in his apartment: his week at the Madhouse, meeting Eva and the others, meeting Marina, seeing Drew again.

"It sounds crazy, but I think I've been happier this last week than I have in a very long time."

"Because you've been active again?"

"Maybe, but trust me, I don't miss that world. I think the thing is, I've been in Vienna for over a year, but it's like I've only been living here this last week."

She raised her glass with a smile and said, "Then let me be the first to bid you welcome."

"Thank you."

He raised his glass too and they drank. He thought she might bring up the question of the next day again, try to persuade him to adopt a different course, but she didn't, and he wondered if that was because she knew how determined he was to see this through in his own way. He was glad of her silence on the subject in any case, because he wanted the evening to end this way, drinking brandy, a shared and mostly unspoken fellowship sitting comfortably between them.

Chapter Thirty-Nine

He thought about checking into another hotel, but he needed to return to the Madhouse at some point, and it was probably better to do that under the cover of darkness than during the day. And besides, everything Freddie had done so far would have left Oberman convinced it was better to meet him as planned rather than try to track him down—he most likely wasn't in a position to lose many more men.

So Freddie took a cab back toward the Madhouse but had it stop a few blocks away so that he could scout the surrounding streets for signs that the place was under surveillance. Apart from a young couple engaged in what appeared to be a light-hearted disagreement, the whole area seemed deserted.

Finally, he walked to the hotel itself. The lobby still had a handful of people lounging about on the beanbags, and a couple came out of the elevator looking like they'd been in the rooftop bar. Eva and Arnold had finished for the evening and there was someone he didn't recognize on reception, so Freddie headed straight up to the fifth floor and wasn't tempted to continue by the lure of beats coming from the bar.

He was tired, weighed down by alcohol and good food and by the vicious hinterland of his day. But he didn't want to sleep, not yet, and didn't want to dream, not of Yemen, nor of the things that might be ready to supplant it in his nightly torments. He had too much to do anyway.

Inside his room, he walked around looking for signs of intrusion, signs that anything had been moved. Spotting nothing, he briefly imagined Oberman had believed him about no longer having a room there. Yet it seemed so unlikely that Freddie opened his equipment case and did an electronic sweep as well. It unnerved him when he once again found nothing, making him question the grounds for such confidence on Oberman's part.

He chased the doubts away, though, realizing he had to concentrate on his own plans, and with that in mind, he made coffee, then sat down at the laptop and created a Word document. Slowly, he wrote a lengthy explanation of everything he believed Lars Oberman had been involved in, what he'd done, and what he'd tried to conceal, from the manipulation of the stock markets to the murders of Jiang Cheng and Wei Jun and Leo Behnke. Once finished, he placed the document in a folder, then pulled images from the footage he still had of Cheng browsing the various company websites and included them.

It had taken him over an hour, but now he went onto the local news sites and scoured through them. There was nothing about the guy Freddie had shot in the thigh, but that only meant he'd managed to get himself back to Oberman and spirited away. The story of the other man, hit by a tram, was well covered, and Freddie felt a new wave of relief when he saw the most recent update saying that he was in a stable condition and that, miraculously, his injuries had not been life-threatening.

But still Freddie trawled on, through ever-more local news, looking for something he did not want to find. He sensed Oberman wouldn't come after him yet, but he still feared he'd try to tilt any meeting even further in his favor by lifting Eva off the street. That's what Freddie was searching for, a story of a young woman failing to return home from work, and even being unable to find such a story did little to reassure him.

He shut down the laptop and walked across to the windows, looking out over the partially floodlit buildings, hoping he was wrong, and that his promise to meet had also extended a temporary protection over Eva. The air was turning misty again, and his mind skipped across the city to their sweetly scented apartment, where he hoped the two of them were relaxing right now, content in their ignorance.

Eventually, he closed the blinds and went to bed, and sleep came quickly and went undisturbed by dreams. For once, the bedding didn't even look like he'd fought a battle when he woke the next morning, and he wondered if that was because he'd talked about Yemen for the first time in five years, exorcising the demons, if only for one night.

He opened the blinds to a dense fog, even denser than it had been a few days ago, and now he thought of Eva again. He wouldn't rest easy until he'd seen her turn up for work, if he hadn't already set off for his meeting by then.

He showered and went down for breakfast around nine, and afterwards he went back onto his laptop. He had every intention of living past the end of this day, but so had Mel and Pete and Talal that day in Sana'a, so he wanted everything to be in order.

The most important was the bank in Zurich, but that was also the most secure, and would continue to function with or without him as long as the money was there. But even thinking about that bank account reinforced in his mind how much he wanted to live. He wanted to live long enough to see that he'd done something good.

Finally, around eleven, he called Oberman. Once again, the phone rang for a while before he answered, suggestive either of game-playing or of hurried gestures to other people in the room, telling them Freddie Makin was on the line.

"Oberman."

"Time and place."

"You really don't believe in chitchat, do you?" Freddie didn't respond. "Okay. Apparently, people take cruises on the river. There are cruise ships specially designed for it. Who knew? *The Danube Prince* is docked on the Danube near the Reichsbrücke, closed up for the season. I'm sure you'll be able to find it. Meet me there at ten tonight."

"Okay. You come alone or there's no deal. Make sure you have a phone with you, some way that you can arrange a bank transfer. And if you don't come alone, you won't see me, but you'll see yourself on every news channel in the morning."

"Is that it?" For a moment, Freddie feared Oberman had seen straight through him, that he didn't believe for a second that Freddie wanted some kind of deal. But then he said, "No instructions about coming unarmed?"

"We're both coming armed, we know that." He allowed the briefest pause, and although Oberman didn't respond, Freddie could almost sense his nerves down the line, and he liked that, liked that he made Oberman uneasy. "The thing is, it's actually not in your interest or mine to use those guns. You use yours and your career will be over. I use mine, I don't get a nice fund to go and retire in the sun."

As with the previous call, Oberman produced a single short laugh, to himself and yet ripe with meaning, suggesting he thought he had the measure of Freddie, and that they weren't so very different.

"Ten o'clock tonight, in the observation lounge of *The Danube Prince*. And yes, I'll be on my own."

"I'll be there."

Freddie ended the call and switched off the phone. Immediately, he went back to the laptop and found the spot where *The Danube Prince* was moored. He wanted to go right now, to check it out, but the chances were they'd expect that, or at least anticipate it, and perhaps have someone down there for the next hour or two in case Freddie showed up.

Instead, he went on to the cruise company's website and looked at pictures of it. Like all the river cruise boats it was relatively low and narrow but incredibly long. From one picture he could see that there would probably be only a single gangway onto the dock, although Oberman could have people hiding out on board already, or land people from the river.

He looked at the deck plans, where the observation lounge was situated, above the restaurant at the front of the boat. He looked at the areas he'd have walk through to get there, the possible danger points. Although, looking at the plans, the entire boat was a danger point. If Oberman was confident enough just to kill him without fear of repercussions, Freddie would have only the slimmest of chances.

Once he was happy he'd learned all he could about *The Danube Prince* remotely, he went for a walk, enjoying the mystery of this opaque morning. He stopped for an early lunch at the vegan café, then took a taxi across town to the wide low wharf alongside the Danube. He would have waited for dark, but given that visibility was down to a matter of yards, he guessed it wouldn't be busy down there and only someone camped right next to the boat would see him.

The driver dropped him near the south side of the bridge, and as Freddie walked onto the wharf he could see the low white superstructure of one of the cruise boats emerging out of the fog. He released the catches on his messenger bag, but when he got to the front he saw that it wasn't *The Danube Prince*.

He walked under the bridge itself, the traffic sounding slow and strangely subdued up above in the fog. There were two boats moored next to each other on the other side of the bridge and he couldn't see the name of the second, although the one alongside the wharf once again wasn't his.

He continued along the dock, the noise of the traffic falling away another notch, and yet all the other sounds of the city somehow reaching him in confused and muffled echoes. There was another boat moored on its own, and on the stern he could see the name he'd been looking for.

He moved alongside it, past the small open deck at the back, past the windows of staterooms. He saw the spot where the gangway would be, but there was only a closed doorway in the side of the boat there now. There were more high windows, albeit with blinds drawn behind them, in what he imagined was the restaurant, and up above them the sweeping glass roof of the observation deck.

There was another small open deck at the front, but the bow curved away from the dock, making it almost impossible to get aboard there. He looked down at the muddy water, then headed back to the rear deck. Unless Oberman planned to get the gangway opened, this was the only place he could board.

Freddie took a quick look around to make sure no one was watching him. There were trees lining the dock, beginning to lose their leaves now but still looming shadows in the gray for the time being. Somewhere beyond them was the rest of the city, apartment blocks and hotels, reduced to stray and jumbled sounds.

In one swift movement, he stepped over the railing and onto the deck. It was wider than he'd imagined now that he was on it, and there were two doors leading off the deck, with steps on each side to an open upper sundeck. He climbed the steps, then opened his equipment case and attached two cameras, one looking at each of the doors. The units would be easy to spot if Oberman came up top, but almost impossible to see from below.

Closing the case, he went back down and looked through one of the doors. There was no sign of it being alarmed. He worked the lock, stepped inside quickly, and closed it behind him, then waited, listening. He'd been right about the lack of an alarm—he supposed kids in Vienna had better things to do.

He took out his last camera unit and left the equipment case by the door. Taking the gun from his messenger bag, he then waited for his eyes to adjust to the near-total darkness before moving on. There was a long central corridor which had no light at all, but he could see that it was brighter at the far end.

As he walked, he checked a few of the stateroom doors, finding them locked, then emerged into what he knew from his earlier virtual tour was the reception. The insipid light here was coming from the picture windows to the river side of the boat, which didn't have blinds drawn, and from the open staircase to the observation deck above.

He checked the restaurant, then climbed the stairs to the observation deck, the glass roof giving it the same amount of light as the gray afternoon that surrounded it. There were some fixed seating units, but all the chairs and tables that could be moved had been stacked at the front of the lounge, leaving a large expanse of floor. There was something desperately eerie and forlorn about this boat, the atmosphere of a nightclub in the morning without any of the pretense of glamor— maybe that was why Oberman had picked it.

Freddie walked to the back of the lounge. There was a bar, devoid of bottles, and a door behind it that opened into an equally empty storeroom. To the side of the bar ran a corridor containing the doors to the bathrooms, and another door at the far end that opened out onto the sundeck at the back.

Freddie had intended to place the final unit in the observation lounge, but instead, he eased open one of the panels above his head and slipped the unit inside, with the camera focused onto the door to the sundeck. If anyone was going to outflank him, it would be from there.

He walked back into the lounge then and stood looking at the blanket of gray beyond the windows. This wouldn't be easy, particularly in the dark. But it wouldn't be easy for them either, and he also had the additional advantage of having very little to lose.

He descended back into the ghostly reception hall, a whole winter of limbo ahead of it, waiting for the next guests to arrive. He retraced his steps, picked up his equipment case, and left the way he'd come.

That day in Yemen he'd been blasé, without stage nerves of any kind, utterly confident that nothing would go wrong. He felt equally devoid of trepidation now, on his own account at least, because as long as Oberman left Eva out of it, it seemed to Freddie the stakes weren't even that high anymore.

Chapter Forty

Freddie walked some of the way, and then stumbled almost physically into a taxi rank in the fog and climbed into the first car to take him the rest of the way to the Madhouse. The driver leaned forward so that his face was almost touching the windscreen, as if that might help him see through the fog. The lights of other traffic moved all about them, although without seeming to actually illuminate anything but the fog itself.

"I've never known it this bad."

Freddie nodded, not wanting to get into a conversation, but feeling he had to say something. "How long have you lived here?"

"Two years now. Before I was in Afghanistan, and now I drive taxi. But this . . ." He gestured with his hand and shook his head.

Freddie nodded again, but didn't say anything more.

When he got out at the Madhouse, he looked up the glass front of the building and could just see the faint glow of the neon sign.

The lobby was empty for a change, and as he entered, Arnold stirred behind the desk and said, "Hi, Freddie!"

"Hi, Arnold."

He felt sick, and was about to ask as casually as he could if Eva was in yet, but in direct response to his first words, a voice sounded in the back office. "Freddie!"

He came close to laughing, with an easy happiness, but most of all with relief. She came out, leaning on the desk next to Arnold, oblivious. Now there was nothing to lose.

"Hi, Eva."

"We're *so* bored, Freddie. Aren't we, Arnold?"

Arnold shrugged at the hopelessness of the situation. "I don't know why people stay home because of the fog. I love the fog."

"So do we, don't we, Freddie?"

He nodded, although he couldn't remember talking to her about it. Maybe he had, or maybe it was just another intuition she had about him—she was right anyway. He strolled over.

"Did you sort things out with your competitor?"

Freddie struggled to think what she might be talking about and stalled by saying, "My competitor?"

She smiled. "The guy who was staring at us, when we met on the street?"

"Oh, him! Yeah, kind of. Although I'm thinking about a change of direction anyway."

Arnold looked disapproving. "No way, you know, IT is . . . it's where all the money is."

"You think?" Freddie smiled. "I think the important thing, and it's taken me a while to see it, you shouldn't be getting out of bed every day because you have to go to work, you should be working at something that makes you want to get out of bed."

"Oh man. I'm writing that down." Arnold wasn't kidding—he grabbed a notepad and started to write, mumbling the words aloud as he did so.

Eva cocked her head to one side and said, "So what would you rather be doing, Freddie?"

Living—preferably here in Vienna, but just living!

"I don't know. But knowing it's not this is a start. I'll see you later."

He headed to the elevator, once again swept up in the sense of relief, because Oberman's people had not picked her up, and by the time she finished her shift, this would be done.

Just before eight, he wired himself up. He emailed the document he'd created about Oberman to both Drew and Marina. Then he sent Drew the link to the feed that would record everything Freddie and Oberman said to each other. He just hoped it would be enough.

It was only a little after eight when he left. Eva and Arnold were busy checking in a group of five guys who looked like a band, although only one of them had a guitar case with him.

One of them was on the phone and as Freddie passed he heard the guy say in English, "Listen, fella, it's bad enough that we got diverted to Salzburg. If the equipment doesn't show up, we can't do the gig. This fog is a joke."

Freddie got a taxi, but had it drop him at the church near the Reichsbrücke, then he took a circuitous route to *The Danube Prince*. None of his cameras had pinged to alert him to any movement on the boat, but he doubted they'd just show up at ten without doing any prep, and he didn't want to bump into them before he even got to the boat.

He saw no one, although that didn't say much in such a deep fog. There had to be other members of Oberman's slightly depleted team in the area. If there weren't, it suggested a confidence on Oberman's part that was a little unsettling in itself.

When Freddie finally reached the boat, he climbed over the railing, and as he stepped in front of the door, he felt the satisfying vibration of the phone in his pocket, telling him he'd triggered one of his own cameras. He still took the gun out before stepping inside, but then moved quickly.

He'd imagined the boat being much darker at night, but despite the fog, the blaze of lights on the bridge and along the waterfront produced an otherworldly glow that seemed to permeate the air inside. In the reception and particularly the observation lounge, it created an almost magical atmosphere, like a stage lit for a theater production.

Once he was happy no one else had arrived yet, he retreated to the restaurant, concealed from the wharf by the drawn blinds. He sat there with his phone in front of him, and waited. He didn't think about what would happen an hour from now, didn't think about what had happened to him this last week, these last years, just waited, listening to the faint noise of traffic and the emptiness of the fog, bathing in the submerged light.

And it was only when he heard a car approaching, twenty minutes before ten, that he realized what he'd been doing as he'd sat there. Finally, after a year of watching Jiang Cheng, he'd managed to exist only in the moment, and he thought, even if nothing else came of tonight, that would be something.

The car drove off again, but a minute later, his phone vibrated and he looked at the feed from the cameras and saw Oberman on his own, stepping in through one of the rear doors. He was wearing a heavy overcoat, but still looked every bit the Wall Street trader, his blond hair swept back and slick, as if he'd taken a shower just before coming out, his skin taut and highly maintained.

Freddie listened now, but before hearing anything he saw the beam of a flashlight dancing around, hitting the glass doors to the restaurant. And only as the light danced away again did he hear the heavy tread of Oberman climbing the stairs to the observation deck.

He heard the steps above him then, so clear that Freddie probably could have chanced shooting him through the floor. Oberman walked forward, and some banging followed, then scraping. He'd pulled one of the chairs free from where they were stacked and placed it on the floor. Then there was silence again, suggesting he was sitting down.

Freddie went back to the feeds over the doors at the back of the boat. There was no movement, nothing even to suggest other people were still nearby. He stood, switched on the wire, slipped his phone into his pocket, and picked up his gun.

He moved quietly, but without hesitation, up the stairs and into the observation lounge. As he'd imagined, Oberman was sitting in the middle of the expanse of floor on a single chair. Freddie was struck once again by how it looked like a set for a theatrical production.

Freddie walked from the top of the stairs and stopped a little way from him, close enough to be sure of picking up his voice with the wire. Oberman didn't get up, but looked at Freddie with a bemused expression.

"I have a theory," he said. "I think the reason S8 keeps a lid on absolutely everything it does is that it also conceals the underlying truth, that none of you guys is really anything special."

"I think I'd agree with that. But I don't know what that says about the number of your men I've put in the hospital. And violence isn't even my thing."

"So what is *your thing*, Freddie Makin?"

Something about Oberman's oily voice, something about the arrogance and swagger he exuded, even sitting still, made Freddie fully understand how much of a smart player he had to be. Oberman had clearly risen through a lot of paygrades, and Freddie doubted very much that it was because everyone liked him.

"You know, Lars, I imagine you're thinking of trying to kill me here tonight. And if you do, you'll find out exactly what my thing is."

Oberman smiled, unimpressed, although Freddie doubted he knew it was pretty much a bluff.

"You're accusing me of murderous intent, and yet you're the one holding a gun. In fact, I would say you're a little out of practice. You assumed, did you not, that I'd pick up your steampunk friend to use as a bargaining chip—the kind of clichéd move I'd never employ. You assumed I'd bring other people, but I've kept my word. You assumed I'd come with my gun drawn, and yet I repeat, it's you who's armed."

"Only for protection."

"You need protection from yourself. I mean, look at you, Makin. What a sorry excuse for an intelligence officer. You messed up the Jiang Cheng operation . . ."

"How did I mess it up?"

Oberman didn't answer. "You're deluded enough to think Drew Clarke would conspire with you against his own colleagues. And most laughably of all, how do you think your superiors will react when they find out you confided all your secrets to our biggest asset in Vienna?"

"What are you talking about?"

"You still don't get it, do you, Freddie?" He smiled with what looked like an attempt at pity. "Marina Mikhailova works for us, and she played you like a cheap fiddle."

Freddie rocked back slightly, as if he'd suffered a physical blow, but he managed to smile and say, "I thought you didn't go in for clichés?"

But Freddie felt the betrayal, betrayed by his own instinct rather than by Marina—looking back, nearly everything she'd ever said to him had been like a declaration that he couldn't trust her. He'd overridden it with his own intuition, faulty again, and so of course Oberman was right in all his criticisms. Because Freddie Makin was certainly a sorry excuse for something.

"I do feel for you, Freddie. The boutique activities of S8 seem to have left you ill-equipped for life in the big leagues."

Freddie frowned. He guessed Oberman was about the same age as him, but he talked like someone from an older generation, or a past generation. There was a patronizing tone to everything he said that really managed to get under Freddie's skin.

"What do you want, Lars?"

Oberman shrugged, as if the answer should have been self-explanatory.

"I just want a guarantee of your silence, and if I can be assured that paying for it is enough, then I'll pay for it. If money isn't the answer, then we have a bigger problem." He smiled, and for the first time Freddie felt uneasy, because he couldn't sense where this was going, or rather, why it hadn't already got there. But Oberman was still needling after something else. "I have to admit, though, I find your behavior this last week a little peculiar. See, I heard you might still be part of S8, and I'll admit that my knowledge of S8 is limited, but I still can't imagine your superiors would be at all happy with some of the things you've done these past few days."

A little bit of Freddie's mind was stubbornly locked into thinking about the things he'd shared with Marina, and he had to force himself to snap back into the moment, to the threat he was dealing with right now.

"So you're worried because S8 knows you've used a highly sensitive program to game the stock market, worried it'll get back to Langley that you killed the CIA asset who created that program."

"I'm not worried about anything, Freddie. I'm confused, that's all, confused that you're acting as if we're on different sides."

"Does Langley know you employed me?"

"I never employed you."

"Okay, does Langley know Marine Finance employed me, a company that you control?"

"You have me there, because I've never heard of Marine Finance."

"Really? It's the same company you used to manipulate the stock price of Walden Inc. and several associated companies."

"I've never heard of Waldstrom Inc. either."

Freddie smiled, because he'd spoken quickly and Oberman had heard what he'd wanted to hear.

"Actually, I said Walden, but in its place you substituted the name Waldstrom, a name you say you've never heard of."

"I misheard you, that's all." But Oberman's smug humor had ebbed quickly away. "And I guess you're recording this, in the hope of using your trickery to make it look like I said one thing when I said another. Trust me, it won't hold." Despite the confidence of his words, Oberman sounded rattled, and Freddie reckoned it *would* hold, not enough to stand up in court, but then this would never go to court. Trying to regain the initiative, Oberman said, "So let's play the same game. How would your superiors feel about the people you've killed and maimed this week?"

"You know, Lars, everything I've done this week has been in self-defense."

"So you'll have told them about it, I'm sure."

"Told who? You don't get it, do you? I don't have any superiors. I left S8 five years ago."

Oberman smiled again, a genuine smile this time, and Freddie realized he'd just made the worst mistake. He felt his phone buzz in his pocket, telling him one of the cameras had spotted movement and activated, and he heard Oberman say, "That's all I wanted to know."

It was what Oberman had been waiting for. He didn't care what information Freddie had. The only thing he'd been afraid of was killing an active S8 officer, and Freddie had finally confirmed that Oberman had nothing to fear at all.

Freddie started to raise his arm, but he was too slow, and didn't know how he could have been too slow. The camera had only just activated, he should have had time, but his gun was nowhere near level with Oberman when the shot tore the air open and he felt the punch in the back of his shoulder blade and his own gun dropped to the floor with a clatter that in this moment of deafness sounded like a stone falling into a well; and at first Freddie thought he could stay on his feet, but his legs buckled and he fell, crashing onto his back, and the pain tore through him, radiating out from the shoulder in jagged pulses.

He was aware of Oberman standing up, approaching. He saw someone else, whoever it was who'd shot him, walking over and picking up the gun Freddie had dropped. He couldn't see his face, only the halo of hazy light around him, and Freddie was lost in wonder that he'd made this so easy for them. What had he expected? He'd always been too complacent, but at least this time only he would die as a result.

The newcomer said, "You should have killed me when you had the chance."

Freddie laughed a little, although even that small convulsion caused another jolt of pain. He couldn't see his face clearly, but he recognized the voice—Bennett James.

"I thought you were just a junior, a nobody."

"No, that's you." It was Oberman and he was standing over him now and Freddie could see his face and was vaguely aware that he too had produced a gun from somewhere and was pointing it at Freddie's head. "It would've been far better for everyone if you'd been in that helicopter five years ago."

He was grateful that Marina hadn't apparently seen fit to tell them about Yemen, and he smiled too, because Oberman was right, it would have been better, and Freddie didn't mind if that flaw in fate's fabric was mended now.

Even so, he said, "There was no helicopter."

"What?" He didn't wait for an answer. The gunshot came, and a neat hole appeared in Oberman's forehead and he fell. Bennett James shouted something, and moved, but a second shot came and he fell, crashing down on top of Freddie, producing such a pulse of pain from the injured shoulder that Freddie cried out.

And yet even now he was trying to think. Bennett James had already been on the boat, somehow, and the ping from Freddie's camera had to be someone else coming aboard, someone else who'd saved him, possibly. It was Drew, it had to be. Despite what Oberman had said, Drew *was* capable of working against his own colleagues, when it really mattered.

The weight of the dead man lifted a little and then got dragged off him, simultaneously offering relief and another sharp, nerve-shredding dose of pain, and then his savior knelt down and cast a professional eye on his shoulder, and it wasn't Drew at all.

"Marina?"

She nodded. "That was closer than I would have liked, but all's well that ends well. I was lucky there were only three of them."

"Three? I thought . . ."

"The third one's floating somewhere in the Danube." She shrugged nonchalantly. "Can you sit up, if I help you?"

He sat up, wincing through the pain, but finding it easier once he was upright. She eased his coat off, then used the bullet hole as an entry point to tear his shirt open. She grimaced, but didn't look panicked, which was something.

"It's a mess, but I don't think it's hit anything important."

"It felt important at the time." She laughed. "But, Oberman said you were . . ."

"Working for him? Yes, that's what he believed. As I said, he wasn't the brightest."

"Not sure what that makes me." He laughed, but immediately grimaced with another stab of pain. "But thanks anyway. I . . ."

"We should be thanking you. And no, I'm not going to tell you what I mean by that. But first off, we need to get that shoulder seen to. Can you stand?"

He nodded and she helped him get to his feet, and he looked down at the two bodies. It was the same situation, five years apart. He'd been the one who'd miscalculated and yet other people had been killed as a result. But at least this time, it was more or less the right people who'd died.

FOUR MONTHS LATER

Chapter Forty-One

Winter was all through the city, with snow on the ground and cold in the stones and the air raw with it. The Café Griensteidl was full, the usual mix of tourists and locals, all steam and warmth and heat and sugar.

Freddie was in his usual spot, but after reading for twenty minutes he put the book aside and checked the time. It was nearly upon the hour anyway, and in truth, he wasn't much enjoying the book.

A group of four people came in and the waiter explained that the café was full and they left again amid much grumbling. The waiter looked across at Freddie and gave him an exasperated look and Freddie smiled back.

He leaned back in his seat then, gingerly, although that was from force of habit rather than because his shoulder was still tender. It had taken two operations and a metal pin, but it was getting better. If anything, he was probably fitter now than he'd ever been.

Drew had visited him in the hospital and he was glad of that because he wasn't sure how he'd have found out about Oberman otherwise—it certainly wouldn't have been from Marina. So thanks to Drew, he knew that alarm bells had been sounding in Langley for most of the previous year, and Oberman's death, while regretted in some quarters, had generally been viewed as the neatest available outcome.

On the other hand, during an evening of intense recuperative boredom, Freddie had done some searching, and discovered that Marine Finance AG was still very much active. He presumed the CIA had taken it in-house and were probably using it to game some stock market or other, just as Oberman had, albeit for different reasons.

He'd received one other official visit in the hospital too, from John Elliott, who many lifetimes before had been Freddie's boss. Astonishingly, given the incompetence he'd once again displayed, John had asked him to come back. But Freddie was done with all of that, and his dreams now were more or less untroubled, and he slept better than he had since . . . well, since he'd stopped sleeping.

As ever, despite the hubbub of the café, the chatter, and the clatter of crockery, he seemed to hear the door open, and so did the waiters. One of them glided over to meet Marina on the threshold and take her coat and fur hat. She chatted with him briefly and then came over to the table and greeted Freddie.

The chess set was produced and they set up, but waited for their order to arrive before starting the game.

As had become their custom, she raised her coffee cup as if it were a drink for toasting, and said, "To Cheng."

"To Cheng."

They started to play, and Marina said, "How's the gallery going?"

"Surprisingly well. I've taken on another two artists. Things are moving. People are talking about it."

"You shouldn't be so surprised." She smiled, teasing. "You had to be good at something." She casually moved a knight in a way that unnerved him—he'd learned that she was most dangerous when she appeared most casual. "But I'm glad you found a reason to stay. And I enjoyed the opening for Eva's show the other week. I enjoyed it very much."

He nodded. "It was a fun evening." Even now, he couldn't believe that he was here, a resident of Vienna, a real resident, part of its cultural fabric.

They played on for another few minutes, but then he glanced across the room and noticed a young woman with long dark hair, on her own. She wasn't even looking at them, but something about her troubled him.

He made his next move. Marina pondered for a little while before countering. He glanced again, and once more the woman wasn't looking in his direction, but he couldn't shake the idea that she was watching. Something was just a little bit off about her.

When he turned back, Marina was smiling at him. "Don't worry, she's watching me, not you." She laughed a little. "You keep forgetting, you're not the only one with a past."

"I keep forgetting I'm the only one who's left it in the past." He made a point of not glancing back at the woman now. "Could it be a problem?"

"Goodness, no." She smiled again, completely unfazed, and looked down at the board. "And much more pressing for you right now is what you plan to do with that bishop."

Freddie looked down at the map of the board as they'd redrawn it and an irritating familiarity came over him. "I've already lost, haven't I?"

She looked at him, then back at the board.

"Probably . . ."

Chapter Forty-Two

Newark, New Jersey

Sabah dropped Aisha at school and then drove on to the Women's Advice Center. But even walking from the parking lot into the office, she could feel the cold piercing through her coat—five years on and she still wasn't used to the winters here, and this one seemed particularly fierce.

She stepped inside and stood still for a few moments, letting the warmth of the building soak into her like a drug, bringing her back to consciousness.

Tracey looked up from the reception desk and said, "Good morning, Sabah, did you have a nice weekend?"

"Good morning, Tracey." She still took pleasure in the sound of these simple greetings in English, and loved even more to hear Aisha speaking the language as a native. "I had a lovely weekend, thank you. And you?"

"Oh, you know. I could use it a little less cold."

Sabah laughed. "I'm glad it's not just me."

She walked through into the office and to her desk, exchanging the same greetings with her colleagues. And as usual, before starting work, she handled a few of her own tasks, then realized it was the first Monday of the month and felt the familiar moment of wonder, curiosity, and anticipation.

She logged into her bank account and there it was, five hundred dollars sent from a bank account in Switzerland, the same as every previous month for the last five years. At first, she'd thought it was from the government, the same government that had so kindly helped her and Aisha come here, but it wasn't, and she'd never been able to find out who it was from.

As with every previous month, she transferred the money into a separate account. She didn't know how long it would last or if someone would come along one day and tell her it was all a terrible mistake and they needed the money back. But she didn't need it day to day, and as she imagined it, perhaps some time in the future it would be Aisha's college fund.

Her gaze drifted sideways, to the photograph, Talal holding Aisha as a baby with such happiness and love in his eyes. She kissed her fingertips and touched them to the glass. Because she knew, and had always known, deep down, that this money was surely from some friend of Talal's, and so in some way it was also from Talal himself.

She would have given everything she had now to bring Talal back, but it still meant so much, every month, to see that someone in the world still cared about him and what had happened to him and about those he had left behind. After all, what greater act of friendship could there be?

Acknowledgments

Thanks as ever to Deborah Schneider and all at Gelfman Schneider/ ICM Partners. The list of people I need to thank at Thomas & Mercer gets longer with each book, but I'll keep it short by saying thanks to Emilie Marneur, Victoria Pepe, Hatty Stiles, Ian Pindar, Monica Byles, and the rest of the extended team. Café Griensteidl is, or was, a real place, one of the most atmospheric cafés in Vienna, but sadly it closed in the summer of 2017—I've kept it in the book as a belated thank you to the wonderful staff and management. And finally, thanks to Eva (hope you like your fictional alter ego!) for bringing me back up to speed on a few things I'd conspired to forget—we'll always have Athens . . .

About the Author

Kevin Wignall is a British writer, born in Brussels in 1967. He spent many years as an army child in different parts of Europe and went on to study politics and international relations at Lancaster University. He became a full-time writer after the publication of his first book, *People Die* (2001). His other novels are *Among the Dead* (2002); *Who is Conrad Hirst?* (2007), shortlisted for the Edgar Award and the Barry Award; *Dark Flag* (2010); *The Hunter's Prayer* (2015, originally titled *For the Dogs* in the USA), which was made into a film directed by Jonathan Mostow and starring Sam Worthington and Odeya Rush; *A Death in Sweden* (2016); *The Traitor's Story* (2016); and *A Fragile Thing* (2017).